THE
ROOM
OF
CONCENTRIC
CIRCLES

A.H. Feral

To Addie – for all her help, patience and expertise

*

ONE

He'd been sitting in the office all morning and most of the afternoon and the telephone hadn't once broken the tranquillity of his day. Yet the very moment he'd decided it was probably safe enough to go and empty his bladder Sod's law decided to intervene. The telephone began to ring loud and clear. Its shrill cry rang out from the office, shot along the corridor, and through the door behind which he stood urinating.

'What the.....!' he muttered. 'I don't believe it. Is this some kind of a joke?'

He hastily shook away the last few drops. Foregoing the nicety of washing his hands, he threw open the door and ran from the toilet as fast as his legs could carry him. Down the corridor, towards the office, he ran, the call of the telephone taunting him. He pushed open the office door and practically fell onto the desk. Reaching across he snatched at the receiver.

'Hello!' he cried enthusiastically into the mouthpiece. 'Beaumaris Investigations!'

Silence, save for a faint breath.

'Hello. Beaumaris Investigations,' he repeated, just as enthusiastically.

With his free hand he was desperately trying to tuck away into his flies what he hadn't had time to in his haste to get to the phone.

Oh,' finally came a tiny voice. 'Is that Pretty Petal Florists?'

5

'No,' he replied, with more than a hint of disappointment. 'This is Beaumaris Investigations.' Then came a glimmer of familiarity. 'Is that you Mrs Sumner?' he stammered.

'Oh!' exclaimed the woman. 'Do you know me then, dear?'

'Yes, of course, Mrs Sumner. It's me, Dylan.'

A moments pause.

'Dylan?'

'Yes.'

'Dylan?' she repeated.

'Yes, Dylan Beaumaris. You know, from upstairs.'

'Upstairs? Mr Beaumaris from upstairs?'

'Yes, Mrs Sumner. This is Beaumaris Investigations. I think you must've found my card, you know the one I gave you a couple of weeks ago, and called me by mistake.'

Another brief period of silence.

'And you're selling flowers now, are you dear?'

A nearby car alarm screeched incessantly rousing Dylan from his sleep. He slowly lifted his head from the desk and wiped the dribble from the edge of his mouth onto his sleeve. Though not yet fully conscious he stood up and turned towards the window, wiping the sweat from his forehead on the other sleeve; April 2011 was set to be the hottest on record. The desolate day and the unseasonal heat had conspired to send him to sleep where he sat. He needed to ease his lethargy and wake up – it was, after all, still only the afternoon.

'Christ, I'm bored,' he said to anyone passing that may have heard, and cared to listen.

No one had, and no one did.

He stared out of the window at the rooftops of Belsize Park, and the glorious sun glinting off the domed skylights of the buildings across the busy thoroughfare. The shards of light shocked him back to life, and although his eyes felt the pain at first, it had done the job. Squinting, but now fully awake, he continued staring out of the window at the passing specimens of humanity below, and the tidal wave that surged along Haverstock Hill from the nearby underground station, hurried and huddled in their movement, like worker ants anxious to return to their nest. Not one soul passing Richardson's the newsagents on their journey home noticed the solitary figure at the first floor window looking down on them.

Sighing he turned back to face the office; the four unembellished walls and the brown, stained carpet that reached out to them; the redundant telephone which he wished would ring, presenting him with something, no matter how trivial a case it may be, to justify his decision to go into the private detection business; the laptop, which was the sole piece of equipment if you didn't include the telephone and the kettle; the desk, which was the one piece of furniture if you didn't take into consideration the two chairs that it came with; and finally, in the far corner of the room, the rusty brown and battered old filing cabinet which had remained vertical only by virtue of the fact that it was being propped up by the two walls it rested against - thanks to the non-existent workload at the moment, its fragility went unburdened by the weight of heavy case files.

'Screw this,' said Dylan. 'I'm going home.'

But of course he didn't.

'So, Jaffah, what's new in oranges then?' was the greeting upon his arrival at the Roebuck pub, his local.

Dylan had once said that Jaffah Shamouti, a name that had began as a joke on seeing an advertisement for oranges in a newspaper, would make for a good nom-de-plume should he ever need one.

'Oh, smaller and rounder, boyo,' he replied, 'Smaller and rounder,'.

Despite all the years he'd lived in London Dylan had not lost the mellow Welsh brogue in his voice. He loved playing up his Welshness and would, in jest, occasionally toss in the word *boyo* to satisfy the perception of the stereotypical Welshman. But this was only in company where he felt comfortable, and certainly never in the earshot of another Welsh person.

He ordered five pints of ale and passed three of these to his friends who were sitting at a table adjacent to the bar. He placed two pints for himself down on the table, the first of which was consumed in one draught.

'Wow! The old private dicking must be thirsty work,' said Jonathan.

'No! Too bloody quiet it is. Sitting on my arse all day scratching I am. Still, I've called up and put an ad in the paper... for an assistant, like.'

'Hold on,' said Aiden. 'What do you want an assistant for if you're so quiet?'

'Well... One of these day I might get a couple of jobs. And you never know, the second might come in while I'm out on the first. You have to plan ahead, don't you?'

'Why not just buy an answerphone?' Nixon the barman shouted across the dirty wood-top bar he was wiping clean with a damp blue cloth. His suggestion fell on stony ground.

'Cos he's got too much money and he doesn't know what to do with it,' piped up Malcolm.

Dylan left the Roebuck at around ten o'clock and walked the few hundred yards to his home in Hampstead Hill Gardens.

The house was quiet, except for the faint sound of tv laughter coming from one flat and the tinkling of classical piano from speakers in another. Dylan managed to make it to his top-floor flat in stealthy fashion without interruption and, more importantly, without being accosted on the first floor landing by the house-busybody, Mrs Sumner.

In the refrigerator he scoured around for something cold to eat, he couldn't be bothered to cook anything. This turned out to be three slices of bierwurst sausage and two slices of cheese in between two slices of unbuttered bread. That would do nicely. He devoured this in five bites and adjourned to the living room where he took a tumbler from the Art Deco drinks cabinet, one which he'd purchased from a little antique shop in the Portobello Road, and poured into it a triple measure of single malt whisky. He then walked to the far side of the room and switched on the small black iPod sitting in its docking station and went round the room gathering everything he needed to prepare his prized hookah.

'Well, Dylan,' he said to himself, settling deep into the comfort of the soft white padded sofa, 'another day, but still no dollar. Never mind though, I'm sure to have a rush on tomorrow.'

He sucked on the tip of the hookah pipe. The soothing smoke from the flavoured molasses filled his lungs. Thoughts of female company swept briskly through his mind and drifted towards Victoria. It was late though, and she'd already be with a client, probably. Dylan wasn't in the mood for rejection tonight, even from lips as sweet as hers.

When he was alone, and filled with the deep melancholy that threatened to pull him under at that moment, his thoughts invariably turned to his late mother. He pictured her face, a beautiful mask behind which lay all the malevolence and decay that had led to her ultimate downfall in those final days of hedonistic destruction – in isolation, many thousands of miles away from where Dylan was boarded and bored.

The sweet vapours and the mellow sound of Chet Baker's trumpet flowed over him. He watched, with glazed eyes, the charcoal as it slowly burned, and soon drifted into the more comfortable oblivion of deep sleep.

The next morning Dylan again stood gazing out of the window. It was now 10:23 and there had been no calls. All was still quiet on the business front. His eyes were soon drawn to one man in particular. Approaching from the direction of the underground station he wore upon his head what Dylan considered to be a proper hat. It wasn't a woollen beanie or a baseball cap, or any other type of modern millinery seen on heads of folk up and down the country every day, it was a trilby. He loved the idea that men wearing proper hats would again, one day, be the norm - not that he was old enough to have remembered when it had been. He was fond of watching old black and white films in which the men wore hats. Intolerance to some aspects of the culture of modern day society propagated many old-fashioned attitudes within Dylan's character.

He had bought a flat cap once, but having studied himself in the mirror he came to the swift conclusion that his face was simply the wrong shape and his hair was too full and unruly to carry it off with any great effect. He had once worn it on a foray to the Roebuck, but the subsequent reaction of his friends had helped form the opinion in his mind that, unless of a certain age, you would just be leaving yourself open to the ridicule of a largely intolerant society. That night he put the flat cap away and it had never seen the light of day since. Even now it lay somewhere in the deep and dark recesses of a cupboard in his bedroom.

Dylan liked the thought of many things not necessarily considered modern society's norm, but he wasn't equipped with the courage or conviction to carry them off himself - even in a place as diverse and accepting as cosmopolitan London. This was why he admired people in society that were not afraid of standing out from the crowd.

He continued watching the man in the trilby who seemed to be looking for somewhere specific. He was walking at a slow pace, scanning each shop as he went, occasionally tilting his head to gaze up at the upper storey windows. And each time he had cause to do this, or if there was a sudden gust of wind, he would hold on to the brim of his hat for fear of losing it to the onslaught of moving traffic. Dylan imagined the man chasing the windswept hat along the pavements of Belsize Park as if it were a piece of tumbleweed being blown across the wilds of the American West.

The man beneath the trilby reached the pavement outside Richardson's and stopped, directly beneath the window from which Dylan had been watching him. His trousers were blowing loosely about his legs like a Bedouin tent in a soft sirocco. He took out a piece of paper from the breast pocket of his jacket, briefly looked at it, then glanced up towards the office of Beaumaris Investigations. Dylan instinctively moved away from the window - like a guilty child caught in an act of mischief. The urge was too great though and a few seconds later he drew himself back towards the window and looked down at where the man had been standing, but both man and trilby were gone.

Returning to his desk Dylan took up the first of the three envelopes delivered that morning, but just as he was about to begin opening it there was a knock on the door. It was strange, he thought, that he'd not heard the door at ground level creaking open, as it tended to do, or the sound of

12

footsteps on the stairs and along the first-floor landing.

Dylan looked towards the door and knew immediately from the silhouette in the frosted glass that the man on the other side of the door was the one he'd just been watching, outside on the pavement. There was the vaguely distorted shape of the trilby. Dylan threw the envelope back down on the desk.

'Come in,' he called out.

The door swung slowly open and the man walked in. He looked around the office, seemingly taking in the despondent emptiness of it all, then turned to face Dylan.

'Good morning,' he said quietly, with a nod of the head. 'I come about the job advertised in the newspaper.'

He spoke slowly and with an accent. He held up the piece of paper he'd been looking at. He was aged somewhere around mid-fifties, or so Dylan estimated, and wearing a dark-brown corduroy jacket with charcoal coloured slacks that were possibly a size or two too big for him – making it look as if he may have lost some weight recently. On his feet he wore well-polished brown brogues.

'Yes, of course,' said Dylan. 'For a moment there I thought you may be a new client. I didn't really expect anyone for the job this quickly - I only phoned it through yesterday afternoon.'

'Ah, no. It is my cousin, Nuncio, you see. He, ah... work at the newspaper. He call last night to tell me about the job. He know that I look for work.'

'Well, I'm not quite sure about the ethics of

that,' challenged Dylan, which was unusual, as his normal tendency was to occupy the moral low-ground. 'But never mind, eh? You're here now. Sit down and tell me about yourself. You want a cup of tea, do you? I don't have any coffee I'm afraid.'

'Yes, thank you. That would be very nice. Milk and one sugar, please.'

'I only drink Earl Grey myself but I have got some regular tea bags for clients. Not that there's been any, mind. I've been in business for two weeks now and I haven't had a bloody bite yet. And I suppose that I should get some coffee in as well really.'

Dylan felt conscious of the fact that he was rambling on a little.

'I see... yes.' A faint smile and a slight nod of the head accompanied the man's almost inaudible response. Dylan got the impression he hadn't completely understood what Dylan had said.

'What's that accent you've got there?' Dylan asked, handing him the cup.

'Italian,' came the reply. 'Oh, thank you very much'

The man went to put the cup down on the desk, but stopped himself. Dylan, seeing his hesitation, motioned that it was okay - the desk had enough ringed stains on it already that one more wouldn't matter.

'That may come in useful one day. You know, if we get a case involving Italians.'

'Ah, no.' The Italian replied. Dylan sensed his anxiety.

'What do you mean, no?'

'I don't speak Italian.'

14

Curious, thought Dylan.

'I don't understand. You have an Italian accent.'

'Yes, this is true, but I do not speak it.'

'So, you have an Italian accent, but you don't speak the language?'

'That is right.'

A timid smile betrayed his embarrassment, and to draw attention from this he picked up the cup of tea and took a long and lingering sip.

'That's a little strange, wouldn't you say?'

'Well, yes, I know, but you have a little bit of an accent yourself, no?'

'Yes, Welsh.'

'So you speak Welsh?'

'I remember a few words, but, granted, no I don't. Not any more at least.'

'So, you have a Welsh accent but you do not speak Welsh. Yes?' he said with a soft precision.

'Well now, I think that's a little different. We were taught it at school, but my mother wanted me to speak English, and I just never really used it that often. I forgot nearly all of what I knew when we moved down to London.'

'I can tell you why I speak no Italian,' the man said, satisfied by Dylan's answer. 'But maybe you will not believe.'

'Try me,' said Dylan.

He explained that he and his family had gone to watch a stage hypnotist in the West End and that the audience had been asked for volunteers. His daughter had raised her hand to volunteer him. According to his story he had been made to forget how to speak Italian. Dylan listened with

15

interest, and more than a little scepticism.

Amongst the other volunteers that had been hypnotised there was one man who had been instructed to request the time from any woman he should meet, and a woman who clucked like a chicken whenever anybody asked her the time. Another man barked like a dog every time he heard a chicken clucking, and yet another man who would mime opening and closing a door every time he heard the bark of a dog.

'Then the hypnotist,' explained the Italian, 'just suddenly collapsed on the stage. And everybody they rush around and in the end they take him away. He was dead. Just like that. And we... we are still in a... how you say... hypnosis? Crazy! And nobody, they cannot find anybody to break this spell. And still up to now, no. And me, I'm speaking only English.

'Did that really happen?' said Dylan, eyeing him suspiciously.

'That is what happen. Really!' he answered, crossing his chest.

'So what about names and food and stuff like that then?' Dylan asked him.

'No, that is okay. Everybody can know names and food. I just pick up slowly slowly.'

He gave a deep, almost, Dylan felt, provocative stare.

'And I was lucky,' he continued, waving a finger in the air. 'Cos still somebody out there make like a chicken every time somebody ask her "Hey, what's the time?"' he flapped his arms and clucked to emphasize the ridiculousness of it.

'Really?'

'Yes, really,' replied the Italian, smirking.

'You know what?' said Dylan. 'I like you. And I suppose everyone's entitled to their little secrets.'

Dylan, for the moment at least, would have to accept his story.

'I haven't even asked you your name.'

'Oh... my name, of course. It is Antonio Spinetti.' He pointed to his mouth, chuckling, as if to indicate saying his name wasn't a problem. 'But everybody call me Tony.'

He took off his hat and placed it on the desk revealing a full head of silver hair.

'Well, Tony, I'm Dylan.'

They finally shook hands.

When Dylan had placed the advertisement for an assistant to help with paperwork and general stuff around the office he knew that he couldn't stipulate any particular sex. Of course, being a thirty-something, full-blooded, heterosexual male, he had hoped that the applicants would be female and, ideally, easy on the eye. He did not expect the first person to walk through the door to be a middle-aged Italian man; one who looked a little out of place and had probably never worked in an office in his life. But this particular middle-aged Italian man had instantly endeared himself to him. Dylan could see potential in their working relationship.

'If you can start right away, we'll see how you get on. But I think that you and me are going to get on just fine. It'll just be good to have someone else to talk to around here.' He looked down at the well-worn trilby laying on the desk. 'And perhaps

I'll get myself one of those too.'

Dylan glanced around the office surveying it for available space in which to locate his new assistant.

'We're going to have to get you a desk. There's a little antiques place in Hampstead I know. Perhaps we'll pop in there after lunch and see what they've got, eh? Now,' he said, turning his attention to the envelopes on the desk, 'let's see what we've got here then.'

Dylan took out a letter opener from the top drawer of the desk. Slicing through the top of a brown rectangular envelope he peered inside.

'Would you believe it!' he cried. 'I've been here two bloody weeks with not a sniff of a case, and already the first bill's come in.'

The ring of the telephone suddenly startled them.

'Blimey, Tony, this could be it,' Dylan cried, excitedly, reaching to pick up the receiver.

The conversation was a brief one and although to Tony it sounded business related there was also something in Dylan's tone which told him it was a touch personal as well.

'Can you come to the flat tonight?' Dylan asked the person at the other end. 'No, that'll be fine. We can have a bite to eat as well.'

'Well, Tony,' said Dylan, ending the call. 'It looks like we could have our very first case. I think you may have brought some luck with you.'

TWO

Dylan stood at the bookshelf and searched for a recipe from one of the three cookery books that he owned. He occasionally liked to think about having a home-cooked meal, but the cooking rarely progressed beyond the thinking stage. In fact he genuinely could not remember the last time he'd cooked anything from scratch. His microwave displayed years of wear and tear but the cooker still had the gleam with which it had emerged from out of the original packaging.

The first book that he took down was a Middle Eastern cookbook. Turning the pages slowly, he perused each dish in detail, but it all looked just too complicated. Having gone through the book from cover to cover, he snapped it shut again and placed it back on the shelf from whence it came.

He picked up the second book: Fast and Healthy Recipes - or so the spine declared. Opened it, closed it, and placed it back on the shelf next to the first.

Finally he removed the third book, his last resort in an exhausted collection. It was a book of recipes which the title suggested would take a mere half hour to prepare. He flicked through it briefly then remembered that his last attempt in preparing one of the thirty minute recipes took two and a half hours and resulted in what to all intents and purposes was the aftermath of a chimpanzees' tea party.

He duly returned the final book to its original

19

position on the shelf alongside the other two and concluded that he would order a Chinese takeaway instead.

*

'So, what is the job, boss?'

Tony had been waiting outside in the street when Dylan arrived. This showed that he was keen, even though Dylan seldom arrived before ten o'clock, and if he did it was, in the current climates of both business and weather, only to sleep at his desk.

'I don't know yet,' said Dylan. 'I'm seeing the client tonight at home.'

'At home? This is a little unusual, no?'

Tony had relieved Dylan of the tea-making duties and was standing by the kettle filling it in readiness for the first cup of the day. However, not having had the chance to assess Tony's level of morality yet, Dylan thought the responsibility of checking e-mails should remain with him - just in case he'd received any deemed unsuitable from his friends.

'She's a friend. She's in the sort of business where you can find yourself in certain situations with certain types of people, if you know what I mean. They may not take kindly if they knew she was seeing somebody in my line of work. So I told her to come to the flat instead.'

'Who is she?'

'Victoria? She's... well... she's a female escort.'

'What, you mean like a prostitute?'

Dylan noticed Tony's eyebrows raise a little.

'That's right.'

Tony made some coffee that he'd bought in and a tea for Dylan and was carrying them back over to the desk. It was still the only desk in the room as his new desk had been ordered the previous day but was not being delivered until that afternoon.

Placing the two cups on the desk, Tony walked over to retrieve the chair that was on the other side of the office. He carried it over to Dylan's desk and sat down.

'Prostitute, eh! Yes, indeed, those girls know some very funny kinds of people. I know, I have cousins who work some girls like this, and *they* know some very funny kinds of people too. Ahhh... it's my cousins so we don't say nothing.'

He gently nodded his head. It appeared his family loyalties were stronger than his disapproval. Dylan stared at him, intrigued by the character that was unfolding. He had expected a more judgemental response but Tony displayed an open attitude which came as some relief.

'Another cousin? You have many cousins, do you?'

'I have one or two. We are a big family,' Tony replied nonchalantly.

Dylan formed a picture in his mind of Tony and his extended family. Gathered around a vast table sharing the fruits of their labours in the Tuscan sun - the patriarch of the family sitting at one end and the matriarch at the other. He envisaged plates being passed along the line of men, ravenous having worked the vineyards in the blistering heat all day - the matriarch loudly

21

demanding they eat more. The home produced wine consumed as though it were water; everybody talking over everybody else, frantically gesticulating with flailing arms and demonstrative hands, and laughing wildly. And through it all the bright Italian sun hung in the clear azure sky that was an artist's delight.

Dylan didn't actually know if this vision of the Spinetti clan was anything like the reality. It was, however, an image of total contrast to anything he could conjure up of his own family - what little there was of it - and it filled him with a certain empathic warmth, tinged with a little envy.

The rest of the day was pretty quiet. Tony's desk was delivered on schedule at between twelve midday and twelve-thirty pm, exactly as the man in the antique shop had said it would be. This led Dylan to consider that the only people nowadays adhering to the old-fashioned values of timekeeping were purveyors of old-fashioned things. Getting a level of service with that kind of exactitude from suppliers of modern furniture was almost impossible in this day and age.

'Si tratta di una bella scrivania' ('It is a beautiful desk'), was what Dylan shouted across the space that now divided his desk from Tony's. He had been practising one or two Italian phrases he'd gleaned from the internet, hoping to catch his new assistant out.

Tony looked back at him with puzzled interest.

'Very good, boss. That is Italian, no? You are learning? Maybe you teach me some?' Tony's smile was, Dylan thought, a little too triumphant.

Not so much mistrustful but rather still unconvinced of Tony's claim, Dylan had decided that he would equip himself with a few choice sentences which, accompanied by the element of surprise, he would throw out there every so often as bait to see if anything could be satisfyingly caught in his trap. And if not this way then one day he was sure to catch him off his guard conversing with one of his many cousins in the full Italian colloquial. The quiet start to Dylan's newly-chosen career made the days drag. So he would take his entertainment anywhere he could find it.

*

As she turned around in the doorway of his flat, Dylan was paying particular attention to how very long and extremely luscious Victoria's legs were. Holding her umbrella outside and away from the doorway, she opened and closed it rapidly in order to shake off the residual water that hadn't been shaken off downstairs.

Dylan considered Victoria's legs to be her finest feature in an ensemble which contained a considerable amount of fine features. He wasn't quite sure why he should have noticed her legs now, more so than at any other time, as they had had sex on several occasions. Perhaps it was the ebony seamed stockings that helped define them so well. Perhaps it was the slit that parted in the back of her skirt as she bent slightly to place the umbrella against the wall near the doorway. Perhaps it was the black and red killer heels that gave her legs the appealing shape that he had difficulty looking away from.

'That's the first spot of rain we've had for a while now,' she said as she turned and made her way into the living room. 'I suppose someone, somewhere, needs it, but I could do without it. Still it should be all good from now on for a while. How've you been?'

Victoria fell back onto the sofa, her skirt riding up a few inches.

'Fine,' Dylan answered, mesmerised. He quickly looked up to her face before she could notice - he hoped. 'You haven't eaten have you? I've ordered Chinese.'

'No. I remembered you saying that we'd eat together.'

Dylan walked to the drinks cabinet and poured out two glasses of whisky.

'So, why did you want to see me? Usually it's the other way round.'

'Straight down to business, eh?'

'I knew that there must be some kind of trouble for you to have called me at the office.'

Carrying the drinks back to the sofa he handed one to Victoria. She rested the glass on the arm of the sofa and proceeded to tell him the story of her friend, Lola, who had met up with one of her regular clients, a man called Gerald De Vere, and had woken the next morning to find him laying next to her, dead.

'She told me that the evening had been going well. She'd drunk a little - Gerry had drunk considerably more - then they went upstairs to have sex. Afterwards they both passed out. The next morning when she woke up, Gerry was dead and she'd been handcuffed to the bed, but couldn't remember Gerry doing it.'

'She knew straight away... that he was dead?'

'She said that she'd had a terrible headache, thought that the drink may possibly have been drugged because she really hadn't had enough for it to have affected her like that. She struggled to open her eyes, but when she did she could see his body out of the corner of her eye. He was just lying there, very still, and she couldn't hear him breathing. And the air smelt bad. She felt him and he was cold.'

'Could it have been a heart attack?'

'She wasn't sure. I've met him and it's a possibility - he was a big man. The sex may have been a little too, shall we say... vigorous for him.'

Dylan looked away from her and down into his lap. Death and other people's sexual proclivities always made him feel a little awkward.

'What did she do then?'

'She tried moving the bed but it was just too heavy, what with Gerry's extra weight on top as well.'

'So how did she get away in the end?'

'She remembered the hairpins.'

'Hairpins?'

'Gerry had given her two hairpins to hold her hair back with. She hadn't thought much of it at the time. Sometimes a client will want you to have a particular look that turns them on. Anyway, when she realised that they were there she knew that was her way out.'

Dylan looked puzzled.

25

'All she had to do was use one of the hairpins to undo the handcuff and she was free.'

'And she knows how to do that?'

'Mmm, it's quite easy. You bend the clip in the lock to make two right-angles and manipulate the small spring mechanism until the ratchet disengages and the rotating arm swings open. We know lots of things. You never know when you're going to need to get out of a scrape.'

'But I don't understand. If this client died of a simple heart attack what do you need me for?'

Dylan struggled to maintain a professional distance, when really the urge to move closer and caress her was eating him up inside.

'Because not too long after this happened, Chas, our boss, received a call from the police saying that Lola had been found dead on the beach at Brighton, drowned. They said she'd consumed vast quantities of alcohol.'

'I'm sorry to hear that, Victoria, but again what....'

'No... you don't understand,' she said, cutting him short. 'There's something wrong. What they're saying can't be right.'

'What do you mean? You don't believe it was misadventure?'

'Not for a minute. Lola never drank so much that she didn't know what she was doing - that was one of the few things she was quite sensible about.'

As Victoria spoke her fingers were drawing loose strands of blonde hair away from her face.

'What police station did the officer who called your boss say he was from?'

'He didn't. And Chas said he was too shocked from the news to think to ask.'

'Well, that's quite curious. What was the last thing she told you when you spoke to her?'

'She said that she was a little shaken about the Gerry business and she was going to meet someone. She asked if I could look after her next client for her. I told her I would.'

'And you don't know who this other person was that she was going to meet?'

'No, she never said and I didn't think to ask. She just said that she'd see me in a couple of days.' At this point Victoria's voice became a little strained. 'She did call Chas a little later. She'd forgotten to tell me something about the client I was covering for her.'

'She didn't call you herself?'

'No.'

'You didn't think that strange?'

'No. She phoned Chas to tell him she was taking a couple of days off and asked him to tell me.'

'I hate to ask you this but, you don't think that Chas may have something to do with it?'

'Chas? No, I don't think so. No. Definitely not.'

'Have you tried phoning her since then?'

'Yes. Her phone is switched off. I've left several messages.'

Dylan could see a tear forming in her eye as she reached down into her handbag and fumbled around for a tissue. He saw a vulnerability in her that he'd never seen before.

'I won't believe that she's dead, I just won't, and just after waking up to a dead client. I think that something is definitely going on, but I can't believe she's dead. You have to help me find out.'

Just at that moment the doorbell rang. The food had arrived. They ate as they talked and Victoria told Dylan everything she knew of her friend's recent movements. He watched as she pushed her food aimlessly around on the plate.

When they'd finished eating - she had eaten very little - she took a packet of cigarettes from her handbag, asking first if Dylan would mind her smoking. He thought this curious as she'd smoked in his flat many times before. He suggested lighting up the hookah but Victoria's response was instant and rebuking.

'No,' she barked. 'I've heard that smoking one of those things is like smoking two packets of cigarettes in one go.' Then her voice softened. 'But I will have another whisky though.'

Dylan poured some more whisky into Victoria's glass and topped up his own. As he did he couldn't help but let his glance linger long enough along the line of her leg so as to be noticed. Victoria smiled.

'You know that you're getting a freebie tonight, don't you?' she said in a husky drawl that, by its mere implication, Dylan thought especially seductive. 'And before you start thinking that I would be expecting the favour returned, I will be paying the going rate for your services.'

'It never even crossed my mind,' replied Dylan. 'Gorgeous you may be but a man has to make a living.' He took a sip of whisky. 'Perhaps we could negotiate a small discount though. Mate's rates.'

She stubbed out her cigarette in the tall stainless steel and marble pedestal ashtray that stood beside the sofa and drained her glass in one swallow. Leaning forward she went to place the glass back onto the coffee table.

'No,' said Dylan, stopping her. 'Take it with you to the bedroom. The night is still young, and I want a deposit.'

With the bottle of single malt and his glass in one hand, he reached down and took hold of her outstretched hand with the other. Pulling her up, he lead her towards the bedroom.

'And besides, there's a bottle of 18 year old Laphroaig that needs sampling.'

THREE

'Of course, maybe he give her the pins for her hair on purpose.' Tony said, as he sat at his very own desk the following morning.

'What do you mean?'

'Well, maybe he want her to escape, but he know that he is not suppose to let her go.'

'Wasn't supposed to let her go?'

'Maybe he was told to keep her there so she cannot get away, but he does not really trust the person who tell him this. So, just for some insurance he give her the pins so if something happen to him she work out how she can get away.'

'I'm assuming that you think it wasn't just a heart attack? You think he could have been involved in something that led to the death, or disappearance, of Victoria's friend too?'

'Could be, boss. Could be.'

Dylan considered Tony's theory. After all, it would be as good a starting point for him as any. If the dead man were involved in some way there may be clues at the house that could point the investigation in the right direction.

Tony piped up again. 'Do you think it is a little strange for the police to call her boss and not her family?'

Dylan thought about this and wondered why it hadn't registered with him when Victoria had mentioned it. It was true. Surely, if someone had been found dead it wouldn't be their boss who was informed, it would be their next of kin. It may not have occurred to Victoria as she would understandably have been in shock at this point. Chas had told her, as he had apparently told Lola, to say nothing about the dead man to anybody; Gerald De Vere was something of a public figure and Chas didn't want the agency implicated in any way. Dylan was now unsure as to the legitimacy of the police officer, either that or Chas was lying, in which case he would be well worth investigating.

*

There had been no reports of a death on any news broadcasts. Victoria had scoured the newspapers looking for anything about Lola's death but there was no mention of either death, anywhere. Not even on the regional news that covered the area where she had supposedly been found. It was then, she said, she'd decided to contact Dylan.

It was agreed that Dylan would begin his investigations by taking a drive out to look over De Vere's house in Hertfordshire the very next day. He didn't mention anything about investigating Chas at this point, as, from the way she had spoken about him, it seemed that Victoria trusted her boss.

Victoria said she would pay a visit to Lola's parents. Sidney and Prudence Douglas lived in the village of Bishops Hendron in Hertfordshire. If they had been notified of Lola's death Victoria could say she was there on the pretext of paying

31

her condolences. If not, she would have to come up with an off the cuff, excuse for her visit and, if appropriate, make discreet enquiries about anything they may know of Lola's recent movements.

Victoria said she didn't really hold out much hope of getting any important information out of Lola's parents as they were blissfully unaware of their daughter's true profession (she had lied to them by telling them that she was something in the City, and Victoria remarked to Dylan that in a way she was - Lola was quite something in lots of places).

Apparently Lola's room had remained untouched since the time she had moved out of her parents' home. Every now and again, when she wanted to escape from the secret life she'd made for herself and return to relative normality, she would go back there for a few nights and her life would revert to conventionality for a brief time. Her parents were totally ignorant of their daughter's life outside of their house in sleepy suburbia.

It was possible that she may have left something in the security of her old room that she didn't feel safe leaving in her London flat; if the mood in the house were favourable Victoria felt she may have the opportunity to look for it, whatever *it* may be.

When she had first arrived at the house, as she later explained to Dylan, Victoria had been surprised by the welcome she'd received. Prudence Douglas hadn't given the impression of being a mother grieving for her lost daughter. She opened the door with the expression of a smiling rabbit caught in headlights.

'Oh... Victoria.... Well, this is a nice surprise. We don't usually see you twice in such quick succession. Don't stand in the doorway, dear. Come on in.' Her cardigan came unbuttoned as her arms stretched out. 'Not that you're not welcome of course, dear. You're always welcome, you know that. It's just that usually we only get to see you every few months.'

Victoria planted a kiss on the older woman's cheek as she made her way through the doorway. She followed Prudence into the living room.

'Sit down, dear. I'm just tinkering about in the kitchen. Can I get you something to drink?'

'I'll just have some juice please. Orange, apple or tomato if you have it. I'm not fussed.'

'Of course, dear. Sidney's just out in his workshop, as usual. He's been very busy lately. He's been getting quite a few orders through.' She spoke without drawing breath as she disappeared into the kitchen.

For as long as Victoria could remember, Prudence had always been a woman on the move. She would be halfway through one domestic chore before embarking on the next; a skilled multi-tasker, her chores would constantly overlap. She would talk on the move, and stopping to chat wasn't an option. This would result in an irrevocable loss in transit of much of the conversation she may be having. Because her swiftness of movement didn't allow her brain to register what was coming out of her mouth, she seldom remembered what it was that she had said. This inability to repeat herself meant that conversations would invariably head off at a tangent until they were lost somewhere in the ether. On the odd occasion that she sat down she would be endlessly fidgeting. Her keen eyes would dart about, constantly in search of the next bit of dust to be attacked by the yellow cloth that she carried religiously.

Victoria could hear her moving about the kitchen as there were tell-tale sounds of utensils and appliances being shuffled about on work surfaces. She could hear the rumble of white goods - the woman was relentless in her washing and cleaning. There were only the two of them in the house, but the nature of Sidney's work undoubtedly ensured that the washing basket was always full.

This had certainly not been the scenario that Victoria had expected to find. It was important, though, to maintain a veil of normality.

'That's great. It'll stop him getting restless,' Victoria called from the living room. 'I'm off on another business trip abroad next week.' She knew as soon as the words were out of her mouth that she had spoken them too quietly.

'Sorry, dear. What was that? I've got the washing machine on in here and it makes a right old racket. Sidney keeps promising to buy me a new, quieter one.'

'No... I was just saying about another business trip abroad next week.'

This time she had shouted it.

'Girls nowadays, honestly. You won't rush

away today though, will you? You will stay for a spot of lunch, won't you?' Prudence implored eagerly.

Victoria considered the proposal. Refusal, followed by departure after just a soft drink, with no reason yet with which to authenticate her visit, may have alerted Prudence to something being untoward.

'Yes, of course I will,' Victoria told her.

Prudence emerged from the kitchen holding a glass of orange juice and stood in the doorway.

'It's only quiche and salad I'm afraid, dear - nothing fancy. But I know what you working girls are like. You probably don't eat lunch at all most days, that's why you're all so stick-thin nowadays. It's no good for you, being too skinny.'

As she turned to head back to the kitchen she suddenly remembered that she was holding the glass of orange juice in her hand. She turned back into the living room and handed the drink to Victoria.

'Urm... there was something, actually,' Victoria said, hesitantly.

'Yes dear, what is it?'

'I-It's just that I need to collect something...,' she stuttered. 'From Lola's room.'

'Lola's room?' Prudence's mind seemed to wander. 'Yes, of course, Lola's room... What is it you need to collect dear?'

Again Victoria stuttered. 'Oh, i-i-it's just... a book.'

She watched the older woman's expression for signs of doubt. Prudence's response was a smile of disappointment, as if she had known that

Victoria's visit, so relatively close to the previous one, would have an ulterior motive. Without a word she casually waved a hand, motioning to Victoria that she was free to go upstairs and retrieve the book she had quite obviously come for.

'You know best, dear. You know where it is. Everything is still where it's always been. I go in there occasionally and dust, but I haven't moved anything. You help yourself.'

Victoria tried not to make her relief too obvious as she got up from the chair. Smiling she made her way towards the stairs.

FOUR

Dylan's drive out to Hertfordshire was a pleasant one. It was a beautiful sunny day and the lanes that he negotiated were particularly leafy and captivating. He enjoyed driving down tree-lined avenues on bright days and glimpsing the sun's rays filtering through branches to illuminate sections of scenery.

He was nearing his destination. It was obvious that the house he was looking for was situated in an area of some affluence: huge imposing houses with gated, sweeping drives on which stood gleaming exotic sports cars. Landscaped gardens, professionally tended trees and topiaried bushes of infinite variety visible through gaps in walls too high to see over. He imagined that behind some of these walls would be the houses of Premier League footballers, hidden away from the scrutiny of the thousands that would watch them on a matchday.

The little blue Honda - bought for the purposes of his investigative work - purred along discreetly amongst the resident Porsches and Ferraris. This was how he liked it. When choosing a car, he had thought to purchase one that would attract the least amount of attention. Small Japanese cars were two a penny, and the shade of blue that he chose was particularly bland and uninteresting enough to ensure that eyelids would not be batted in its presence.

He had nearly reached his destination and as

37

he turned the final corner he could see the length of wall that ran along the front of Gerald De Vere's house. He slowed down as he got to the point where the wall began, staring at the set of black wrought-iron gates.

Dylan stopped on the opposite side of the road, a few yards past the gates. Craning his neck to look back at the house he could see that, once through the gates, the driveway veered to the right. Even if he moved further along another few yards he would still be able to see the front door and main sweep of the house, whilst hopefully avoiding the kind of suspicion that being parked directly opposite the entrance would attract. At least, that was his thinking.

He moved off at a snail's pace keeping a check on his angles. When he reached what he thought to be the optimum position he stopped again and killed the engine. It was still too early and too light to consider making a move. Although it was quiet, it was still generally a busy time of day and, unsure as to whether anybody would be in the house, he decided to wait.

Ahead of him, a little way down the road, he could see what looked like a pub sign. Displaying the image of a stag it beckoned him, as did all pub signs. Dylan being Dylan, he considered a stakeout from a pub infinitely more appealing than a stakeout whilst sitting in a car. Besides which, he could test the new gadget he had purchased for just such eventualities.

Reaching over he opened the glove compartment and took out a small black device shaped like a stumpy cigar. He looked back briefly towards the house, then reached back into the glove compartment and took out an attachment with a sucker pad on the bottom of it. He attached this to the bottom of the cigar-shaped device and positioned it on the dashboard so that it pointed towards the gates and the house beyond. From his inside jacket pocket he retrieved his mobile phone and searched for the application that he needed. He pressed on the touch screen in order to launch it and after a few seconds the screen cleared to form an image of the scene outside of the car. He manoeuvred the micro-camera into a position enabling him to monitor comings and goings through the black gates and around the visible section of the house.

Once he was satisfied that the camera was in position he abandoned the car, and glancing around to make sure that nobody had spotted him made his way to the pub.

The top-of-the-range spy camera came at a price. He was assured that it would work within a range of a quarter of a mile and the pub was certainly closer than that. He could have a drink and a bite to eat whilst keeping an eye on the house from the comfort of the hostelry. Now that was a plan, Dylan thought to himself.

*

The interior of The Stag looked cosy. A typical old village pub that enticed and provided comfort for as much time as the price of a pint could buy. He ordered a pint of McMullen AK and a ham ploughman's and settled down at a table in a quiet, unobtrusive corner. He was well away from the small throng of people congregating around the bar area, who he assumed were locals judging by their familiarity with the landlord.

Looking around, he took in the pub's pleasant ambience. The sun streamed in through the lead-latticed windows and reflected off of the brassware that hung from the oak beams just beneath the ceiling. Pictures of hunting scenes hung alongside photographs of scenes of the village from days gone by. There were also a few tacky photographs of celebrities, including one or two Premiership footballers, in an over-the-shoulder embrace with the landlord as they enjoyed his hospitality.

Three hours of covert surveillance passed and Dylan had witnessed no-one either entering or leaving the De Vere house. It was time to move - there was only so much soft drink that he could stomach. On top of this the landlord's cat had firmly attached itself to him, emotionally; sensing Dylan's love of all animals, it purred and mewed and rubbed itself up against him. He'd obliged by stroking its black and white fur continuously and soon grew quite attached to the creature. When the urge came upon him to liberate the furry bundle from its pub drudgery and take it home to a life of feline luxury in Belsize Park, Dylan knew it was probably time to leave. He gave the cat a last couple of strokes and then shooed it off. The cat hurried away, disappearing behind the bar, bemused at the swiftness and ease with which the human mood can turn.

Dylan would have to make his move and take a

chance that the house was empty. He picked up the couple of drained glasses that were still on the table and deposited them at the end of the bar.

'It's not like the old bottles y'know,' the landlord shouted from the other end of the bar. 'You don't get money back on the empties,' and he let out a big guffaw.

A couple of people standing at the bar joined in with the laughter. With just a smile and a nonchalant wave of the hand behind him, Dylan walked out of the pub.

*

It was now quite dark outside. The moon was pale and low and afforded hardly any light. The orangey-blue roof, painted by subdued street-lighting, was the only thing Dylan could make out of his car. He looked across and along the line of the wall laying boundary to the house. From where he stood he could see no light at all beyond it. It seemed to be in complete darkness.

As Dylan walked in the direction of the car he was looking to see where the easiest point of entry to the house might be. Climbing over the gate, he thought, was sure to make a noise. This was a quiet neighbourhood so the slightest noise was sure to bring one or two of the local residents meerkatting from behind their curtains. Besides which, there were extremely sharp looking finials running all along the tops of the gates, and the last thing he wanted was to get stuck on one of those - again. Having been trapped on an intrusive finial once before, during his childhood in

Porthmadog, the experience had remained with him.

Dylan remembered how he and a group of friends had broken into the school playground during the holidays one summer, for a game of football. Unknown to them they had been spotted by some of the local busy-bodies who had then gathered together to discuss what action was to be taken regarding the flagrant violation of municipal property. The police were subsequently called and their arrival caused a mass exodus of children back over the railings. On Dylan's attempt to evade capture, a stray finial had become painfully lodged in the button fly of his trousers and he was unable to get away. He didn't want a repeat of that acutely embarrassing incident. The mocking laughter of the police officers that helped him down was still ringing in his ears, even after all these years. He was also a lot older now, and the areas to which an errant finial could do severe damage had since expanded.

There was no getting over the wall either - it was around seven feet high - and being a little on the cumbersome side he wasn't a natural climber.

His line of vision followed the wall to the left of the gates but there was no gap between it and that of the neighbouring house. Although it was now quite dark, he followed the line of the wall to the right of the gate and could just make out that the wall came to an abrupt end, or at least carried on at a right-angle along the perimeter of De Vere's property.

Dylan continued walking and when he reached

his car he didn't stop but carried on past, a mere cursory glance ensuring that neither the car, or anything in it, had been tampered with. The nearer he got to the other end of the wall, the clearer he could make out the tall Leylandii hedge which stretched all the way along the frontage of the neighbouring house, effectively hiding it from view. This was it. There had to be a gap, if only a small one, between the wall and the hedge next-door.

There was.

When he broke through the hedge into the neighbouring front garden he saw that the wall carried along the side of De Vere's property, completely cutting it off from its neighbour. These were big, expensive houses and the residents fully exercised their entitlement to security and privacy.

Dylan noticed that there were one or two lights on in the neighbouring house, and coming from inside he heard the gruff growl of a dog. Judging by the sound it wasn't a small dog he could hear, and he felt it may be prudent to find a way over the wall before the owners decided that it was time for the dog's evening walkies.

He looked around for the best place to attempt his ascent, and as he turned his head he could not believe his luck. Resting against a nearby tree was a small wooden ladder. At the bottom of the tree there was evidence of branches having been cut down. It had obviously gotten too dark to carry on, so the ladder had been left there in order to carry on where they had left off, the next day. It wasn't very good practice where security was concerned, but it was certainly an incredible stroke of good fortune for Dylan.

The tree was a little exposed where it was; there were two security lights that were positioned on opposing corners of the house - just beneath the line of the roof - that illuminated the front of the property and cast a dull light around the area of the tree as well. Dylan felt that, if he were quiet enough, he should be able to retrieve the ladder and carry it the short distance to the wall without being detected. He could then make his way over without too much of a commotion. This was exactly what he did - climbing the few rungs once the ladder was in place as quickly as he could. From the top of the wall he stopped and looked around him. There was no indication that anyone had been alerted. He'd been pretty quiet when moving the ladder which, being wooden, wasn't as noisy as a metal ladder potentially would have been. He could still hear the dog barking inside, but most importantly there were no faces at the window. He pulled the ladder up slowly, and as quietly as possible, and slid it up and over the wall. Carefully lowering it back down the other side, he propped it up against the wall and pressed on it with his foot to make sure that it was firmly planted on the ground. He didn't want it to slide away as soon as he set foot on it.

He looked around the grounds of De Vere's house; there were no particular features to be seen as everything was in darkness. One or two faint edges of the house were visible, as was the pale outline of the bank of trees, made possible by remnants of light from the neighbouring property and a distant and dull, amber street light. There was no light showing at all from the front of the house itself. He looked towards the back of the house to see if there was any indication of an interior light reflecting into the back garden, but here too there was nothing to be seen.

This is it, thought Dylan to himself. This is where my very first case really begins.

Just then a rare moment of bravado came upon him and Dylan decided that he would jump down from the wall instead of using the ladder. It didn't look too high, just a few feet. Unfortunately the fall was heavier than he had anticipated, and as he met with the uneven ground beneath he stumbled, causing an awkward landing on his left foot, and resulting in what felt instantly like a spraining of his ankle.

He lay in the dark on the cold grass for several minutes, clutching at the damaged ankle. The pain was quite intense and Dylan could do nothing but bemoan his sudden change in fortune.

FIVE

Victoria's later description to Dylan of her visit to Lola's bedroom was almost clinical. She had described to him the small plaque on the door which simply read *Lola's Room,* saying that she was a little surprised that it had not been removed by her parents.

She looked around her. It was all so painfully tidy. She had remarked to Dylan that it would never have been in its current state of tidiness had it still been occupied.

There were a couple of framed prints on the wall, an antique floor standing mirror in one corner, a wicker waste-paper basket and a dark oak dressing table against the wall next to the window, which looked out onto the back garden and Sidney's carpentry workshop beyond. There was a single free-standing wardrobe, also dark oak, and a small bedside table, all made by Sidney's own hands. On the bedside table stood a lamp, and next to this a patterned-duvet-covered bed partially obscured by a number of scatter cushions. There were no other loose items anywhere. All surfaces, including the window shelf, were smooth and uncluttered, and quite obviously easier for the fastidiously tidy Prudence to dust and polish.

Victoria walked to the wardrobe, opened it and looked inside. There were items of clothing, but no internal compartments. She then moved over to the dressing table and opened each drawer. Apart from the usual stuff that women kept in dressing tables, there was nothing to arouse suspicion. Moving over to the bed, she sat delicately on the edge and looked down at the small bedside table which had one small top drawer and a larger compartment underneath. She opened the top drawer. The first thing she saw was a paperback of Graham Greene's collected short stories. She took the book out of the drawer, placed it on top of the table and perused the cover for a few seconds. She then looked back inside the drawer. There were bits of chewed gum and wrappers that had been tossed idly into the drawer - a teenage trait that had never been grown out of. It was clearly evident that Prudence respected her daughter's privacy when dusting around in her abandoned room, as the rubbish remained undisturbed. At the back of the drawer Victoria could see a personal CD player. Pulling it free of a piece of hardened gum attached to it she opened it to reveal a disc of the music of Elgar and Vaughan Williams by the Scottish Chamber Orchestra.

There were quite a few pieces of hardened chewing gum stuck to the inside of the drawer. With the hint of a smile and a disapproving shake of the head she pulled the drawer out a little further, following all the smooth pieces of pink synthetic rubber. She remembered reading somewhere once that this was exactly what chewing gum was made from – synthetic rubber.

Just then she saw it. On the back panel of the drawer was something small and black. She pulled the drawer out completely, revealing a micro SD card pressed into yet more gum, quite obviously in order to conceal it. Victoria smiled to herself. This was just what she was looking for. She tried to pick the miniature plastic card from the solidified resin but it held fast and she didn't want to damage it. Instead, she decided to prize the gum away from the panel with a nail file, with the card still on it. The card could be removed from the gum later when she had a little more time - she didn't want to spend too long upstairs, fearing this may arouse Prudence's suspicion.

Victoria put the small drawer back and slid it closed. The larger compartment beneath was opened to reveal several books on generic art. She told Dylan that she had thought this strange as Lola had never really shown much of an interest in art before. She took them out one at a time and flicked briefly through each, then, placing the last of them back, she closed the door to the compartment. She could hear Prudence downstairs, cheerfully humming a tune. It was vaguely familiar but she couldn't quite place it.

Victoria pressed the SD card, complete with gum, into the pocket of her jeans, noticing that she had left the paperback on top of the table. Reaching down to pick it up she saw that there was a very small gap in between two of the pages. As she opened the book something fell out onto the bed. It was a ticket for entry to the zoo at Regent's Park.

'Victoria, dear, lunch is ready,' she heard Prudence call out from the bottom of the stairs. 'Don't be too long, dear, otherwise the quiche will have cooled down.'

It gave her a start and she quickly picked the ticket up from the bed where it had fallen and placed it back in its original position in the book. Holding onto the book, she got up from the bed and made her way back down the stairs. Cold quiche? Perish the very idea, she thought, entering the kitchen. Whatever next? Was this really the woman who had named her daughter after a Kinks' song?

*

The tiled path that led by the side of the house was in darkness and Dylan trod very carefully as he made his way to the rear. His ankle - having been rested for a while - was still uncomfortable, but the pain had subsided a little and he was able to put some weight on it again.

He got to the back of the house and could make out the trees at the far end of the garden backlit only by the vaguest shaft of light, but now clearly defined. He considered that this may be another exit route, if required. However, what concerned him more at that moment was finding an entry point. Through the pervading half-light he could just make out the shape of a set of French windows. When he reached them he tried to push down the handle of one of the doors but it wouldn't budge. He tried the handle of the other door and to his amazement it moved and he felt the door loosen. Unbelievable, thought Dylan. His very first case and this really was just too easy. Perhaps somebody, somewhere, was trying to tell him that this was indeed the job that he had been put on this Earth to do; all afternoon in a pub, a conveniently abandoned ladder, and now an open door - sprained ankle aside, of course. He was the little boy again, riding a bike unassisted for the first time. And besides, little boys sprained their ankles falling off bikes all the time, he beamed to himself.

With the renewed confidence that this little piece of good fortune had brought with it all the initial trepidation he had felt, at taking on his first case, just fell away from Dylan like the shedding of a heavy, oppressive skin. With a defined boldness he swung open the door and stepped defiantly inside the gloomy house, having abandoned due consideration to discretion.

Inside, it was dark. Very dark.

SIX

Dylan carefully closed the door behind him. Peering through the darkness he reached into his pocket for his mobile phone. The phone had no torchlight facility, but as it was so dark the light given off by the screen was sufficient enough to allow him to see a fair distance in any direction. He could just make out a section of wall around twenty feet or so in front of him on which hung several paintings in perfect symmetry. He was by no means an expert on art, but to a philistine such as himself they looked expensive; they were not paintings of dogs playing poker or a local artist's depiction of the pub over the road.

He made his way hesitantly through the room avoiding the coffee table replete with champagne bottles, one of which was on its side, and half-full glasses, a sofa and chairs, and the odd stiletto shoe that had been discarded in the heat of passion. He emerged into the hallway. Spotting the kitchen to his left, he peered inside. There was nothing to be seen even in the relative gloom, except for kitchen related furniture, appliances, crockery and utensils. There were of course drawers that could be searched, but who keeps anything incriminating in the kitchen, he thought, rightly or wrongly. Should he have time, and the inclination, he would have a quick look around on his way out. This was how Dylan rolled.

He turned around and headed for the other remaining doorway which led off the hallway.

Looking inside he saw that this was quite clearly the main reception room as it seemed infinitely more formal than the room through which he had just entered the house. He didn't linger for long though, as through the murk he could see the staircase, and he had already decided that he would start his search upstairs and get that out of the way first, then return to search the lower floor afterwards. If there was something incriminating to be found, it would always be found in a bedroom drawer or closet. That was fact. And, it was Dylan's thinking that, if interrupted, it would naturally be easier for him to make good his escape from the ground floor than it would be from upstairs. Of course, this rather relied upon the unexpected interruption occurring later, rather than sooner. After all, in the films they were never interrupted at the beginning of a search. What would be the point of that? They always had the time to have a good look around first before they were disturbed.

It was always best to have a plan A with which to start any operation, even though on occasion recourse to plan B may be necessary in order to finish it. Dylan's plan B was a simple one – *run*. Wherever you are just run. Overwhelming moments of bravado, such as the one that resulted in the spraining of his ankle, were a rare occurrence in Dylan's life. Dylan the Dauntless was never to be an epithet by which he lived his life; gormless on occasions maybe, but very rarely dauntless.

As he made his way up the stairs, lighting his way before him, he could see that there were a further two doors coming off of the section of the hallway on the other side of the central staircase. These two rooms he would also inspect upon his return to the ground floor.

Dylan also noticed, even in the semi-darkness, that all of the walls in the house were adorned with artwork, both classic and modern. He concluded that Gerry was obviously a collector. Victoria may have mentioned this to him, but in his defence, on occasions that her lips were particularly rouged and alluring, he was not always receptive to the words that came out of her mouth. He would never have admitted that to her though.

For now it was onwards and upwards and Dylan cautiously climbed the steps, like a modern-day Dalek with vertical movement capability, his free hand on the rail for stability. Approaching the top of the staircase he lifted the phone in order to illuminate the landing and could make out five doors, all of which, except one, were ajar to varying degrees. He completed his ascent to reach the top and was immediately hit by an unpleasant smell. Making his sweep from left to right he arrived at the first room and pushed the door slowly open so that the gap was just wide enough to comfortably allow his, not too insubstantial, frame through. Dylan would have been the first to admit that, although he didn't considered himself to be overweight, he did have a fair amount of flesh on his bones, due mainly to his varied diet, both liquid and otherwise.

Waving the phone around the room in random

fashion, he could clearly see that this was a guest bedroom. Everything was pristine, neat and tidy, and there were absolutely no possessions of a personal nature to indicate that it was a bedroom in regular use. It was certainly a large room because he could only just make out the wall at the far end, but not large enough to be the room that Victoria had described to him. He also noted that this wasn't the room that the smell was coming from because, even though it was present in the room, the odour was not as strong as it had been out on the landing. He had a quick look around the few pieces of furniture inside and, finding nothing of any significance to draw his attention, made his way back out onto the landing.

He found the second room to have a similar layout and décor as the first, and it too was bereft of anything suspicious or incriminating, or particularly odorous, so he moved onto the third room.

This was the room around which the smell seemed strongest. Dylan stood in the doorway with one hand over his nose. Whatever it was that was contributing the foul smell was almost certainly in this room. He swung the phone in an arc from left to right, its light falling in-turn upon a full-length mirror, an easy chair, some built-in wardrobes, a dressing table, a large bay window with its curtains drawn and partially hidden by a screen, and finally another easy chair. They were all quite a distance away as this room was far larger than the previous two.

Suddenly wary that there may be somebody

hiding behind the screen he trained the light back towards it and could see to his relief, through the few inches gap between the bottom of the screen and the floor, no evidence of shoes or human feet. The phone then continued on its arc, making out an Ottoman which was nestling beneath the window at the farthest end of the room.

As the faint light continued its sweep it hit the foot of the bed and crept slowly further up. In that moment Dylan saw something that he would never forget, something that instantaneously provoked an icy chill that rose up within him with such ferocity that it froze every inch of his body, effectively rooting him to the spot on which he stood, incapable of movement. He had located the source of the smell.

On the bed lay two bodies, pale and exposed, and ultimately lifeless. One was a man of immense proportion who seemed almost peaceful in repose; the skin stretched across his body was faintly marbled and displayed slight blistering in places - the other, a young woman, brunette. Her body did not look to be in the same state of decay as the man's. She had one arm by her side and the other stretched behind her, handcuffed to the brass headboard.

Taking a few seconds to thaw from his initial shock, Dylan moved tentatively towards the bed, the light held firm on the shapes of the two bodies lying peacefully, side by side. The man was surely Gerald De Vere, thought Dylan, and commanding exactly the same position that Victoria said Lola had found him in when she awoke a couple of days ago. As he approached the bed he concentrated his gaze on the female by his side. Although the light was gloomy he could see that she had been beautiful, only death now seemed to have given her beauty a strange, ethereal quality.

With a composure he struggled to maintain, he slowly reached into the inside pocket of his jacket and pulled out the small photograph that Victoria had given him. He looked at it in the dull light then squinted back at the dead girl on the bed for confirmation. It was not a great picture - a little out of focus and taken from a distance it was the only one that she had, but it looked enough like the girl whose body now lay before him to convince Dylan that it was one and the same person. He had no time to stand and ponder; he had to take a photograph as verification for Victoria. He was being paid to find the proof after all.

It was just at that moment that the screen on the phone, which was set to five minutes, decided to timeout, and for a short while he stood at the foot of the bed on which lay two dead bodies. The barely unbroken darkness pressed in on him. Dylan's anxiety began in his feet and shot quickly up through his body to his head which was silently screaming cacophonous thoughts.

Standing there in the dark he found himself back in the slate mines at Blaenau Ffestiniog. Down in the depths of the mine, Dylan and his friend Ianto had decided to break away from the rest of the group of children on a school trip, and look around a few of the tunnels that had been closed off to visitors. Sneaking off, they headed down into one of the restricted tunnels and were spotted by an employee of the mine. Appreciating a joke himself, the man caught up with the two boys and thought he'd teach them a lesson by turning out the lights in that section of the mine, effectively leaving them in total darkness. The sheer panic they had felt in the already claustrophobic atmosphere of the tunnels was made worse by the booming voice in the darkness which eerily welcomed them.

'Hello boys,' it called out, deep and other-worldly. 'Come to visit me in my tunnels, have you?'

This tipped the two boys over the edge. When the lights were switched back on moments later they didn't dare look behind them to where the voice had come from, but ran instead, as fast as their legs would carry them, back in the direction from which they'd come, and the security of their teachers and schoolmates.

For what seemed an eternity, but was in fact just a few seconds, Dylan sensed himself to be in that same darkness, and he quickly reached across with his free hand and shakily pressed the power button on the phone. The restored glow of the screen took more than a few moments to relieve his anxiety. He quickly took the photograph.

Just at the moment when the flash completely illuminated the room, Dylan thought he heard the sound of a creak coming from somewhere in the house. It sounded as if it may have been from one of the rooms downstairs, possibly one of those that he had noticed at the beginning of his ascent of the staircase. Although it may have just been the wind, or pipes, it was also possible that there was somebody else in the house. He froze again as thoughts of his next move scurried around his head. There had to have been someone else in the house in the last day or so, a someone who placed Lola's, now defunct, body back next to that of De Vere's. Maybe, thought Dylan, whoever it was had only just completed the task before he'd arrived and, unable to leave, was still lingering somewhere in the dark. They could be skulking in the shadows waiting to make their move at this very moment.

Dylan came to the swift conclusion that his constitution was not robust enough to deal with unforeseen and potentially unfriendly confrontations at that moment – or at anytime really - not on top of what he had just seen. He decided to put plan B into effect. He ran. His search was over. He had found the object of his quest.

Pointing the swathe of light directly in front of him he made his way surprisingly quickly out of the room. He still felt the pain from his ankle but he was now moving on pure adrenalin, and could think about pain at a more convenient time. Now, with the possibility he may cut through a murderer with the glow from his phone, the darkness seemed somehow more ominous.

He made his way hurriedly back down the stairs and across the room through which he had entered, giving the coffee table an agonising thwack en route, sending the bottle of champagne that was on its side rolling onto the carpet. More pain, but really no time now he thought, as he stumbled on. Swinging open the French windows he staggered out.

Once he was outside in the garden he decided to slow his pace - the aggravated pain in his ankle, and the new coffee table-induced injury to his right shin, helped him to come to this decision. He thought also that his screams, if he had to resort to it, would at least be heard outside.

SEVEN

'That's not her,' Victoria whispered.

Dylan showed her the picture that he had taken of the two bodies on his phone. The relief was evident on her face.

'Not her?'

'No. I'll admit,' she conceded, looking at the photograph, 'it does look very much like her. But, it's not her.'

'Are you a hundred per cent sure? I mean... the light wasn't very good in there.'

'Yes. Absolutely. I'm sure.'

'Then the question is, why has somebody gone to the trouble of placing the body of a girl who looks like Lola next to De Vere's body? And perhaps more frighteningly, was she killed and put there just because she bears a resemblance to your friend?'

A prolonged silence ensued until Dylan finally broke it.

'You really are sure it's not her?'

'For the last time,' Victoria cried. 'I know that it's not Lola in the bloody photograph, lying there in that bed. I know because Lola's got a small tattoo of a rose right next to her... her intimate part.'

Dylan zoomed in on the aforementioned part of the dead girl's body.

'Oh, right..., no. The lighting's not great, but I'm pretty sure there's no tattoo on any intimate part of this body.'

Dylan lingered longer on the photo than Victoria thought was strictly necessary.

'Having a bloody good look!!!'

He quickly and awkwardly wrenched the phone away from his gaze and practically threw it onto the coffee table.

'I was just making sure,' he said defensively. 'I'm not a bloody pervert. And anyway, a body starts changing once it dies; chemicals and stuff start working, and destroying it from the inside; the skin changes. Chemicals may have rubbed out the tattoo. You never know.'

'After a couple of days? She would have to be a skeleton before that tattoo disappeared.'

'Fair enough,' not wishing to prolong a battle he knew he could not win, and to avoid an icy atmosphere forming in the room, he yielded. 'My ankle has started hurting again. Give it a rub for us, will you?'

A smile, albeit faint, returned to Victoria's winsome features.

*

By the next morning Dylan's ankle had swollen to almost twice its usual size. Victoria had stayed the night, recounting the story of her visit to the Douglas' house. She had wrapped the ankle in an elasticated bandage and applied a cold compress. He was to keep it elevated with the support of a cushion.

Knowing this would put him out of what action there was to be had for a day or two, he telephoned Tony and told him to come by the house in order to collect the office keys. He hadn't yet got around to having a spare set cut for him.

When Tony arrived, Victoria opened the door to let him in. He stood in the doorway perusing the beauty before him from beneath the rim of his Trilby. He removed the hat and tilted his head.

'Good morning, young lady,' he said respectfully in his smooth anglicized Tuscan cadence. 'I come to collect some keys from the boss.'

Victoria melted in the Latin heat of his voice.

'You must be Tony. Do come in. That is a lovely accent you have there. Whereabouts in Italy are you from?'

'Montalcino, near Siena. Famous for the wine, one of the finest in all Italy, Brunello. Do you know it?'

'No, I'm afraid not. Not the place anyway, but I have drunk the wine.' She let out a tiny giggle. 'Please, follow me.'

She led him into the living room where Dylan lay prostrate on the sofa, with his bandaged ankle resting at a forty-five degree tilt on the cushion.

'Ah, Tony. Allora, cosa sta succedendo?' (Ah, Tony. So, what's happening?)

Tony looked down at Dylan, bemused, and started rotating the Trilby around in his hands. A possible sign of nervousness, thought Dylan.

'You been practising, boss. Very good. What does it mean?'

Tony maintained his composure, and the edges of his mouth curled to a faint smile.

Dylan joined in the game, if indeed it was one,

and smiled also. He decided not to dwell though, and changed the subject.

'Is that today's paper you have there?'

'Sure, boss. I had a quick look through, but I leave it for you and I pick up another one on my way. I think there is something which you perhaps find very interesting in there.'

Tony threw the newspaper onto the coffee table, and in the same move picked up the keys.

'I drop off the keys after I finish work. I hope you feel better soon, boss. And don't worry, anything I don't know I will call you at once.'

Dylan felt there may have been the slightest hint of sarcasm in his tone, but he couldn't be totally sure. Then again he couldn't be sure about anything regarding his new assistant, yet. It was early days, but there were certainly more layers to the Trilby-wearing Italian that were yet to be peeled back.

Once Tony had left, Dylan picked up the newspaper and started flicking through it. When Victoria returned from the kitchen, where she had been preparing two steaming hot mugs of tea, she found the newspaper opened out on the coffee table.

The page displayed, in bold lettering, the headline: FAMOUS ART DEALER FROLICS WITH CALL GIRL.

There were three photographs of the famous art dealer in question, Gerald De Vere, with a young girl on a beach. Dylan recognized De Vere as being the male body on the bed.

'That's the client, Gerry,' Victoria said. 'The

dead guy. And that... is Lola.'

She looked away from the photograph, visibly upset.

'I recognized the man, but how can you be sure that's Lola and not the dead girl? They're not exactly clearly focused pictures. Obviously taken from some distance.'

'Just call it women's intuition. And I'm sure that if you had a magnifying glass you would see the tattoo that I mentioned.'

Dylan reached over and pulled the newspaper towards him, leaning in to have a closer look.

'Hey!' cried Victoria, resentful of her best friend having been laid bare in the pages of a sleazy tabloid.

'I was just looking for the tattoo... honestly.'

'But what do you think this all means?' asked Victoria. 'That is definitely Gerry. And that's Lola with him. The dead girl that you saw laying next to him wasn't Lola, just someone who looked like her.'

'Then we have to work on the basis that your friend is still alive, Victoria.'

She slumped down onto the sofa, just missing Dylan's foot by inches. This caused the cushion that it was resting on to bounce up then down again, causing him to wince. He tried to hide this from her, but she noticed the pained expression on his face.

'Oh, I'm sorry,' she said softly.

Her eyes were starting to moisten as she tried desperately to fight back tears of frustration. It was a losing battle. Lifting both legs off of the sofa and placing them gingerly on the floor Dylan sat up and placed his arm over her shoulder.

'Look, I know that you're upset, but I promise you that I will get to the bottom of whatever is going on here. After all, that's what you're paying me for. It's my first case so if I screw this one up I may not get another one. But I must say that you have to be prepared for what we might find, because it may not be nice, one way or another.' Then he intuitively added, 'I have a sneaking suspicion that the story in the newspaper will be followed up in the next couple of days.'

Victoria lifted her head, which had been nestling in the hollow of his shoulder, and looked deep into his eyes.

EIGHT

Dylan's intuition, such as it was, didn't let him down. The very next day the same tabloid newspaper carried the story of the art dealer, fresh from the previous day's frolicking, found dead, together with a prostitute, at his Hertfordshire home.

Tony picked up two broadsheets and a tabloid from Richardson's and was making his way to Dylan's flat to collect the keys. He assumed that Dylan's leg was still quite painful and this was the reason he hadn't opened up the office. Today Tony would be getting a spare set cut at the key cutter on Haverstock Hill.

Just as Tony passed one of the many fast-food restaurants in the area, that ensured the indiscriminate diners of Belsize Park did not go hungry, he saw the familiar figure of Dylan hobbling along towards him.

'Hey, boss! Where you think you going?' he reprimanded a panting Dylan.

'I'm going in to work, Tony. Victoria's gone and I can't stand another day at home. Help me, will you? My bloody foot's killing me.'

Tony quickly moved to support him. Dylan rested his arm on Tony's shoulder to alleviate some of the weight that he was putting on his injured ankle. They made it to the door on the ground floor and Tony helped Dylan slowly and warily up the stairs. When they got into the office Dylan sat down in his chair and threw the set of keys to Tony.

'There you go, old son. Go and get a spare set cut... actually, make it two sets, will you? Just in case we need them at some point.'

Tony caught the keys. Moving towards the door he was halted in his stride.

'Hold on,' called Dylan. 'Leave the papers here, will you?'

'Oh, yes... of course. I bought them for the office.' Tony lay the newspapers down gently on Dylan's desk and, tapping the top one, said, 'Very interesting, boss.'

With the parting words 'I go now,' Tony turned and left the office.

Dylan watched the older man leave, and for several moments after he had gone he watched the space that he had vacated as he listened to him going down the stairs. He was a very intriguing man, thought Dylan. Very calm and unassuming, everything he said or did was done so in a precise way, as if premeditated, yet natural. He was appealing and distinguished; a man that, Dylan understood, could hold a certain attraction for women. Not just for his accent or his silvered hair, but for the way he conducted himself and the way he treated everyone around him with great respect. Dylan knew this from the way that Victoria had been around him - a giggly schoolgirl with a teacher crush. Dylan had admitted to himself at being more than a little jealous of her reaction. In the three short days that he'd known him, Dylan assessed Tony to be a man staid in his ways, but so, because he knew through experience those ways to be right. In situations that required careful handling, there were the wrong people, those that lacked fortitude, and with aggression as their automatic response, and there were the right people, people like Tony. Dylan admired the very restrained, all-knowing Tony, and saw him as the potential father-figure that had been missing from his life. But first he had to gradually unravel him and ensure that he was indeed the man he thought him to be. A man he could rely upon implicitly. After all, he had literally just walked in off the street. Because of his relationship with his mother, and a father that he had never known, Dylan had always found difficultly in trusting the older generation, choosing instead to rely on his peers. There was still the mystery of Tony's lost language of course, but that alone did not a dishonest man make. And even the most virtuous, he felt, should be allowed the recreation of mischief sometimes.

Dylan pulled the uppermost newspaper towards him - it was the tabloid. So he was sure to start with the more sensationalist slant on whatever the interesting story was that Tony had alluded to. He flicked quickly through and on page 5 was the story in question. ART DEALER FOUND DEAD AFTER SEX GAMES ran the headline, and underneath, a photograph of De Vere taken at some function or other.

This was the story that Dylan had expected, he knew it was coming, he just hadn't anticipated it coming so early. He thought that there may have been a few more days between the revelations of the seaside frolic and the breaking of this story. Any investigation now would have to be carried out much more stealthily as the police would surely be looking into it as well.

The story alluded to the deaths having occurred as a result of a sex game that had gone wrong - classic tabloid, Dylan thought. They gave no indication that there were any circumstances surrounding the deaths seen as anything other than misadventure. The implication was that it was the same girl as in the previous days photographs and that she had died by suffocation during some sort of fetishistic sex game shortly before De Vere had had a heart-attack and died himself; a clear-cut, open and shut case with no extenuating circumstances.

They were judge and jury. They had summed up in four words, "Sex games gone wrong" and it was now only left for a senior hack to announce the verdict and spew out some inane journalistic rhetoric that the unfortunate De Vere would be forever remembered by. Surely, even with the dark secrets hidden behind his public persona, De Vere did not deserve this rubbish.

Dylan scanned the two broadsheets for a contrasting viewpoint but was unable to find anything at all. He flicked through each paper three times but found nothing. Strange, he thought, that one solitary paper should carry a story as sensational as this, surely the press as a whole would have been notified. Maybe the others would carry the story tomorrow. Maybe they had all received it too late to go to press for this morning's edition.

He read through the story in the tabloid again, this time with greater brevity. This wasn't difficult as the quality of the piece did not demand a great level of concentration. Analysing it, he came to the conclusion that it was indeed a very scant piece of reporting, put together from very limited information. Its sensational headline gave it the desired effect - designed to ensnare any passing reader and leave them hungry for a more in-depth story, which would inevitably follow in the next day's edition. Dylan seldom felt his cynicism unjustified, but when it came to the press, never.

'Ah,' said Tony, upon his return, 'you have been reading it.'

'Yes. But I was just trying to work out why the story is in one newspaper only.'

'What? You looked through the other two?'

'Of course I did. I couldn't find anything.'

Tony flicked through the first broadsheet and opened it out on the desk when he had located the page he was looking for. He did the same with the second broadsheet, and left it at an angle to the first.

Dylan pulled the top broadsheet towards him, and tucked away in the bottom left-hand corner of one of the pages he noticed a single paragraph story with the headline: CANADIAN OIL SANDS DEAL IN JEOPARDY. He read how negotiations for the sale of Canadian oil to Britain were in danger of collapsing after one of those involved in securing the deal was found dead at his home, namely Gerald De Vere. Written in a very low-key way, it was the reason why he had not noticed it at first glance.

He opened the second broadsheet. Again the

story was covered in much the same way as the first. Two paragraphs this time, no more. There was no mention of anybody else having been found. The indication was that De Vere had died alone at home, the victim of a heart-attack.

Dylan looked over at Tony who was now standing by the kettle waiting for it to boil.

'Why the two different stories d'you think? It makes you wonder who's been feeding these newspapers.'

'But we know which one is true, boss. You see with your own eyes.'

'Yes, but technically neither is true. The tabloid story is trying to make out that the girl found with him was the same girl that he was photographed with on the beach, but we know that not to be true.'

Having looked through a few other on-line newspapers, it seemed that the official story was that De Vere had died alone. The original tabloid had cried out in big bold lettering that he had not.

'You know what I think, boss? I think that maybe somebody, or somebodies, got a secret... what is the word?... Ahhh... agenda. That's it.'

'I tend to agree with you, Tony. But who are they? And what are we gonna do about it? And what's more, our job is to help find Victoria's friend. How is she involved with all this?'

An idea then occurred to Dylan.

'Hey, hold on a minute, you have a cousin who works for the newspaper, don't you?'

'Yes, Nuncio, but he only work for the local paper, not the big ones.'

'But maybe he has some contacts at one of the

71

nationals. Can't you ask him? Maybe he can make some discreet enquiries as to where they got the story from.'

'Sure. I give him ring now.'

Dylan watched Tony dial the number and waited for him to speak, hoping that he would slip up and speak to his cousin in his native tongue. However, Tony was either too good at the game or genuine.

Disappointingly, Tony spoke only English, but Nuncio did indeed have a contact that could possibly find out what they needed to know and said he would call back as soon as he had some information. This sounded encouraging.

Just after twelve o'clock midday, the telephone rang. In the hope that it was his cousin, Tony answered it. It wasn't. Tony handed the phone over.

'I'm worried, Dylan.' He sensed the trepidation in Victoria's voice. 'I've just spoken to Chas and he said he had a call from someone who told him that Lola's decided to go away for a few days. Chas said that it sounded like the same person that claimed to be the policeman. Charlie's not happy. He knows now that the original call was definitely a hoax, but he doesn't know if it's Lola messing around or someone's messing around with Lola. Either way he's pissed off. He even said that he was going to call the police, which is *really* not like Chas. But I've managed to stall him. I had to tell him I had someone looking for her, though. He wasn't much happier after that because he hates anybody poking about in his

72

business.'

'Good girl. Look, it could be nothing. She may have just decided that it was best to get away for a little while, until this whole thing blows over. If she's innocent she won't want all the exposure she'd be getting, will she?'

'But why wouldn't she call me and let me know?'

Dylan looked over at Tony whose attention seemed to be drawn by something he was watching out of the window.

'Dylan, I'm really worried now that she's got herself into real big trouble and won't be able to get herself out of it. She's strong in some ways, but she can be weak in others and I can't understand why she would have got involved in whatever it is. And without me knowing about it. She's my best friend. I still don't know for sure whether she's alive or dead.'

'That's what I'm going to find out for you. We don't actually know yet if she's not just a victim in all of this.'

Dylan was desperate to allay Victoria's fears, but he had already resigned himself to the opinion that her friend was no victim but smack bang in the middle of whatever it was that was playing itself out before them. The police would soon figure out that the girl in the beach photographs and the girl found dead with De Vere were not one and the same. They would then start investigating the first girl and sooner or later come up with Lola's name. However, he couldn't admit that to Victoria, at least not until they had found some sort of evidence that was cast-iron guarantee of Lola being complicit in the affair.

'Oh, by the way,' said Victoria. 'There was something I forgot to tell you about the other night. Something I found in Lola's room. I only remembered when I was going through my pockets before putting my jeans in the wash and found it.'

'What is it?'

'An SD card that I found at the very back of one of the drawers. It was deliberately stuck there with chewing gum so it's obvious it was something that she didn't want anyone to find.'

'What's on it?'

'I don't know. It's too large for my phone. I thought that I could bring it over to the office and we could look at it together.'

'Why don't you come over tonight?' I've kinda got used to having you stop over in the last few days.'

'I can't tonight. I've got a client.'

Although she couldn't see it, Dylan's morale had just collapsed onto the carpet.

'I've got to work. I'm a working girl. I have to earn money to pay you for a start.'

Dylan's head suddenly reared up.

'Give up the escort business and come and work for me.'

He knew already what her answer would be.

'What? You are joking. I'm the only client that you have at the moment. To be truthful, I don't even know why you need Tony. How can you afford to pay him?'

'You know that I've got money.'

'Yes, but not to throw away.'

'I won't be throwing it away. The work will come, I know it. And there will be work where I can use a beautiful girl like you.'

'What! I'm no honey-trap, Dylan.'

'No, not like that. Well... not exactly.'

'Look, let's just see what happens with this case. And anyway, I don't want to piss Charlie off any more than he is right now. He's just as confused as me about this whole Lola thing. Look, I'll be in your office around three. And I'll see you then.'

The line went dead.

Dylan slowly placed the handset back down, and still deep in thought looked across at Tony who was still looking out of the window.

'What are you looking at? You've been staring out of that window for ages now.'

'I'm not sure, boss, but I think there's somebody watching the office. Since early this morning, I keep seeing the same guy every time I look out of the window. He's across the road sitting outside the café. Every time I look, he's there. And thing is, I think he keeps looking up here. There,' he said, pointing out of the window at something Dylan couldn't see from his desk, 'he just look now.'

Tony edged quickly away from the window, for fear of being spotted, as Dylan pulled himself gingerly up from the desk and made his way to the window. There was only one person sitting at an outside table at the café. Dylan wasn't sure whether the man was trying to look conspicuous on purpose or not, but he would have looked more at home in Belize than Belsize Park. He was wearing a stone coloured suit, light blue shirt and a particularly flamboyant multi-coloured tie. He was reading a broadsheet newspaper from which he would periodically look up towards the window from which he was being watched. If his remit called for discretion he was sadly lacking in his task.

After a few seconds he lifted his head and, slowly putting the newspaper down on to the table, gave the pair a full-on stare. There was a distance between them of two wide pavements, wide enough for several café tables and chairs, whilst still allowing ample room for passing pedestrians, and a busy main road. However, the brace of investigators standing either side of the window were convinced they had been spotted, enough so as to instinctively, and simultaneously, jerk their heads backwards when he looked up.

Having left a few seconds grace they looked first at each other then back out of the window again. The stone coloured suit weaved its way in between the stream of cars as it crossed Haverstock Hill and came towards them. Both men turned apprehensively towards the frosted glass of the office door and listened for the inevitable creak of the door at ground level, followed by the advance of footsteps on the stairs.

NINE

Dylan's mother, Angharad Morgan, had been an object of great beauty and distraction to the men of the town of Porthmadog, or at least to those with intention in their eyes. The reputation which she had built from a young age, she was to wear around her neck like a millstone for the remaining days of her life. A reputation built on providing succour to one sex whilst systematically making it her mission in life to alienate the other.

Having won the title of Miss Gwynedd, she had become the face of commerce for the region, and it was widely agreed that she had thereafter thrown herself wholeheartedly into this task. Her duties, which included opening stores and meeting visiting dignitaries, had one day brought her into contact with a Saudi Arabian businessman visiting Wales in order to negotiate the purchase of top quality slate for building projects back in the Middle East. Relations between the two had soon transcended mere commerce, although it could be said that it was commerce of sorts, and one night, in a hotel on the Isle of Anglesey, alcohol inevitably interacted with uncontrollable lust and Dylan was conceived. Having concluded his business in the area, the businessman departed to return to his home and family.

However, he had never forgotten the Welsh beauty, or his responsibility to the child that he had fathered. What Angharad had not realised was the extent of the businessman's wealth and the esteem in which he had held her. Upon his unfortunate, and premature, demise Angharad had been prominently named amongst a list of his beneficiaries. Subsequently, it transpired that he had left her a considerable sum of money and a rather large property in the Hampstead area of London – one of many properties he owned throughout the world. It was, she was informed, a token of his enormous affection and a legacy for the child to whom his duty was unbound.

Taking courage from her new found wealth, Angharad tore through Porthmadog society expressing the utmost disregard for family, friends and relative unknowns. Having made sure that she would leave behind as much emotional upheaval as possible she gathered what few belongings she possessed that would be suitable for her new standing in life and, along with the reluctant thirteen year-old Dylan, departed for their inheritance in London.

In the ensuing years it was true to say that she had spared no expense in her quest for enjoyment. Nor so in compensating for her absence from her son by ensuring that the most belligerent nannies and the austerest of boarding schools were secured in order to oversee Dylan's journey towards manhood. But time passed and hedonism took its toll, and whilst still only in her middle years she had arrived at the terminus that all things living are inevitably destined for.

Dylan, who was by now fast approaching his thirtieth birthday, had thought to be by his mother's side when notified of her impending death, but the thought quickly passed. California was quite a distance. And so, unsure whether his commitment would've lasted long enough to have been by her side during her final days, Dylan had instead decided to drink to her declining health from the comforts of the snug in his local pub.

Following her death he arranged for her body to be shipped back to Wales for a quiet ceremony and burial in a small cemetery just outside of Porthmadog. He knew that this was what she would have hated.

Very few of her family and friends had attended the church. Dylan gave a small speech, having ransacked his subconscious for one or two favourable things to say about his mother. Then, promising the people of Porthmadog it was his intention they should benefit financially from her demise, he concluded matters and left once more for London.

The money he had inherited from his mother's estate was spread around many worthwhile causes - the inheritance was such that the spread was quite wide. Dylan had not forgotten his promise to the people of Porthmadog either, donating large sums to Angharad's family and friends as well as local hospitals, hospices and animal shelters. The house in Hampstead Hill Gardens, which he considered too large and unnecessary for his requirements, was converted into separate flats. Keeping the penthouse for himself, the remaining four flats were sold off.

Allowing for adequate financial resource with which to live quite comfortably, but without extravagance, he thought about a business venture. After many unsuccessful attempts he came to the conclusion, having played at being an amateur sleuth in his youth, that the life of a private investigator would be quite an interesting one. Dylan dropped his surname of Morgan, but retained his middle name of Beaumaris. He then set about locating nearby premises to use as his office, which he found above a newsagents shop on Haverstock Hill - a mere stone's throw from his flat.

When the day came, he had watched with swelling pride as the sign-writer painted the words *'Beaumaris Private Investigation Agency'* on the glass pane in the door.

*

Dylan watched the frosted glass pane as the beige silhouette pushed the door open and entered the office without even a cursory knock, but a fair amount of arrogance.

Once inside, and without waiting for an invitation, it made its way across the office and purposefully towards the chair by Dylan's desk, and sat itself down. Dylan looked over at Tony and then back at the stone coloured suit.

It seemed an eternity before the silence was broken, but Dylan felt it should be he, as host, who finally broke it.

'Take a seat... please. Make yourself comfortable.'

Dylan waited for a response.

The stone coloured suit, not rising to the tone of sarcasm in Dylan's voice, remained silent as the two colleagues exchanged surreptitious glances.

The stone coloured suit eventually spoke.

'You, I take it, are Mr... Beaumaris?'

Although talking to Dylan he was not looking at him, glancing instead around the office. This display of contempt was not lost on Dylan, and he took his time to muster a suitable response. However, that small pleasure was to be denied him for the moment as the stone coloured suit continued his speech. He was now looking out of the window at the rooftops opposite.

'Beaumaris, the Jewel of Anglesey. From the French name Beaux Marais – beautiful marshes. Did you know that the French builders of the castle so named it because of the castle being built...' here he paused for a few strategic moments, '...on a marsh?'

He stretched his arms out and back, bringing his shoulder blades closer together, and arched his spine in an attempt to alleviate stiffness. He continued looking out of the window as he spoke.

'Tell me, Mr Beaumaris, what claim do you have to the name you have chosen to operate under?'

He finally turned to look Dylan directly in the eyes.

'After all, it's not your own. Is it?'

Dylan was ready for him now.

'Well, actually Mr... Stone, it is my own. It's my middle name, see. Properly christened and everything, I was.'

This was greeted with a quizzical look.

'Mr Stone?' the man muttered to himself, then

looked down at his suit 'Ah, I see. Most amusing.'

'Yes, I was christened it because that's where I was conceived, you see. I don't know where exactly, but at a guess I would say it was in one of them nice rooms at the Bull's Head Inn. Mammy used to take me there sometimes, when I was growing up, like. Oh, lovely days they were. Do you know, we'd buy a portion of chips each, lots of salt and vinegar of course, and by the time we'd walked around to the Bull's Head, we'd finished them and we were ready for a drink. Gasping we were.'

As Dylan spoke his words grew angrier and angrier.

'Mammy would get herself half an ale, and a fizzy pop for me, and we'd sit at one of them tables, surrounded by all that antique weaponry on the walls. I used to love all that, you know. Well, kids love any kind of weapons, don't they? And Mammy would sip her drink and stare longingly up and almost through the ceiling to where the magical room was. Ohhh, great big beds they have, some of them – four-posters and everything. Ripe for a spot of old rumpy pumpy they are. Do you know the place, Mr Stone?' He didn't wait for an answer however. 'Yes, I can see my mammy and pappy now, doing the dirty deed up there in one of them big old four-poster beds.'

He was in full flow and he could see, past the stone coloured suit, Tony smiling to himself.

'Oh yes. Then nine months later, almost to the day so I'm led to believe, there was little old me, red and raw, like. Ripped from the comfort of my mammy's belly and crying out loud to high heaven, I was. And my mammy must've looked down at me and said to herself, "What am I going to call this little bundle of throbbing gristle here then? I gotta call him Morgan, obviously, 'cos that's my name. I won't bother with his father's name, mainly 'cos I can't spell it. And I think I'll call him Dylan, 'cos I like that Bob Dylan, or is it that rabbit off of Magic Roundabout that I like? Or maybe that Under Milk Wood chap. Oh well, see you, it'll be a bit of a mystery for him anyhow - and it is Welsh, after all. And I simply must give him a middle name. Oh, I know, Beaumaris, that's a nice name, isn't it? After all, me and his pappy had a real good time there, that night. Bloody comfortable it was too, bouncing about in that four-poster... that's sorted then. Write it down. It's official, Dylan Beaumaris Morgan it is.'" This was followed by a prolonged period of silence as both men just stared at each other.

Mr Stone smiled and began a slow and sarcastic hand-clap. 'Very good, Mr Beaumaris,' he said. 'Very good indeed.'

'Thank you, thank you,' Dylan responded, theatrically.

'A word to the wise though,' offered Mr Stone. 'You try your hardest to keep hold of that sense of humour because I get the funniest feeling that you're going to need it.'

Dylan had grown tired of the game and stood up to gain a position of superiority. He felt the sharp pain in his ankle and flinched.

'Sit down, Mr Beaumaris. You don't want to aggravate that ankle of yours. You'll need as much mobility as you can get in the coming days.'

As Mr Stone rankled, Dylan's composure was starting to show signs of tear. Stone then tore a gaping hole with his next words.

'You touched upon your father during your little soliloquy there, Mr Beaumaris. A Middle Eastern gentlemen, wasn't he? Didn't hang around too long, I understand.'

The hole was now large enough to climb through.

'Look, enough of all this,' Dylan snapped angrily. 'Who are you and what the bloody hell do you want?'

'As the entertainment appears to be over, Mr Beaumaris, let's just say my name is Mr Stone,' and he let out an irksome huff. 'And what I want is for you, and your assistant here, to give up the pointless quest that a certain attractive female acquaintance of yours has you running around on.'

He had done his research.

'In the next few days you will be receiving a few offers of work, Mr Beaumaris. I know that you've been very quiet up till now, and it will certainly be enough to keep you busy for a while. I suggest that you take what jobs you are given and concentrate wholeheartedly on them. And, I suggest also that you terminate the job you have on at the moment... whatever the incentive is to see it through.'

Smiling arrogantly, he rose from the chair and made his way to the doorway, then swivelled round to look at both men in turn. 'I strongly urge you to do as I have suggested otherwise you will come into contact with persons and situations that will almost certainly be beyond your capability.'

Both Dylan and Tony remained silent.

'Mr Beaumaris.... Mr Spinetti,' said Stone, placing emphasis on the name Spinetti to assure Dylan he had done his homework and was not to be taken lightly.

With a parting nod of the head he turned once more and was gone. All that remained were the diminishing footsteps along the corridor and down the stairs, until they were finally silenced by the creaking of the door on the ground floor as it opened and then closed with a terminal groan.

'Well, Tony,' Dylan cupped his hands together with a clap, 'we better brace ourselves for all this work we're going to be getting soon.'

'You going to drop it, boss? You going to drop the job?'

'Not on your life. I'm not going to drop anything. The fun's just getting started. I'm just going to have to be a less conspicuous about it. And you're going to be a lot busier with everything else.'

He banged both fists on the desk, rhythmically.

'Perhaps you might want a word with that network of cousins of yours 'cos you may need some help here and there. I'll take the bastard's work if he wants to give it to me.'

Tony nodded his head positively at this.

'And speaking of which, chase up that cousin of yours at the paper, will you? See if he's found out anything yet. Perhaps something that might even tell us who this Mr Stone character really is.'

Dylan turned and looked out of the window. The sun was now high in the sky and dazzlingly bright.

'There's not many people in this world that I don't like, Tony, but when I find someone that I don't like, I really don't like them. And I *really* don't like him, with a bit of a passion if I gotta be honest. And what he didn't hang around long enough for me to explain was that, unlike most people, I really don't have anything to lose. And see, what he's obviously forgotten is that maybe the castle was built on a bloody marsh, but after seven hundred years it's still standing.'

TEN

Having inserted the SD card that Victoria had found in Lola's room into Dylan's mobile phone, they were unable to retrieve any information as it had been secured with a password. Two hours of fruitless attempt and several cups of tea and coffee later they finally admitted defeat.

'I have to go,' Victoria informed a disappointed Dylan. 'I'll keep thinking of what the password may be, but I really have to go and get ready for this client tonight.'

'Don't go,' Dylan pleaded. 'Who is this client? Do you know him? Is he new?'

'What's with all the questions?'

Dylan told Victoria of Mr Stone's visit and of his concerns that they wouldn't be able to trust anybody.

'It's okay, I know him. I'll be alright.' Victoria reached across the desk and placed her hand on Dylan's. 'Look, I appreciate you looking out for me and everything, but you learn to look after yourself in this game.'

He wanted desperately to make the point that Lola hadn't been so good at looking after herself, then considered that maybe she was.

'Look...,' said Victoria. 'I would understand if you wanted to drop the investigation. I want to find her, but the more it goes on, the more I think that she's got herself into some sort of mess and that she'll have to get herself out of it - if she wants to get out, of course. I'm just thinking... if she's that desperate she knows I'd help her in any way that I could, but I don't even know what's going on. And I really don't want anything happening to you or Tony because of it. I've known you long enough now to know that you're not really cut out for the rough stuff. I wouldn't have got you involved if I'd known it was going to be this complicated.'

This was a red rag to an emasculated bull.

'Okay, Vicky. I understand that you've got to go to work tonight. I really do. But I've already decided, Tony too, that we're going to carry on with the investigation. We're going to find out what's happened to Lola, one way or another. It's a matter of principle now.'

He pushed himself up to a standing position, edging his way around the desk.

'But I want you to seriously consider my offer. I really meant it.'

Victoria stood up to leave. 'I know that you did, and I will think about it.'

With a suppliant glance towards Tony, which he read as 'look after him', she departed.

Dylan waited for the creak of the street door then slowly edged back to his chair. As he sat down, Tony called across the office to him.

'You should walk around, otherwise your ankle is gonna seize up.'

'Yeah, you're right. Listen, would you mind closing up the office? I'm gonna head off. I think I'll have a night out with some friends tonight - a drink and a bite to eat somewhere maybe, something to get my mind off all this for a few hours. Do me a favour though, Tony, try your cousin again. See if he's found out anything, will you?'

'Sure thing, boss. You want I should let you know tonight, or leave it till the morning?'

'No, the morning will do. I don't want to think about anything else but enjoying myself tonight.'

*

Dylan had arranged to meet his friends at his favourite restaurant. Sofra in Winchmore Hill, was a place he liked not only for its fine Anatolian cuisine, but also for the fact it had an area sectioned-off outside for those wishing to smoke a hookah pipe with their after dinner Turkish coffee or tea. This was something Dylan particularly enjoyed - though not so much the coffee. He had tried this on his first visit, until he found, the day after, that the grainy residue was still stuck to the roof of his mouth. From then on he stuck to the more delicate tea.

When he arrived he found his friends from the Roebuck already there. He was greeted at the door by the owner's daughter Aygul, a pretty girl who stood a shade over five foot and possessed the most hypnotic brown, almond-shaped eyes.

'Hello, Mister Dylan. It is good to see you again. Mister Malcolm, Mister Jonathan and Mister Aidan have been waiting for you.'

She had arrived from Turkey just a handful of years previous, but her heavily accented English was excellent and Dylan had remarked upon it in the past, which had pleased her immensely.

'Thank you, Aygul. It's always a pleasure to

see you my little moon rose.'

This, she had once told him, was the meaning of her name. Dylan thought this appropriate as she had been blessed with a face that was round and illuminated in its welcome, and a smile which bloomed so readily that he imagined her having emerged from the womb with it. Indeed, he was very fond of Aygul, and of the place itself; the staff, the décor, the traditional hanging lamps and authentic Turkish kilims on the walls, the belly dancing - all made for an ambience in which he felt comfortable, and now, as he could no longer be certain of anything around him, strangely safe.

'Aygul, will you do me a favour please?' he asked, looking down at the girl; Dylan stood at just under six foot tall so the difference in their heights was marked.

'Yes of course, Mister Dylan. What is it?'

'If you see anyone tonight that looks a little suspicious will you come and tell me - but quietly, without my friends hearing, eh?'

Frantically waving for him to join them he pacified them with a wave.

'Is there any trouble, Mister Dylan?' Aygul asked, concerned.

'No, don't worry there won't be any trouble. But if you do spot anybody like that just please let me know, yeah?'

He attempted to allay her concerns by placing a hand on her shoulder, but instead this had a contrasting effect.

'Yes, of course I will, Mister Dylan. And you don't worry either.' Her tone was charmingly sweet, but serious. 'If there's any trouble here tonight, Kemal, Alkan and the rest of the boys will be out very quickly, and with many knives to sort it out.'

He looked for tell-tale signs that she was joking, but her smile only served to compound the sincerity of her pledge.

'Well... that's good to know, Aygul. Thank you.'

Grinning nervously, he walked off in the direction of his friends, his ankle still causing him mild discomfort.

*

The four friends ate, drank and talked ceaselessly. Aygul kept the food and drink coming. The conversation was light and helped to take Dylan's mind off of whatever else was going on in his life. There was also a fair amount of interaction with people on other tables, and pretty soon something of a party atmosphere had developed.

There were two women sitting at an adjacent table who had ventured out on a balmy Friday night with the intention of enjoying a quiet meal and a girlie chat about the stresses and quandaries of their week. They were soon forced to accept that this was not how their evening was destined to go. One, in particular, was unable to extract herself from the constant attentions of Dylan's friend, Aidan, who considered himself something of a ladies man. At first both women seemed quite obviously irritated by the intrusion, but they too eventually gave up and joined in.

One by one the majority of the customers were

sucked into the whole and it wasn't long before the group that had brought everyone together soon became the butt of most of the witticism.

It was discovered that the sum total of Dylan and his friends amounted to no less than a traditional British joke; collectively they were Jonathan the Englishman, Malcolm the Scotsman, Aidan the Irishman, and of course Dylan the Welshman. There was no stopping the tidal wave after that. Taken in good heart by the four lads, pretty soon each of them were telling humorous anecdotes at the expense of the other three.

The eating, drinking and merriment began slowing down at around half-past eleven as people started to leave. Just before midnight Dylan announced that he was going outside for his customary smoke. His friends, all having commitments in the morning, said their farewells and departed in search of a taxi.

'You want to smoke nargile now, Mister Dylan?' Aygul asked him as he sat looking abandoned and the worst for wear. She smiled her gentle smile and he, hearing the magic word he knew to be Turkish for hookah, responded with a drunken grin.

'Ohhhh, yes please, Aygul. I can't leave here without a smoke... and another one of your lovely smiles.'

She smiled again.

'Okay, Mister Dylan. You must sit there and finish your drink while I go and get it ready for you. And then I will come and get you. And I will also get you nice Turkish tea to go with your nargile. Okay?'

'Yes of course, my little moon rose. I will wait right here,' he slurred, as he dug his finger into the table cloth. He giggled like a child, occasionally emitting a barely audible hiccup.

The solitary figure of the Welshman sat waiting, his upper frame rocking from side to side in the chair as he tried desperately to steady the body that he was fast losing control of, with alien limbs and stiffened rump. He finished off the dregs of his beer and laughed, without comprehension, at any jokes made by the small group of diners still remaining. But through it all he maintained the smile, borne of having consumed too much of everything, that looked as if it were chiselled into his features.

He tried desperately not to let his mind wander to Victoria, and what she may have been doing at that precise moment in time. He tried. An alcoholic haze had obliterated any capacity for control, bringing to the fore thoughts uppermost in his mind for most of the day. Despite disappearances, dead bodies and visitations from gentlemen bearing threats, the one thing that he couldn't eradicate from his mind was the image of Victoria and her client rolling about on a big soft bed, morphing the shape of their joint bodies from one position of the Karma Sutra to the next.

Whilst he was fighting his inner turmoil, Aygul returned to lead him outside. The diminishing but still present pain in his ankle, together with the alcohol-induced disorientation he was suffering, meant he had cause to use Aygul as a crutch in order to get to the outside area where the hookah awaited him.

The area which was set aside for the purposes of smoking was quite cosy, only large enough for three small tables with a couple of chairs at each. It was a corner plot separated from the public making its way along the cracked weather-beaten pavement by a three foot high railing along its perimeter. Although they were only ever kept outside for short periods, between the time the customer had finished with them and the time that they were collected by one of the staff, Dylan had always wondered why it was that the ornate smoking implements were never taken. Then he remembered the knives that Aygul had mentioned, and their implication, and concluded that this probably served as fair deterrent. Certainly to any locals who knew the management, or of them.

Aygul sat Dylan down in a chair next to the edge of the back wall and handed him the hose of the hookah. As he sucked on the small tip of the pipe the water in the bowl burbled away satisfyingly. One of the waiters came out carrying a small silver tray on which stood a thin glass of tea with two sugar lumps by its side on a saucer. He placed the tray on the table in front of Dylan, smiled, and hurried back inside. Aygul followed him, turning one last time to ensure Dylan was okay before disappearing through the doorway herself.

On a balmy spring night there were not many other places that Dylan would rather have been than right there - enveloped in the vaporous delights of an intimate Turkish tea garden. Looking out at the silhouetted trees, and beyond them the moonlit tapestry of the wispy lapis lazuli North London skies, he was content. He smiled away happily to himself and felt the enervating flavoured tobacco warming and soothing him. He vaguely remembered reaching out for the lumps of sugar and letting them drop into the glass of brownish-red tea. So engrossed was he in the moment that he did not notice the gloved hand that appeared from around the other side of the wall until it was upon him; a hand which held a chloroform-laced napkin to his mouth until the feeble struggle that he managed to offer up in opposition gave way to a darkness blacker than the bank of trees that were his final memory before surrendering to unconsciousness.

ELEVEN

Tony opened up the office on the Saturday morning. Dylan hadn't arrived yet, but in the short time that he had been working for him, Tony had already worked out that Dylan wasn't really a stickler for punctuality, by virtue of the fact that he'd had to wait for him each morning on the doorstep. Now though, Tony had a set of keys, and it was agreed that whoever arrived at the office first would naturally open up, but more importantly, put the kettle on. Then the mail would be opened, although the postman sometimes didn't deliver until after ten o'clock.

On this particular morning, the postman had already been as there were half a dozen envelopes lying on the floor as Tony pushed open the door downstairs. He picked them up with a sweep of the hand before climbing the stairs to the first floor. Unlocking the office door he stepped in and walked straight up to Dylan's desk, throwing the envelopes down together in a heap.

Tony still liked to give his boss the first option for opening the mail even though Dylan didn't have a problem with his assistant doing it before he got there. The fact that Dylan didn't have much of an ego or sense of self-importance was self-evident, and was one of the reasons that Tony had taken a liking to the young Welshman when they had first met. Before he'd arrived at the office, on that first day, he had felt a little trepidation as to the kind of man he would be working for. Being the first job that Tony had ever had which didn't involve working with family, he was more than a little apprehensive.

When he'd asked Nuncio - the cousin who worked for the local newspaper - to keep an eye out for interesting jobs advertised in the North London area, he never expected to be offered one of a private investigator's assistant. He had been reluctant to apply for it, but his cousin thought it ideal. Taking a few hours to think about it, he called Nuncio back later that evening to advise him that he would apply in person for the job the very next morning. Now, here he was, walking over to his very own desk at the Beaumaris Investigation Agency - via the kettle, of course.

He removed his hat and threw it down onto the corner of the desk with a gesture that indicated a feeling of comfort with his new surroundings. Once the initial nervousness of arriving at a new place of work had passed, it hadn't taken him very long to know that he would enjoy working alongside Dylan.

He had never met anybody quite as laid back as Dylan before. It was not a characteristic commonly associated with the people he fraternised with; Italians tended to be highly passionate about everything they said or did, and therefore situations were usually dealt with in much the same manner.

He sat down in his new high-backed leather swivel-chair, listening to the steadily increasing hiss of the kettle, and looked back across the room at the letters on Dylan's desk. Perhaps he wouldn't wait - perhaps, today, he would open the post himself. After all, this was the largest amount of post they'd received in one go since he'd been there. It was not inconceivable in fact that this was quite probably the largest amount of post received since Dylan had started the business.

Tony noticed immediately that although all five had stamps on them none were postmarked. Not particularly familiar with the workings of the Royal Mail, one thing he felt sure of was that it was pretty unusual to have this many letters in one delivery with no postmark. He started opening them. The first was from an insurance company, suspecting a policy holder of having made a fraudulent claim. The second, from an East London based food company, wanted them to investigate some funds that had gone missing. The third and fourth related to the serving of summonses.

The final letter was from a man who was convinced his wife was having an affair with her cousin's husband. Enclosed were two photographs of the woman along with a list of the places she would be visiting during her travels on any given day. Tony thought this strange. If the man knew the whereabouts of his wife throughout the day the indication was that he'd had her followed in the past. In which case why had the investigation been terminated? Alternatively, she may have told her husband of her movements. However, if she was having an affair surely she would be lying. So, why would her husband give details of these places knowing them to be highly improbable as places she would actually visit? It just didn't add up.

Another thought crossed Tony's mind. Even though he had been in the private investigation game for just a handful of days, he felt certain that it wasn't common practice that offers of work were made in such an impersonal way. Initial contact in such matters were made either in person, or at the very least over the telephone. When he then noticed that all five envelopes were written out in the same hand he drew the indisputable conclusion that this was the work of Mr Stone.

*

It was just after ten o'clock and Dylan had still not arrived. Tony tried calling Dylan's mobile phone - it was switched off and went straight to voicemail. He chose not to leave a message as, no matter how simple the intention of the message, he always struggled to get the right words out. He tried the landline but there was no answer and, again, it went to answerphone. He decided to leave it until eleven o'clock and if Dylan hadn't turned up by then he would take the short walk to his apartment.

Shortly afterwards the telephone rang. Before he could answer he heard the voice of a young girl calling frantically down the line.

'Mister Dylan, Mister Dylan, is that you?'

Her voice full of panic, she spoke with an accent.

'Ah no, sorry. This is not Mister Dylan,' replied Tony. 'He is not here.'

'I am looking for Mister Dylan. Do you know where he is?'

'No. He has not come into the office yet. Who's calling please?'

'My name is Aygul,' she said, excitedly. ' I am trying to find Mister Dylan. He was eating at our restaurant last night. I took him out to the tea garden to smoke nargile pipe... and when I went out again, he was gone. He was a little drunk... or maybe very... and I thought that maybe he just left without letting us know and he went home. I have been trying his home but there is no answer.'

The anxiety in her voice grew.

'I try to call his friends and I manage to speak to one of them. He told me that he has not seen Mister Dylan since last night at the restaurant,' she said, tearfully. 'He may still be asleep of course. Do you think that he is still asleep? Sorry... I didn't ask... who are you?'

There was, thought Tony, a mercurial charm in her voice.

'I am Tony, I am Dyl... Mister Dylan's assistant. Look... young lady, he has not come into the office yet, but if you leave me your telephone number I will try to find Mister Dylan and I call you back. Who have you spoken to already?'

'I speak to Mister Malcolm.'

She tailed away briefly and Tony could hear the voice of a man speaking in the background, in a language unfamiliar to him.

'Okay. You leave it to me. I will go to his apartment and I will call you when I find him.'

'Oh, thank you very much. I am most grateful.

We are all worried for Mister Dylan. I hope that he is okay. Oh... Mister Tony, I should also tell you that Mister Dylan was worried about something and he ask me to tell him if I notice anyone strange in the restaurant. I didn't see anything, but just so you know – in case it is important.'

*

Tony stood at the top of the steps leading up to the front door on Hampstead Hill Gardens. He pressed the button alongside Dylan's name on the intercom for a third time, this time leaving his finger there for longer. Still there was no response. Now, close to midday, he was starting to worry that Dylan was not simply sleeping off a hangover but that, with everything else that had been going on, there was a distinct possibility he may be in some kind of trouble.

Looking down the list of occupants of the other four flats, next to Flat 1 was the name Bowden. He pressed the buzzer and waited, but received no response there either. He pressed the buzzer for Flat 2, alongside the name McGuiness.

'Hello?' came a weary Irish voice over the intercom.

'Yes... hello. Can you help me, please?' Tony stuttered into the speaker. 'I am looking for Mr Beaumaris from the flat at the top.'

'Silly question, fella, but have you tried his buzzer?'

'Yes, a few times already, but no answer.'

'I heard him go out last night, but I didn't hear

101

him come back... hold on there a minute, fella.'

There was a moment's pause then Tony heard a buzz and the door clicked open. As he stepped into the doorway he saw the door to the flat on the right-hand side of the hallway open. A man wearing lounge pants, a t-shirt and Homer Simpson slippers emerged.

'Ah, there you are,' he called out.

Tony was leaning back in order to take another look at the name on the intercom.

'Mr McGuiness. That is you, yes?'

'Ah... yes. That's me. Now you were saying that you were looking for Dylan up on the top floor. Well, as I say, I heard him go out last night – probably around seven thirty it was – but then I went out myself and got in after chucking out time. I didn't hear him come in after that, but then I was out sparko soon after I got in.'

Tony wasn't familiar with the term but had a fair idea what he meant.

'My wife was in all night. She had a couple of friends over for a girlie night in and they were still up when I went off to bed. Unfortunately I can't ask her at the moment as she's out doing a bit of shopping. I haven't heard anything from him so far this morning, though. Have you looked in the Roebuck? He's always in there.'

Tony walked further into the hallway and looked at the door of Flat 1.

'There's no point knocking there, fella. Don works on a Saturday so he won't be in. So does Bikram at number four. But I tell you what, if anyone's heard anything,' and here he lowered his voice to a whisper so that Tony could only just hear him. 'It'll be Mrs Sumner in number three.'

The Irishman looked at the top of the stairs, pointing the way with his eyes.

'She's the eyes and ears of this place alright.'

Tony instinctively turned and tilted his head to look up the stair.

'Okay. Thank you very much, Mr McGuiness. I will speak to the lady upstairs.'

'Are you a friend of Dylan's then?' He looked Tony up and down, the faint stress in his voice betraying his doubt that Dylan could have a friend this much older than himself. This was not lost on Tony.

'No, I am his assistant.'

'Oh, right. The old private investigation stuff, eh? Dylan gave us all a card when he started the business a few weeks back...'

A telephone starting ringing. He hurriedly swivelled round and started moving back inside, turning briefly.

'Mrs Sumner upstairs. She'll help you, if anyone can. If not, check the Roebuck.'

He disappeared back into the flat shutting the door behind him.

Tony made his way up the staircase and to Flat 3. He gave a couple of soft taps to the door, and this was answered within a few seconds by a nervy female voice on the other side.

'Yes? Who is it?'

'Mrs Sumner? My name is Spinetti, Tony Spinetti,' he said to the door. 'I work with Mr Beaumaris... who lives upstairs. Can I speak with you, please?'

'What for?'

'I think that maybe something has happen. I try to find out if anybody has seen him today.'

'Who?'

'Dylan.... Mr Beaumaris, Mrs Sumner.'

'Mr Beaumaris?' she called out. 'Yes of course, dear. Wait there and I'll be out in a tick.'

He could hear her muttering to herself. A piece of furniture scraped along the floor as she pulled it away from the door.

'Just one minute, dear... nearly there...'

There was the sound of a key turning in the lock, then the muffled chinking of a chain. She opened the door and pulled it as far as the chain would allow. When she saw Tony standing outside - quite obviously not the person she was expecting to find there - she was taken aback.

'You're not Mr Beaumaris,' she said, anxiously. 'Who are you? What do you want?'

She wore make-up, heavy and haphazardly applied, reminiscent of Bette Davis as Baby Jane. She pushed the door, closing the gap a little, so that only one side of her face remained visible.

'No, Mrs Sumner. I am not Mr Beaumaris,' Tony's voice remained calm and placatory. 'My name is Tony Spinetti and I am...'

'Spinetti?' the old woman interrupted him.

'Yes, Spinetti. I work with Mr Beaumaris. In his office.'

'His office?'

'Yes, his office. On Haverstock Hill.'

'He's a lovely man, Mr Beaumaris,' she said, growing a little more confident. 'Is he with you?'

Her head stretched out from behind the door so it was almost completely visible and looked passed Tony out onto the landing.

'No, Mrs Sumner. He's not with me. That is why I am here. I am trying to find him. Nobody has see him since last night. The man downstairs, he told me that you might have see him or heard him.'

'Can't find him? Top of them stairs, dear. That's where he lives.' Confused, half her face disappeared behind the door again.

A sense of despair was laying siege to Tony's face, but he remained equanimous. At that moment a familiar piece of music drifted into earshot and he began making exaggerated expressions with his hands, whilst his head weaved from side to side in mock rapture.

'O Mio Babbino Caro. One of my favourite.'

He sang a few bars in an attempt to capture the old lady's interest on another level.

'Puccini? You like Puccini, dear?' Her ears pricked up.

'Of course, Mrs Sumner. I am Italian, from Tuscany. How can I be from Tuscany, the place of Puccini's birth, and not like Puccini?'

He reeled her in. Her whole face reappeared from behind the door.

'You are from Tuscany? Whereabouts in Tuscany are you from, dear?'

'I am from Montalcino. It is very near to Siena.'

'I've not been to Montalcino. Very nice wine though. Brunello, isn't it, dear?'

'Indeed, Mrs Sumner. One of the finest wines in all of Italy.'

The old lady was beginning to let her guard

down.

'Yes... very nice... but I've not been there. I have been to Tuscany though.'

'Really? Where did you stay?'

'Oh, not far from Siena, dear. Now what was the name of that place that my friend Mary and I stayed at? I remember it had a bouncy little name. Oh yes, that was it - Poggibonsi. Do you know it, dear?'

'Yes I know it. I visited a few times when I was young, but I don't know it very well. It is around the same distance from Siena as Montalcino, but in the other direction.'

The old lady stared at him in an awkward silence eventually broken by a deflated 'Oh....'

She released the door from the security chain and swung it open.

'Now, what was all this about Mr Beaumaris having disappeared, dear?'

After several more minutes of superfluous conversation, Tony established that the old lady had absolutely no idea as to Dylan's whereabouts. She had however heard him talking to Mr Malhotra from number four on his way out yesterday evening and that was the person he should be talking to. As Tony had already established that Mr Malhotra was unavailable for questioning, he left to make his way back to the office, looking in at the Roebuck, just in case. He wasn't there. Nixon said that he hadn't seen Dylan for a couple of days.

Walking back along Haverstock Hill Tony couldn't quite put his finger on what it was, but a sense of being watched overwhelmed him. As he walked he scanned the area, trying to spot any observers. He reached the pavement in front of the office and looked across the road at the café but there was nobody sitting outside. When he got into the office he went to the window overlooking the main road to check again, but even though there were many people milling around nobody stood out as being an obvious suspect - certainly no Mr Stone that he could see.

Once Tony had reassured himself that nobody was watching the office he thought about calling all the hospitals in the area. If Dylan was drunk, and had tried to make his way home on his own, then it was just possible that he may have been involved in some sort of accident. In which case, he may be lying in a hospital bed somewhere.

He got the telephone directory from the bottom of the filing cabinet and made a list of hospitals that were located somewhere between the restaurant and Belsize Park. One by one he called them all, making sure to give them Dylan's full name as, in all probability, he would have been registered as Morgan. He described the Welshman as best he could: early thirties; just under six foot tall; lobe length, dark, curly brown hair; a bit of a drinker's girth. There was no record of anyone of that name or description having been admitted to any of the hospitals he rang. He considered the possibility that they were not permitted to give out information over the telephone, but all were able to reassure him without revealing any personal details.

At the last hospital he called, the one which stood a hop, skip and a jump from Dylan's apartment, a very friendly woman, with the warm Caribbean sun in her voice, advised Tony that she thought it would be a good idea for Dylan, upon his return, to be looked over by a doctor. It would depend on the circumstances of his disappearance, of course, but she said that her daughter had disappeared for three months once, and when she had returned she had done so with child.

'Of course, I know dat dis won' 'appen to your friend, darlin', what wid 'im bein' a man, but y'mus' know dat dis London 'as become such a wicked place, where all sort of bad ting 'appen to people agains' dere will. Y'mus' be sure, y'know. You aks 'im to come see the doctor 'pon 'im return. 'Ave a proper check-up, jus' in case. Y'never know, y'know.'

TWELVE

Dylan could hear the soft piquant note of a saxophone gently dissipating. The pulsating corridor in which he stood wound its way dreamily into the distant haze. He could feel the walls, which seemed to be contracting and expanding in syncopation with each breath he took. Before him he saw several white doors, and from behind one of these came the resonance of an Indian tanpura accompanied by the rhythm of a beating tabla.

Dylan stumbled along, his clammy palms pressed into the soft and beating walls, as something carried him towards the door behind which the music seemed to be coming. The door opened slowly, and almost immediately an overpowering smell of sandalwood incense hit him. He stood, gazing in at a large white room covered in wall rugs of a thousand colours. On the deep lush carpeted floor there were cushions of a thousand colours more, laid out in a pattern of concentric circles. In the middle was the largest of these cushions, around it an inner circle comprising four smaller cushions, and finally eight even smaller cushions completing the outer circle.

Sitting cross-legged on the middle cushion was an elderly Indian man in a state of meditation. Long, grey, straggled hair cascaded from his head and hung like a silver shroud over the red and gold kurta he was wearing.

There was something familiar about him. Then it occurred to Dylan - he bore a remarkable resemblance to the image of the sitarist, Ravi Shankar he'd seen on album covers in Bikram Malhotra's flat – only older.

The hoary old gent looked up and smiled, indicating he had been expecting Dylan. He spoke in a tiny, unobtrusive voice.

'Ah, won't you come in, young man? I have been waiting. Now, are you one of the four, or one of the eight?'

Dylan's reply was slow and laboured.

'I'm not exactly sure where this is,' he said. 'Or who the four and the eight are.'

'Then you must come in from the doorway, so that I may take a good look at you.'

Dylan began walking towards where the cushions lay on the ground. Unlike his speech, his movement was effortless - almost as if he were gliding on air.

'Let me see,' contemplated the old man. 'Ah, yes, I know. You are indeed one of the four. Your place, young man, is in the inner circle,' he said, indicating with a motion of his hand.

'And you must sit directly in front of me. This is most important.'

The old man's head rocked gently from side to side to emphasise this.

'Why?' asked Dylan.

'Because every cushion here before you has a relevance. Even the simple shape of a circle may have points which are of more importance than others.'

'How so?'

110

'Consider that you are looking at a compass. It is circular in shape, yes? But can you truly say that any point on that compass is any more, or any less, important than any other? Yet, you will find that for each person who looks at that compass, there will always be one distinct point which will have more significance than the others. It may be a point which is relative to where they have come from, or one significant to their most desired destination in life.

'The same also goes for a clock, does it not? If it is one's overwhelming desire to fill one's belly always, then the points on a timepiece which will hold greater importance, but which are of seeming parity to others, are those which correspond with the times at which one feeds the belly. And so on and so forth. And therefore, as you are the one at the centre of that which is to unfold, your place is there.'

He indicated again the cushion directly in front of him.

'But you are at the centre, Ravi.'

The old man was again very calm in his response.

'As is the pin that secures the hands of a clock and gives them stability, allowing them to perform their primary function, the telling of time. This you will agree is its only purpose, yes? Yet, it is not the pin that we look to, but the hands of the clock which are of most importance. It is to where they point that we look. For is this not the clock's reason for being?'

He gestured again towards the cushion and Dylan lowered himself down onto it.

'Now we wait for the others. But you must remember at all times that things may not be quite as they would appear.'

His voice trailed off into the distance, and as it did Dylan's thoughts turned to the sound of the tanpura and tabla. Strange, he thought, that the music should be quieter inside the room than it was from outside - as if the distribution of signals to and from his brain were being tampered with.

Dylan noticed there was now someone on the cushion directly behind the old man. He could just make out the periphery of a human frame. He leant over to get a better view and saw that it was Victoria. She was wearing the little black dress he had always liked so much. Her long blonde hair was draped loosely about her shoulders like a shawl. Her eyes, surely bluer than usual, were vacantly staring past everything, and at nothing in particular. She sat still as a porcelain figurine.

Then he saw Tony. He was sitting on the cushion to his right. Eyes fixed firmly on the white-maned figure in the middle. He, like Victoria, sat as if sculpted. Finally, Lola appeared on the cushion to Dylan's left.

'Now that we have the four we can invite the eight,' said the old man. 'At this point in time they will all, except two, be a mystery to you, and even of them there will be many things which you do not yet know.'

In the blink of an eye all eight cushions in the outer circle were occupied. As the old man had spoken, all but two figures were featureless - that of his mother, Angharad, and the man he knew as Mr Stone. The others were faceless and formless to the point of indeterminate gender.

'And now we may begin.'

The old man's voice, echoing around the room, was now accompanied by the notes from a sitar which had appeared in his lap. His playing grew increasingly frantic and reached a ferocity his fingers were struggling to sustain.

Dylan watched as Lola rose from her cushion. She held out her hand invitingly to him. Dylan reached up and took it, and with incredible ease rose to a standing position. She led him out of the room and they made their way down the vacillating corridor. Dylan noticed that the volume had increased once again as he watched the music in the air around him moving in waves above his head.

They reached one of the doors and stopped. Lola turned to Dylan and in his mind he heard her speak.

'This place has many rooms,' her soft voice came. 'Although all the doors are white and may look the same each hides a different secret, and your conviction alone will determine which of them may or may not remain undiscovered.'

She opened the door and led Dylan inside. There were no windows, but the room was flooded with an artificial light. In the middle there was a large, ornate four-poster bed. This was adorned with hand-carved posts, flutings and an overhanging deep forest-green canopy decorated with gold Prince of Wales feathers.

Releasing Dylan's hand Lola walked over to the bed. Dylan stood for a few moments in the doorway and observed her, entranced. Framed by the posts, the canopy and the bed itself, she looked as enticing as Botticelli's Venus.

He moved towards the bed just as the loose turquoise and black, silken dress she was wearing slipped slowly from Lola's shoulders. Falling away from her rounded breasts, the dress then slid unhindered down her smooth body, crumpling to the floor and leaving her completely naked. Sitting him down on the edge of the bed, she carefully undressed him with one hand, gently pleasuring him with the other. Dylan followed the rhythm of her hand as she caressed him. He made no attempt to hold back the tidal wave that was building up inside of him. He was filled with a concupiscence not to be abated. Lola had a beautiful body and she was offering it to him. Why should he not enjoy it? They made love and he knew, somewhere in the back of his mind, that this should have been wrong, but his will was not his own - he was powerless. With not a single thought of Victoria during the love-making, he let his hands and his mouth explore every crevice and curve of Lola's body. Whatever pleasure he took from it was not to be a guilty one.

Afterwards, Lola led Dylan back to the room of concentric circles. The music had now settled at a more comfortable level, the old man's playing more sedate. Eyes still closed, his face still shone with the same indelible smile. Lola, naked, sat back down on her cushion as a vacant expression returned to her face.

Before Dylan could sit back down he saw Victoria rise. She did so in one single flowing movement and extended a hand out to him. Dylan

114

became suddenly conscious of the fact that he, like Lola, was still naked. Dylan's hand reached out to meet Victoria's. Silently, she led him outside into the corridor and to another door. As they stood outside Dylan watched Victoria's rouged lips. She seemed to be mouthing words, but Dylan could hear nothing.

Victoria opened the door and they entered the room. She motioned towards an armchair facing a large leaded window, looking out upon a scene of abstract beauty.

Dylan rounded the armchair and saw that sitting in it was the man whose dead body he had found so difficult to rid from his mind. Gerald De Vere rose from the chair and offered his hand. They shook in greeting. Between them flourished an inexplicably unconfined joy. Dylan felt De Vere pass something to him. When De Vere spoke it was through still lips.

'The brightness beyond the dark can be deafening if you do not guard your eyes. But also, the truth can be so abstract it eludes you if you do not open them wide enough.'

The mound of flesh that was Gerald De Vere sat back down in the armchair and continued his gaze out of the window at the indiscriminate haze.

Dylan looked down into the palm of his hand at the old coin that De Vere had passed to him. Above the date of 1890 was a depiction of St. George slaying the winged serpent. Just as he was about to turn the coin over Victoria motioned for him to follow her, and so he placed the coin on a small gate-legged occasional table by the door and together they left the room. She led him back to the room of concentric circles.

The music, and the old man's playing, was quieter still and slower of pace. What was before the overpowering smell of sandalwood incense was now barely perceptible. Dylan instinctively looked towards the figure of Tony, expecting him to rise up as Lola and Victoria had done. But he didn't. He sat stone still, smiling. Turning his head, Dylan saw that standing just outside the doorway was the figure of Mr Stone beckoning him. Dylan turned for one last lingering look around the room of concentric circles and made his way out.

Mr Stone had not waited. He was already making his way towards the far end of the corridor. Dylan watched the stone-coloured suit getting smaller as it grew more distant. It eventually came to a stop outside another doorway. It occurred to Dylan that the distance between them did not correspond with the brief amount of time it had taken Mr Stone to reach the door. It were as if he had somehow contravened all laws of time and space.

A distant Mr Stone spoke. His voice seemed to come from just behind Dylan's right ear.

'Venturing into a cave there inevitably comes a point when it is no longer obvious which is closer: the entrance or the exit. The time is then upon you to decide in which direction it is safest to head as you stumble along in the darkness.'

Mr Stone walked through the doorway and behind him Dylan could see an expanse of trees and dense vegetation. He could hear the unmistakable cries, growls, and screeches of wildlife. He reached the doorway and saw that on the other side was a deep, verdant jungle. The heat was so stiflingly intense the air itself was shimmering. Indigenous primates were swinging from the protective cover of one tree to another.

Without hesitation Dylan walked through the doorway. Mr Stone was now nowhere to be seen and there wasn't, as far as he could see, a path of any sort. Wandering aimlessly between the trees he brushed aside vegetation, constantly wiping beads of sweat from his face. The flies grew in number. With no inclination to kill or even harm them he attempted to gently waft them away, but found this soon to be a fool's task. He stumbled deeper and deeper into the jungle without direction or plan.

It was as he was breaking through one particularly large clump of vegetation that he noticed an undulating shape out of the corner of his eye. Moments later he felt an excruciating pain just above his left foot. Looking down he caught the momentary slither of a small blue snake as it shifted and disappeared into the broad natural cover of the undergrowth.

Dylan fell heavily against the nearest tree, consciousness fast abandoning him. He desperately held on for as long as he could but his limp and naked body finally lost all co-ordination and he fell, crashing to the ground.

*

Unable to open his eyes, Dylan heard a soft Indian voice imploring him through the darkness.

'Wake up, Mr Beaumaris, wake up. It is now time for you to go back.'

THIRTEEN

When Dylan woke it was light and the chill of early morning made him shiver as he took hold of both lapels of his jacket, pulling them firmly together. It took him a few moments to work out that he was still sitting in the chair he'd fallen asleep on - in the tea garden of the Sofra restaurant.

'Ohhh,' he whispered, closing tight his eyes before opening them wide again. 'Bloody dream.'

His head ached, it was pounding like a bass drum. What had Aygul put in that hookah? Surely it had only been flavoured tobacco. Or was it the drink? He remembered a considerable mix of drinks last night. He had felt like a human cocktail shaker. Efes beer, raki, whisky, brandy, exotic cocktails and a selection of other spirits offered up for tasting by fellow customers. Dylan could take his drink certainly, but even he had to concede that on this occasion he just may have overdone it.

He looked around him. The hookah that he had been smoking had gone. Along with everything else, it had been placed back inside the restaurant at the end of the night - everything, that was, except for Dylan. Crazy! Who would leave a customer sleeping outside and shut up shop for the night? Why would they have done that? Surely Aygul would never have left him out there and gone home. She could at least have offered to take me with her, he thought - Dylan was never too far gone for a salacious thought.

He looked through the glass doors. There were no signs of life inside the restaurant. His watch told him it was 6.17am. It was still not fully light. If anybody were in there, surely they would have some lights on. He tried to stand up, pushing down on the table as he lifted his body, which felt heavier than usual. His hands were too close to the edge of the table and caused it to tip over onto his lap, which in turn sent Dylan crashing back down on the chair.

Lifting the table back up, he could feel the pain in his ankle again, only now it seemed more acute. Aggravated by inactivity, he reasoned. Unsteadily, he attempted again to stand up, this time placing his hands in the centre of the table. He edged along, with the palm of his left hand flat against the back wall for stability, until he reached the double doors. He pressed his face against one of the panes of glass, eliminating any reflection, but there didn't seem to be any sign of light or movement inside the restaurant. He let out a very audible sigh of frustration.

Making his way steadily back to his chair, he sat back down. Once he felt more competent, and his head was again acclimatised to reality, he would make his way over the small railing then slowly home. The Sofra restaurant would certainly be getting a call from him later that day telling them exactly what he thought of them. He was incredulous as to how they could treat a customer this way.

The blue of the morning sky was gradually growing lighter in shade. Dylan sat watching some early morning commuters. Then he noticed a more familiar figure approaching in the distance.

When the figure finally got close enough he saw that it was Aygul, making her way from the direction of the station. She crossed the road and approached the front of the restaurant. As she fumbled around trying to get the keys out of her handbag, and was about to disappear from his line of sight, Dylan called out to her.

'AYGUL!'

She heard his feeble call and turned her head towards the direction it was coming from - the tea garden. She took a couple of steps back. Craning her neck she caught sight of someone sitting at one of the tables. Her expression was a picture of confusion. She stood staring at him, unsure. Then it dawned on her that it was Dylan, and she sprang into action. She rushed over, excitedly calling out his name.

'Mister Dylan,' her cry rang out, breaking the early morning calm. 'Mister Dylan.'

She reached the railing, stopped and stared at the dishevelled and disorientated Dylan sitting at the table.

'Mister Dylan, where did you go? I was very worried. Where have you been?'

The concern in her voice was lost on Dylan, who'd been itching to launch into a tirade.

'Where have I been? Where have I been? What do you mean where have I been? Sitting in this bloody chair all night, asleep - right where *you* left me. Why did you leave me out here last night, Aygul? I don't understand why you would do that.'

His throat felt quite raw. It was paining him to do so, but he had to speak out against the injustice of it all.

The girl just seemed even more puzzled.

'I don't understand, Mister Dylan. It was not last night you were here.'

'What do you mean it wasn't last night? Of course it was. I was with my friends, remember? And afterwards you brought me out here so I could have a smoke. Then you just bloody well left me here.'

Still perplexed, she said, 'But that was not last night, Mister Dylan. That was three nights ago. You have been gone for two whole days. Everybody was looking for you. We didn't know where you were. We were all very worried.'

'What?' cried Dylan. 'Two days? I've been gone for two days? That's impossible!'

'No. It's true.'

'What day is it?'

'Monday morning. You were here on Friday night.' She made her way to where Dylan was sitting. 'I came outside to look for you but you were gone and I thought that you must be drunk and you had climbed over and gone home. It was too late to call anybody, so I waited for the next morning and called your friends. They told me they don't know where you are and they have not seen or heard from you since when they left here.

'We try all of Saturday to call you on your mobile and your home telephone but there was no answer and I call your office and speak to Mister Tony but he didn't know where you were and he say that he would try to contact all the taxi company and hospitals and the police and then he call me back and told me that you were nowhere.'

Dylan could not believe what he was hearing. He saw that Aygul was getting quite agitated.

'Okay, sweetheart, I believe you now. I'm sure you did all you could.'

The young girl carried on. Her excitement had subsided.

'My father has been sleeping at the restaurant for these three nights, just in case you came back here.' She looked through the double doors as if to demonstrate the fact. 'I think that he is still sleeping upstairs.'

Dylan was now arched over the table with his face in his hands. This was not what he had expected to hear. Two lost days. *Two lost days.* Where had they gone? He couldn't remember anything apart from the remnants of a dream, and in truth he couldn't remember much about that, just a vague recollection of cushions.

Aygul was now getting back some of the breath that she had neglected to take in her excitement. Resting one of her hands gently on his shoulder, she said, 'I will open up the restaurant then I will come through and help you to get inside.' She spotted the patches of dried vomit on his clothing. 'Then we will clean you up and have some coffee. And maybe you will be able to remember something after that.'

*

Some time later, cleaned-up and reinvigorated by

several cups of sweet Turkish coffee, Dylan made his way home. He had thought to phone Tony and let him know of his return but discovered that his mobile phone was missing. He'd searched every pocket but, unable to find it, began to doubt having actually taken it out with him on the Friday night. Probably in his other jacket, he thought. His wallet was still in his inside pocket, contents intact and complete. Whatever the motive for his apparent abduction it certainly didn't seem to be financially motivated – but the way things were going at the moment, being mugged was the least of his worries.

On his way home from the station he thought to pop into the office and put Tony's mind at rest. When Dylan walked in Tony was sitting behind his desk concentrating on some official looking letters lying in front of him. On the window sill a portable radio played classical music. Dylan stood in silence. Without looking up from whatever it was he was immersed in, Tony motioned towards the small kitchen worktop with his forefinger.

'Just put it over there.'

'Put what over where, boyo?' boomed Dylan. The rawness of his throat had eased.

Tony looked up with a start. When he realised who it was his eyes widened. He stood up, bringing his hands together in a loud clap.

'Boss! It's you!' he cried, making his way towards Dylan. 'Where you been? I look everywhere - I phone everybody. Nobody know where you are.'

Dylan was unable to move, overcome by the display of open emotion as Tony hugged him.

'So? Where you been, boss?'

Dylan stared at him blankly.

'I don't know, Tony. I really don't know. That's the truth.'

Dylan slowly walked to his chair and sat down, his elbows on the desk and his forehead resting in his hands.

'I left here on Friday night to go have a meal with some friends and I think that I may just have had a little too much to drink. I was sitting outside the restaurant having a smoke on my own and I must've fallen asleep. When I woke up, the girl, Aygul, told me that it was Monday morning. And I can't remember anything that happened in between.'

Tony walked over to the radio to turn it off.

'No,' said Dylan, stopping him. 'Leave it, I like it.'

Tony explained how he had phoned all the hospitals in the area and that by the Saturday afternoon, as Dylan hadn't returned, he decided to report him as missing to the police. The police officer he'd spoken to was quite dismissive at first. He said that as the missing person had gone out drinking perhaps he should wait until that evening, then if Dylan didn't turn up after that to contact them again and they would then file a missing person report. Half an hour later, he'd had a call back from a Detective Inspector Cranshaw who seemed rather more interested in Dylan's disappearance. He apologised profusely for the dismissive attitude of the officer on the desk, and wanted to know everything about Dylan and his movements.

This intrigued Dylan.

'Why would a DI be so interested in an ordinary missing person?'

'That's what I think, boss. And he start to ask questions about what you been up to in the last few days.'

'So what did you tell him?'

'Nothing much. I tell him that we had some cases on at the moment and that you were always out investigating those.'

'Did he ask you what sort of cases?'

'Sure, so I tell him. A... how you say?.... adultery case, a missing person, some false insurance claims, blah, blah blah. Stuff like that.'

'Nice one,' said Dylan, impressed by Tony's initiative. 'Wish we bloody did though. This Lola thing seems to be a little overwhelming at the moment. I'd like a bit of a diversion.'

'Well, that's just it, boss. We do have the work.'

'What?'

'Yes. We have a few jobs come in on Saturday and one or two more just this morning.'

'Oh, right. Mr Stone?'

'Is possible, boss. And... it is possible that this Mr Stone kidnap you?'

'I don't know, Tony. It's possible I suppose, but why would he send us this work, then kidnap me? Ahh, I'm sure we'll get to the bottom of it sooner or later. Anyway, tell me more about these jobs.'

Dylan was certain that the work was Mr Stone's doing, but as long as he was being paid, and it was legitimate work, he didn't really care. It was all experience that he needed.

'By the way, did your cousin ever find out who sent those photographs to the newspaper?'

'No, boss. He was told they are sent in anonymously. No clues.'

'No clues? Great. And they just used them?'

'Hey, you know this newspaper, what they are like.'

'Okay, let's have a nice cup of tea shall we? I need to get rid of the taste of that Turkish coffee from my mouth. Then we'll take a look at all this work that we've inherited.'

Tony shook his head. 'Oh no, boss. First you get yourself down to the hospital and get checked out. You don't look so good. You been gone two days. Anything could have happen.'

Too weak to argue, Dylan agreed.

'Who did you think I was when I walked in, when you asked me to put whatever it was over by the sink?'

'Oh, no, it is my son, Nico. I bring him in to help. I send him to get some lunch but he's no back yet. I think he has gone to bookies with the money I give him.'

It occurred to Dylan that Tony, thinking it was his son standing in the doorway, had spoken English, not Italian.

'Have you spoken to Victoria, by the way? How was she about my disappearance?'

Tony hesitated.

'I don't know, boss. She never ring here and I don't have a telephone number to call her.'

Dylan tried to hide his disappointment.

'No, of course, I forgot that we still haven't got a client phone book. I'll er... I'll have to get one.

127

Especially now that we've actually got some more clients, eh?'

Intuitively Tony knew how Dylan was feeling.

'Go to the hospital now, boss. I think that it is going to be very busy.'

FOURTEEN

The Royal Free Hospital was a stone's throw from the house in Hampstead Hill Gardens, and so, also quite close to the office. Within twenty minutes, Dylan was standing at the reception desk of the Accident & Emergency department. The woman on reception was a little irascible, telling Dylan that he should have gone to his GP first, and that A&E, as the name inferred, was for accidents and emergencies. She was placated however, when Dylan explained his reason for being there.

Dylan sat in the waiting area looking around at the assembled casualties of misfortune in various states of physical impairment. There were people slunk forward in states of lament, heads in their hands, looking vacantly up to the ceiling, and others with their faces stuck firmly in a book or a magazine. There were arms in slings, legs in plaster, and crutches firmly wedged in armpits. There were bawling children nuzzled into cleavages, and frustrated mothers attempting to pacify them. Each of them eagerly listening out for their name to be called. Some, it had to be said, more patiently than others.

Nurses rushed frantically through one door only to disappear just as frantically through another. A doctor, her head down and eyes trained on the clipboard she was holding, emerged from a small room and called out a name. Dylan looked around, but nobody responded. Others twisted their heads to look. The doctor called out the name again. Still nobody responded, so the doctor turned on her heels and disappeared back into the room. Orderlies nonchalantly pushed trolleys from one place to another, slowing down occasionally to chat to a colleague.

As well as the cacophony of sights and sounds there were the smells: chemical smells of medicinal spirits, anti-bacterial hand gels and disinfectants; smells of food wafting in from the cafeteria and the kitchens; and somewhat more disagreeable than all of those were the unfortunate and downright funky human smells from some of those that sat in the stuffy and over-crowded environment of the waiting area.

Then there was the young girl who particularly intrigued Dylan. Somewhat Bohemian in appearance she was wearing a loose flowing cambric-print dress, dark blue knitted shrug, and had short French-braided hair. She wore no shoes, and every time she lifted her feet to reveal the soles Dylan could see the dirt that she had obviously accumulated on her travels. Her nose he thought a little large for her pixie features but it was a face that was not unattractive. He would turn every now and again to watch her as she sat busily having a conversation with those around her. All the time that Dylan had watched the little group that she was sitting with he had not actually seen anybody acknowledge her attentions, or even turn to look her in the eye. On the contrary, in fact. Desperate to look anywhere other than straight at her, they moved restlessly upon their chairs, looking around them for alternative places to sit. But none of them, or at least none capable of doing so easily, actually made the move. Perhaps, Dylan thought, this was out of fear of drawing more attention to themselves should she then have followed them.

The girl however, was seemingly oblivious to this. She doggedly carried on the one-way conversations, undeterred by their total disregard for all the splendid words she was regaling them with. And Dylan, from a safe distance, thought it all highly amusing; occasionally laughing to himself, he was provoking stares from those seated nearby.

The first person sitting in the vicinity of the young girl to be called took the long route to get to the room that he had been called to, as opposed to the shorter route which would have meant passing directly in front of her. The nurse that had called his name stood, bemused, watching him as he wound backwards and forwards through rows of chairs, as if trying to find his way out of a maze.

One by one all the others sitting near the girl did the same; the same relieved expression displayed on their faces as they hurried off.

Dylan thought this great entertainment, or at least he did until the last person around her had been called and she began looking around for an alternative audience and caught sight of him watching her. She stood up and started walking eagerly towards him. In a wild panic Dylan turned and looked around, and to his dismay he saw that there were now quite a few unoccupied seats close to him which she could select from; as time had gone on the crowd had thinned out considerably. To Dylan's relief though, at that very moment a nurse came out of one of the rooms to his right and called out his name. He stood up with great speed, forgetting the pain that still dogged his foot, and made his way hurriedly towards the room. As he did he couldn't help but glance back at the girl who was making her way to where he'd been sitting, her face a picture of profound disappointment.

*

Dylan's physical examination showed that the pain in his ankle had been exacerbated by tiny needle entry points around the site. The nurse was quite alarmed by this, especially when Dylan told her that he had no idea how he'd got them. She called for a doctor who requested immediate blood and urine tests. Dylan's case had become an emergency.

Hah! Should have gone to the GP first - what did she know? Dylan felt vindicated after what the woman on the reception desk had said.

After having his blood taken, with a short stop in the toilet to fill the specimen bottle he'd been given, there was a further period of inactivity in the waiting area. Fortunately the young girl had moved on by then and pretty soon Dylan was ushered into the doctor's office.

'Mr Morgan, do you use recreational drugs?' asked Doctor McKiddie, looking down at Dylan's notes.

'No, doctor. To be honest I do smoke a hookah occasionally, but that's it. And I do like a drink or two.'

'You smoke a hookah?'

'Well, yes, but only flavoured tobaccos.'

'I see. Then, have you had any kind of treatment recently which necessitated the use of an anaesthetic or sedatives? I can't see anything in your notes here.'

'No, doctor. Why?'

'Well...' he hesitated, '...because we've found, amongst other things, traces of sodium amytal, ketamine, benzodiazepines and chloroform in your blood and urine.'

'Are they dangerous?'

'Yes, they all can be if given in enough quantity, especially chloroform which can be quite fatal even in relatively small quantities. But I suspect by the amounts that we found that whoever administered these substances must have known what they were doing. I think that they just wanted you out of it for a while, for whatever reason. How have you been since you woke up? Have you had any hallucinations for instance?'

Dylan shook his head. 'No.'

'Do you remember any vivid dreams or nightmares from when you were asleep?'

Dylan told him he had, but couldn't recall much.

'Any heart murmurs or nausea?'

The doctor reeled off a list of symptoms, all of which received negative replies.

'Your heart-rate is a little on the quick side, and your blood pressure is a little high, but apart from that I think that you may have escaped any serious adverse effects. However, symptoms may start to show in the next few days. So I advise you to make an appointment to see your GP, just so we can keep an eye on you. He'll arrange for you to have a series of tests, just to be on the safe side.'

'Okay, doctor. Thanks very much.'

As Dylan stood up and turned to leave, the doctor called after him.

'Oh, and I hope that you will appreciate, Mr Morgan, that I will have to notify the police about this.'

Dylan stopped in his tracks and turned around again to face the doctor.

'Why do you need to do that?'

Dr McKiddie leaned forward in his chair.

'Because I think it would be unethical of me not to do so, Mr Morgan. Surely you must understand that the police would need to know that something like this has occurred. Whoever did this to you has committed a criminal act. Injecting drugs into someone against their will with the intent of incapacitating them is against the law. You must know that? And you must also understand that it is my responsibility, as the examining doctor, to notify them in case you do start showing symptoms, your situation worsens and something happens to you - if only to cover myself. It's none of my business of course, but do you have a reason for not going to the police yourself?'

'It's complicated, doctor. You're not here to listen to my problems.'

'Yes, but when it could become my problem it's in my best interest to listen. So you better sit back down and give me the super quick condensed version.'

Leaving out the bits of the story that he felt may not go down too well with a law-abiding doctor, such as the discovery of dead bodies, Dylan gave Dr McKiddie a brief version of the events. If hindered by police involvement at this stage it would slow down his investigation. The doctor made it clear to Dylan that his responsibility was towards his patient, but agreed that he would only tell the police the bare facts. Whatever else they were to hear would be up to Dylan himself. Dylan once again stood up and shook the doctor's hand. Having found someone else to share his woes with somehow made his burden feel lighter.

'I must admit though to being quite fascinated by your line of work, Mr Morgan. If you ever need any medical advice to do with a case you're working on, please contact me. I'll be happy to help.'

He took out a card, on it the number of a private medical practice, and handed it to Dylan. 'As long as it's all ethical and above board, of course.' He waved an admonishing finger.

'Of course, Doctor... McKiddie,' said Dylan, looking at the card. 'thanks again.'

*

The sky was dark when Dylan got out of A&E so he decided to head straight for home. Walking the short distance to his flat the pain in his ankle was a sharp reminder of the needle marks found in his foot. Thoughts were swimming around his brain and he was still a little dazed and confused. He hadn't noticed it before, as it was still daylight when he had got to the hospital, but now that it was dark the lights of the cars were dazzling, forcing him to squint. He hadn't had a problem with bright lights before and thought it could be a side-effect of the drugs that had been introduced into his body.

He contemplated the implications of what had happened to him. Visitations from mysterious men in baggy summer suits was one thing, but being abducted, kept unconscious, and losing two whole days was bordering on the surreal. Was he out of his depth, he wondered? It did seem that this may just be too big a case for a rookie private investigator. Perhaps he should sidestep the case after all, Victoria would understand if he did - especially after this latest development. When he had agreed to take the case on it was just about finding a friend who had been falsely reported dead and had possibly gone missing. He had been eager to do so as it was his first case – and, of course, it was Victoria. Since then things had spiralled out of control and on to a whole new, unmanageable level.

As he entered the house on Hampstead Hill Gardens and made his way up the staircase he heard a door being opened on the first floor. As he got to the top of the stairs and was making his way along the first-floor landing he was confronted by Mrs Sumner.

'Oh, Mr Beaumaris,' she said excitedly as she

pawed at his jacket in her usual tactile manner. 'I didn't get a chance to speak to you yesterday and I wanted to make sure that everything was okay. Your friend was here on Saturday evening. He was knocking on all the doors and asking if anybody had seen you, but nobody had and he seemed very concerned. A very charming man he was. A lover of Puccini, just like myself.'

She smiled as her gaze disappeared off into the distance. She pressed herself up against him, her hands clutching at the sleeve of his jacket.

'Yes, Mrs Sumner, that would've been my friend Tony. Unfortunately I had to go away and I totally forgot to inform him.'

'Yes, dear, most concerned he was. I was so worried after he left.' Her expression, at first concerned, changed to a smile as she continued. 'But then, I heard you moving about in the early hours of yesterday morning and it put my mind at rest. I was still in bed when you left yesterday and you must've got home very late last night. I would've already been tucked up fast asleep so I didn't hear you. But here we are, dear. So you're alright are you?'

She tightened her grip on his sleeve and Dylan looked up towards the top floor.

'You heard me moving about yesterday morning you say? You're sure it was yesterday morning?'

'Well, to be truthful, dear, it was more like banging about but I didn't want to say anything. You're usually a very quiet young man. I thought that you may have had a visitor, or something,' she winked. 'But it was definitely yesterday morning. I may be getting on a bit but I haven't lost my marbles just yet, dear.'

'Of course.... I've just remembered,' he said animatedly, 'I did have a guest over. In fact it was her I've been with for the last couple of days. As I say, I just forgot to tell my friend. I hope that you weren't too inconvenienced.'

He looked towards the stairs and, ever so carefully, began to pull away from her.

'Not at all, dear, but I do worry about you.' He managed to escape her clutch. 'You need someone to look after you, dear. I'm only downstairs you know.'

Dylan flashed her a winning smile and started towards the stairs.

'I know, Mrs Sumner. Thank you.'

He climbed as quickly as the discomfort in his lower leg would allow him. When he reached his door he found it locked. If someone had paid him a visit they hadn't forced entry through the door. He put his ear to the door, listening out for any noise from within. Nothing. He doubted whoever had broken in would still be inside anyway. They would be long gone.

Cautiously, he took his keys from his jacket pocket, careful not to let them jangle as he did so, just in case. He inserted the key in the lock very gently and pushed the door open ever so slowly, scrutinizing each section of the hallway that came into view as the gap widened. It looked as it had when he had left on the Friday evening; the pictures still hanging up on walls and the plant pot still on its stand. There were no initial signs of any disturbance. He reached just inside the doorway and carefully took down the nearest of the pictures hanging on the wall. With both hands he gripped it. It was his intention to smash it over the head of the first person he came across.

He could see the living room door was ajar. He walked into the hallway, leaving the front door wide open - just in case it turned out that there was someone still in the apartment and he needed to make a quick exit. Like Michael Jackson, he was a lover not a fighter.

He walked cautiously into the living room and glanced around. Everything looked normal - no upturned furniture, no open drawers, no papers on the floor, nothing. The glass he'd left on the coffee table stood exactly where he had put it down, and still with a small amount of Scotch in it. He checked each room in the flat, one by one, with vigilance at first, but as each room was found to be clean and seemingly untouched, subsequent rooms were entered with increased confidence.

Having checked every room Dylan found no indication of violation. He walked back to where he had taken the picture off the wall and placed it back on its hook. The intruder (or intruders) were extremely neat. If anything, he thought, the apartment was possibly tidier than when he had left it. Although he conceded that this may just have been his imagination.

The next course of action was to go round and check for bugging devices. It sounded crazy to him, even as he was thinking it, but if someone had been rooting around his flat, and he had no reason to disbelieve Mrs Sumner's claim that she had heard someone in there, then he could see no other reason for them doing so. He didn't know what sort of people he was dealing with so had no idea what they could be capable of. He looked behind wall hangings, he looked underneath lamps, he checked in drawers, he looked inside ornaments, he unscrewed ventilation grilles, he looked in every conceivable place. He found nothing.

It had been a long and tiring day, he decided to put his feet up. He would have a drink or two, order a takeaway and reflect on the past few days' events, even though he had no recollection of most of it. Oh, and perhaps try and get in touch with Victoria.

As he'd thought about phoning her, he remembered that he had to check the other jacket which was hanging in his wardrobe, for the mobile phone. When he went back into the bedroom he noticed the phone laying on top of his bedside cabinet. He examined it. It looked like his phone. Maybe he had taken it out to transfer it to the pocket of the jacket he was going to wear and had forgotten to - easily done. The phone still being there did confirm, however, that the intruder must have been more than just common or garden burglars breaking in for something to sell on.

After he'd eaten he tried to phone Victoria, but there was no answer and the call went straight through to voicemail. He left a brief message asking her to contact him, as he didn't want to mention anything about his abduction in a voicemail message. Too tired to do anything else,

140

he fell into bed and shortly after into a deep
sleep.

FIFTEEN

At seven o'clock the next morning Dylan was noisily awoken by an alarm on his mobile phone, an alarm which he hadn't set. Eyes wide open, he lifted his head from the pillow and looked towards the phone which vibrated to the sound of sonorous bells. Dylan sat bolt upright and tried to stretch off the sleepiness. Reaching across to turn off the alarm, he noticed that there was an accompanying message requesting that he *Listen to voice recording.* Needless to say Dylan was curious. The intruder hadn't taken or planted anything, as far as he could tell anyway, but it seemed they had set an alarm on his mobile phone and left him a voice recording.

Curiouser and curiouser.

First however, he would make his usual morning visit to the little boy's room in order to expel the residue of the previous day's ingestion and hopefully, during the course of the short journey there, the morning's glory would return to its normal state of flaccidity.

So the question was: who had made this recording? He returned to the bedroom, picked the phone up and clicked on the voice recorder icon. Selecting the only message available, he sat on the bed and listened. The first few seconds were just dead air then a male voice started to speak.

'Hello, Mr Beaumaris. You don't know me and you don't need to, but if you want information as

142

to the whereabouts of a certain young lady meet me at the café in the grounds of Kenwood House on Hampstead Heath at one o'clock this afternoon, Tuesday 19th of April. When you get there just wait and I will find you - unless of course you have received this message too late, in which case I assume that I will be dining alone.'

Dylan considered the message. Looking down, it occurred to him that the tiny air bubble in the top right hand corner of the phone, trapped beneath the screen protector, had gone. Whoever this character was that had been breaking into his apartment, leaving messages on his phone, and was in all probability responsible for his abduction, had at least got rid of that blasted bubble that he himself had been unable to, despite repeated attempts. He clicked on the record button and spoke into the phone.

'Note to self: Remember, when you meet, and just before you hit the bastard, you must shake his hand and thank him for getting rid of the bubble.'

*

Dylan parked the little blue car in the car park just off of the Spaniards Road, making a point of popping into Jack Straw's Castle before proceeding to the meeting point at Kenwood House. There was a small psychological trigger in Dylan's brain which invariably drove him to meeting points early if he knew that there was a pub nearby. And as Jack Straw's Castle was a particular favourite, the opportunity was one just too good to miss.

143

The path that led from the entrance to the heath, nearest to the Castle, followed a course through woodland and across the West Meadow to meet up with the path that ran along the anterior of Kenwood House. It was close to one o'clock and the heath was buzzing with an assortment of folk.

Excited, colourful tourists were enjoying the unusually clement British weather that they probably hadn't expected when arriving from whichever far distant shore they'd been flung. Shirt-sleeved workers from nearby offices were out for a lunchtime jaunt in the glorious April sunshine before having to return to work. Screaming, uniformed children ran around manically chasing each other, rolling about on the grass and generally attempting to evade the attentions of the teachers there to keep a guardian eye on them. The teachers for their part were indifferent to it all, chatting amongst themselves and slyly puffing away at cigarettes, which they would hide as soon as a child approached.

Several pairs of alfresco lovers, oblivious of those around them, were making no attempt at stealth and were quite openly utilising the soft April pasture lands or the trunk of a fallen tree in order to answer the calling of their casual carnality. Owners were walking (or being walked by) waggy-tail dogs that were happily relishing the new smells that the mid-spring heath was offering up.

Dylan's eye was drawn by the colourful spring flowers that were blooming in banks along the edges of the path; the brilliant blues of the bluebells, the reds of the campions and the vibrant yellows of the ragwort. Watching a group of black and white birds chattering noisily as they scavenged the pasture lands, Dylan wished he'd had better knowledge of the flora and fauna. He thought that in all probability these were magpies, but couldn't, with full conviction, say so for sure. He knew that reading a few books and showing more of an interest than just a cursory glance would have made him more learned on the subject, but this required more dedication than Dylan felt he was able to give. He showed equal aptitude in a lot of things. He would have loved to have been able to cook for instance, and had three books on the subject, but when it came down to it the commitment was lacking. Money from a relatively early age had shielded him from the requirement of knowledge of all things he felt to be non-essential for his lifestyle.

As he walked he kept lookout for anyone appearing as suspicious. Not knowing what the person he was meeting looked like, but they knowing what he looked like, obviously had him at a disadvantage.

When he arrived at the cafeteria he saw that the tables outside were starting to fill up; on a bright sunny day most people's preference would be to dine outside. He hurried inside to purchase his food and drink so he could get back out quickly. The voice on the message hadn't specifically requested him to sit outside, but voices carried further inside, and therefore not conducive to what was sure to be a very private conversation.

The queue for food was long, but included a few children who were just standing with their parents. As Dylan joined the rear of the queue he looked around him to see if any of the people in the cafeteria invited obvious suspicion, but quite what he was looking for he wasn't sure. A man sitting in a corner wearing a trench coat, fedora and sunglasses would of course have made Dylan's position a little less tenuous, but there was no such individual at hand.

The crowd steadily increased and space to move was at a premium. People were barging through the queue in order to get to the toilets, and several brushed past Dylan at a proximity that could be considered extremely intimate. Dylan made jokey comments to one or two of the female interlopers which were received as they had been intended, but decided it was perhaps best not to say anything to any men brushing against him for fear of his words being misconstrued.

Finally reaching the front of the queue, he bought and paid for his food, carried the tray outside and sat at one of the few remaining tables. Dylan ate and drank slowly, keeping one eye on those around him.

At half-past two Dylan was still waiting. The mystery person was yet to put in an appearance and an empty plate and drained teapot was making his continued occupation of a much sought-after table untenable. Something had either gone wrong or somebody was playing tricks on him, but he couldn't justifiably sit there any longer.

Then the thought occurred to him that this

146

whole charade may have just been a ruse to get him away from his flat. Whoever had broken in in the first place may have needed to return for some reason. He rose hurriedly from his chair and was making his way out of the grounds of the cafeteria, when he heard a young voice calling out from the crowd of diners.

'Oi, mister. Hold on a minute.'

He turned towards the voice and saw a boy in school uniform, aged around twelve or thirteen, rushing towards him, screeching excitedly. In his hand he was holding something flat, black, and rectangular in shape.

'Sorry, mister - I nearly forgot that I was supposed to give you this.' He handed Dylan the mobile phone he was holding. 'Phew! I might've been in trouble if I hadn't seen you get up to leave just now.'

Dylan looked closely at the phone then felt the inside pocket of his jacket where his phone had been. It was gone. His pocket must have been picked whilst standing in the food queue. It was the only place it could have happened. One of the people that had brushed past him in order to get to the toilets, possibly even someone he'd joked with. It was expertly done however, as he hadn't felt a thing.

He looked down at the phone. He was sure that it was his, but why would someone take it only to return it to him almost straight away? Was this the only reason for bringing him out here? Dylan looked down at the boy.

'What's your name, young man?'

'Josh.'

'Well, Josh... may I ask who gave you this phone and told you to give it to me?'

'Some man. I don't know who he was. He came up to me earlier and pointed you out while you were queuing up in there.' He pointed towards the cafeteria. 'He said that I should leave it as long as possible, but I had to make sure you got it before you left. He said to tell you he's sorry that he took it. He said it was a mistake because he thought you were someone else. And he gave me twenty quid,' he said excitedly.

'What did this man look like?'

Dylan wasn't really expecting a photo-fit description. A rough description may have been enough to go on if the mystery man was still somewhere in the area.

'He was a bit weird looking,' said the boy. 'Like he had some sort of disguise on. I thought it was funny at the time, but then he flashed the twenty pound note at me, so I didn't really care.'

'What sort of disguise was it?'

'Well...' The boy tried desperately to cover his tracks, 'it might not have been a disguise I just said it looked like one. But he had a black beard and a moustache and these really thick glasses. It just didn't look real. It could've been, I suppose. And he was wearing a really colourful hoodie, with the hood up. He looked too old to be wearing something like that.'

Dylan hadn't seen the people that were brushing past him in the queue too clearly, but he thought that he would definitely have remembered someone of that description.

'Did any of your mates see him?'

'I don't think so. Too busy messing about.'

'Well, what about your teachers? Do you think any of them saw anything?'

The boy laughed. 'Nah! The teachers only see what we want them to see.'

This made Dylan smile.

'Okay then, Josh. Thank you very much. You've done a good job.'

As Dylan walked away the boy called to him. 'Oi, mister. Ain't you gonna give me any money for returning your phone then?'

'Of course I'm not. My mate's already paid you, hasn't he?'

*

With no urge to rush back Dylan chose to return to the car via an alternative path - one which ran behind Kenwood House. He stopped off at Dr Johnson's summerhouse, where he liked to sit and while away time on visits to the Heath. The summerhouse itself was long gone, having been burnt down many years previously. Now, in its place lay a concrete slab on which stood two benches. Dylan had always found it a very tranquil place to sit and think; overhanging trees providing the perfect seclusion.

He climbed the few steps that led up from the path and saw that both benches were empty. As he sat down on one of them he reached into his inside jacket pocket and pulled out the mobile phone. He called Victoria's number, but again there was no response. 'Where could she possibly be?' he whispered, tormenting himself. The client that she'd spoken of the last time he'd seen her had quite obviously whisked her away, probably somewhere romantic like Paris. Perhaps I should do that, Dylan thought. Perhaps I should take her away on a romantic weekend somewhere when all this is over. But he knew deep down that something like that would not have swayed Victoria. Whether it was a posh hotel in Paris, or a flat in London, for Victoria it was just doing the job. He knew that. One day she would lose her heart to somebody, be it Dylan or somebody else.

Disappointed, he pulled the phone away from his ear and looked down at Victoria's caller ID photo. He pressed the 'end call' button and as the screen went blank he noticed something strange about the phone; the small air bubble in the top right-hand corner had reappeared. He was both annoyed and confused. This was definitely his phone, and to confirm it he started browsing through the different screens to make sure that all the apps, widgets and shortcuts that he had customised the phone with were still there. They were. If this was his phone, which he was sure it was, the phone with the message but without the bubble couldn't have been. Somewhere along the line there must have been at least four switch-overs. His phone must have been taken at the time of his abduction, even though he thought he had forgotten it at home. The dummy phone was planted in his apartment with the message on it. The dummy phone was then pick-pocketed from him at the cafeteria. And finally, his original phone returned to him via young Josh. For what reason though? Why all the dramatics today?

Surely, whoever wanted his phone could have done whatever it was that they did with it during his abduction and just slipped it back in his pocket before depositing him back at the restaurant.

Dylan's head was reeling. He closed his eyes.

Just then he heard a voice, as a hint of incense blew on the gentle breeze.

'There are many things to consider, young man.' The voice came in a soft, calm Indian lilt.

Startled, Dylan opened his eyes and looked across to the seat opposite on which sat the figure of the Indian gentleman who he suddenly remembered from the cushioned room of his dream. Without thinking about it Dylan asked:

'What sort of things am I to consider, Ravi?'

Dylan's manner was settled and serene, and the old man answered in similar fashion.

'You must consider the concentric circles of life. You must consider the ripple in the water. You must consider that the most important circle in a ripple is the one in the middle – the one from which all other rippling circles emanate. And you must determine which circle you are and your importance amongst all others in the matters which affect you.'

'But you have already shown me,' said Dylan, suddenly remembering more of his dream. 'I am in the second circle and you are in the middle.'

'Oh, but I am not in the middle, young man,' said the old sage. 'I have no importance in the matters which concern you. As I have already told you, I am merely a guide. You must determine for yourself who is in the middle and who is most important in these matters. You must then determine in which way their importance comes to bear relevance in the things which are troubling you, in order that you may ease their burden...'

So saying he was gone, almost in a blink, and Dylan was left staring at the empty, weather-worn bench.

Slipping the phone back into the inside pocket of his jacket, Dylan stood up to make his way back to the car park. As he slowly descended the steps back down to the path, he noticed two police officers standing just beyond the bottom step.

'Are you Dylan Beaumaris Morgan?' the slightly taller of the two officers asked, his face tilted upwards toward the approaching Welshman.

Dylan regarded the two officers with caution.

'That's me, officer.'

'Then I wonder if you wouldn't mind coming down to the station with us and answering a few questions, sir.'

SIXTEEN

'...We *know* that you were at the house on the night of April thirteenth, Mr Morgan. We have the evidence.'

Detective Inspector Cranshaw pushed a less than clear, black and white, 8x10 photograph towards Dylan, turning it to ensure the image was the right way round.

'This looks like it's been taken by some infrared camera or something. It looks a little like me, I suppose, but those things always make people look a little vague. What makes you think it's me?'

'We don't *think* it's you. We *know* it's you, Mr Morgan – or Beaumaris, if you prefer.'

'No, no, constable. For the purposes of this exercise, Morgan will suffice.'

Cranshaw maintained his composure, allowing only the vaguest of smiles.

'Mr Morgan, we know that it was you in Gerald De Vere's house that night because not only do we have this, admittedly slightly blurred, image of yourself by the bedside, but we also have infrared film footage from not only the bedroom, but from other rooms around the house. And not only that... we have CCTV footage of a car registered in your name which was parked outside the house for several hours that evening, too. And what's more, I have written statements from some of De Vere's friends and neighbours stating that a gentleman fitting your description spent a fair chunk of the afternoon and evening sitting at a table in a quiet corner of The Stag public house, within spitting distance of the De Vere residence. "And to all intents and purposes", the landlord himself told us, "he appeared to be waiting for somebody or something."'

Dylan left a long pause before responding.

'Well, I have to say, it looks like you got me bang to rights. It's a fair cop. But if you've got all this footage from cameras all over the place, you must know that I didn't kill him.' His entreat sounded less than desperate. 'And, before you try to lay some retrospective drink-driving charge on me, I was only on soft drinks that day. Well... I may have had a couple of pints, but that was it.'

'Unfortunately, the camera footage from the actual time of the murder has gone missing.' Cranshaw's tone was accusatory.

'Ooooookay then... well, that's obviously another point that's not in my favour.'

Cranshaw, silently toying with Dylan, allowed him time to work out what was happening before putting him out of his misery.

'We know that you didn't do the murder, Mr Morgan. What we're trying to find out is who did. What I need to know is what you were trying to find and who you were trying to find it for?'

Dylan knew that he couldn't give him Victoria's name. She had knowledge of the crime and didn't report it, but she was innocent. Even if she only had the limited information given to her by Lola, giving Cranshaw her name may make her a chief suspect.

'I can't give you the name, Inspector. Client

154

confidentiality.'

'Client confidentiality, eh? Okay, you're pulling that one out are you? So what is it that you were looking for, then?'

'I can't tell you that either. Again, it's client confidentiality.'

Cranshaw noticed that Dylan was starting to look uneasy, his jauntiness slowly melting away. Looking past Dylan, at his fellow officer who was standing against the wall by the door, he smiled.

'Alright then, Mr Morgan, let's try something else. Perhaps you can tell me what your client may have had to do with the art dealing, man about town, Gerald De Vere.'

'Look, Detective Inspector... I'm sorry, but I can't tell you that either for fear of compromising my client's position.'

Cranshaw lifted himself up straight in the chair.

'Mr Morgan, let's not beat about the bush any further, eh? Especially as it is your compromising positions that you have to thank for your current situation. If you can't tell me anything, then perhaps I can show 'n' tell you a thing or two.'

Cranshaw's whole manner had changed and he now looked like a man who was prepared to throw himself fully into his mission. Sitting on the table was a file from which Cranshaw pulled another blown-up photograph. He slid this across to Dylan who'd been vigilantly watching his every move, only this time he didn't turn it around, an indication that his patience was now at a premium. Dylan pulled the photograph the rest of the way towards him, turning it ninety degrees.

He looked at it quickly, already having realised that it was the photograph he himself had taken of the two bodies on the bed. He instinctively knew that the man in front of him knew where it had come from. Quite obviously the result of the recent mobile phone merry-go-round, he wondered if this could have been the only reason for it all, or was there more to come? He knew already that Cranshaw was too shrewd a man to lie to, so Dylan decided to remain silent. He moved his gaze back up to the policeman's face.

'I take it that you're aware of where that photo came from, Mr Morgan?'

'Would it help my case at all if I was to say that my mobile phone was stolen recently?'

'You can say anything you like, Mr Morgan. However, the fact remains that we know that the photograph on the table in front of you was taken by the camera on your mobile phone. The fact that the mobile phone may have subsequently been taken is neither here nor there. Were it not for the fact that we're already in possession of more than enough evidence against you then we may, or may not, have been worried about the origins of this one picture. The reality is though, that this evidence...' he pointed down at the photograph, '...along with all the other overwhelming evidence we have, puts you incontrovertibly at the scene of the crime.'

Dylan looked down at the photograph then back up at Cranshaw. 'Maybe, at the scene of the crime, but not at the time of the crime. Those bodies looked like they'd been there for days...' His words tailed off at the realisation that he had just admitted being in the house that night. Even though they already knew it, Dylan had helped them by overcoming their first obstacle - that of getting him to admit his presence at the crime scene. He had opened the door and foolishly walked into the trap all by himself.

'So you admit that you were in Gerald De Vere's house on the evening of April the thirteenth?'

'Yes,' was all Dylan could bring himself to mumble.

Cranshaw let his arms slump onto the table and pushed his upper torso back into the chair, stiffening and raising his shoulders. He stretched his neck, twisting it from side to side on its axis, which produced a crack, indicative of tension. Then, with a voice gentle enough to betray his rough exterior, Cranshaw finally spoke.

'Mr Morgan...' Dylan noticed an instant softening of expression. '...I've got a few years left before I retire, it's not around the corner, and however many years remain I'd like to try and do it my way. There are some of my colleagues out there who would be sitting here threatening all sorts in order to get some sort of confession out of you. Some of them prefer to employ the hard approach as a means to an end. You know, bad cop and worse cop. I, on the other hand, like to think that there's a place in this world for all sorts of policing. And, go ahead if you want to and label me as some sort of namby pamby "New Copper"...'

Cranshaw actually made speech marks in the air as he said the words, which quietly amused

Dylan, though he didn't dare show it.

'...It's just that I like to think that I'm a good judge of character. God knows I've met enough 'characters' in all my years in the job so I like to treat them how I think that they deserve to be treated.'

'Well, that's... very fair of you, Detective Inspector.'

'Oh, I can certainly be tough enough if the situation dictates - don't be fooled into thinking otherwise. Just look at me - what else could I be with a face like this? I'd make Marty Feldman look good.'

Dylan let out a small huff of a laugh, even though he wasn't entirely sure who Marty Feldman was.

'So I can do tough, Mr Morgan, but in all honesty I don't think you deserve it. I'm a reasonable man and I'm sure you'd prefer that this little matter was brought to a quick and mutually fulfilling conclusion, without too much pain all round.'

Cranshaw took a deep breath and reached into the folder on the table. He pulled out two further photographs and pushed them towards Dylan. Dylan looked down and saw that they were of a couple having sex. The body on top was definitely female - a brunette, whose face was hidden from the camera - whilst the body underneath was, to his horror, Dylan himself. He reached out and pulled both photographs towards him.

'Mr Morgan, what do you know about these two photographs?'

It was clear to Cranshaw that the expression on

158

Dylan's face was not an act, but that of a person who had just gazed upon the scene in the photographs for the very first time. Dylan looked up from the photographs.

'Hand on heart, I genuinely know nothing about this,' Dylan said softly.

'You agree though that the gentleman in those two photographs is you?'

A piece of the missing section of Dylan's life had just been revealed, and this had ripped something from him.

'Yes. It does appear to be me, doesn't it?' he replied feebly.

'What do you mean 'appears to be', Mr Morgan? Do I understand from that statement that you have no recollection of the encounter with the girl in the pictures?'

It may have been his imagination, brought on by the conflict of emotions that were currently dancing around the maypole of his mind, but Dylan thought that he sensed a certain inflection in Cranshaw's last few words, an inflection which implied that he was subconsciously willing Dylan to reply in agreement.

'I have no recollection of it whatsoever.'

'Do you know who this girl is?'

'No.'

'Do you have any idea who it may possibly be?'

'No.' He lied. Although he couldn't be sure that it was definitely Lola.

'You're sure?' The inspector asked him. He knew.

'Yes.'

'Well, let's see if this one helps you at all.'

Cranshaw reached into the folder once more and pulled out a third photograph.

'Now, in this photograph, Mr Morgan, you will see that we get a shot of the girl from the front. Unfortunately, whoever took the photograph went to great efforts to ensure that her head was out of shot. However, if you look closely at the area at the very top of her right thigh you will see that she has a tattoo.' He pointed out the position of the tattoo in the photograph. 'We've had a close look at it and we're pretty sure that it's a small rose. Tell me, Mr Morgan, do you know of, or recollect having had sex with a brunette with a rose tattoo close to her... well, you can see exactly where it's close to...?'

Even though the situation was not conducive to rapid thought, Dylan knew that he would have to think extremely quickly. Should he admit that he knew who the girl in the picture was, even though he had no conscious memory of having met her, and certainly no clue as to how he had managed to compromise himself with her in such a way? But if he did, he would have to tell Cranshaw everything.

Or maybe not.

If he gave Cranshaw Lola's name he wouldn't necessarily have to give him Victoria's. Maybe they were trying to tie Lola in with the De Vere murder because of her similarity to the girl found next to him. He knew he could clear that one up for them, remembering that the dead girl didn't have a rose tattoo.

'Yes. I do. Well, I don't know her... despite

what those photographs may be telling you, Inspector, but I do know of her. And I can't deny that is me with her in the photographs. I'm pretty sure that she's the girl I'm looking for... for my client. And if it is, her name's Lola Douglas.'

Dylan felt a sense of relief at having given the inspector something, although he knew that wouldn't be the end of it.

'Well, it looks to me like you've already found her, Mr Morgan,' he said, pointing at the photographs spread on the table.

'That's just it, Inspector. I didn't find her. She must've found me. When I said that I have no recollection of the encounter in these pictures I was telling you the truth. I really don't remember a thing.'

'Was she the reason that you went to De Vere's house?'

Cranshaw's question suddenly sparked something in Dylan and he considered that all may not yet be lost.

'No. It wasn't for that. I went to De Vere's house on another case that I'm working on. I have more than one case you know.'

'Oh, and what case is that?'

'It's an insurance case. My client claimed that Mr De Vere had made a fraudulent claim, and I was there to investigate it.'

'At night? In the dark? By breaking and entering? Is that how you conduct all your investigations? Well, the ones that you're fully conscious for, at least?' Cranshaw spat venomous sarcasm.

'For the record, Inspector, I did not break. The

161

door wasn't locked. I just opened it and went in.'

'Okay, Mr Morgan. So, just trespassing then?'

'I would have knocked, but I'm not sure the owner of the house would've heard it.'

Dylan immediately regretted joking at the expense of the dead De Vere.

Cranshaw, whose body posture had caused him to slide down in the chair again, pulled himself back up and came back at Dylan.

'So, we've established that you're a sensitive soul. We've also established that you're prone to incredibly casual sexual encounters during blackouts. We've established that you have more than one case that you're working on at the moment, and that these jobs on occasions make it necessary for you to break the law. And we have established that the person with you in this, less than memorable, assignation bears a resemblance to the body found alongside Gerald De Vere. Some coincidence, wouldn't you say, Mr Morgan?'

Shuffling the photographs around on the table Dylan seized his opportunity.

'Ah, well, Inspector. You noted yourself that the girl in this picture had a tattoo of a rose... just there.' He pointed to it. 'But if you look at the girl's body that is next to De Vere you will see that *she* has no such tattoo. It can't be the same girl.'

Dylan felt such satisfaction; he was the defence lawyer who had just blown to smithereens the prosecution's cast iron case with the one simple piece of evidence that had been in front of everyone's eyes all along. Dylan's satisfaction was short-lived however.

'We know that it's not the same girl, Mr Morgan. In fact, the girl in this photograph, next to the body of De Vere, is not a girl at all.'

This was most unexpected.

'What do you mean? It's a man?' Dylan was incredulous.

'No, Mr Morgan, it's neither male nor female. It's actually a rubber doll,' replied the inspector quickly. 'A life-size, silicone sex-doll, to be exact. Made, quite obviously, to look like your young lady... from another case.' Another spit of sarcasm.

'But its eyes are closed. Surely those dolls would have their eyes open?'

'I don't know, Mr Morgan. Perhaps it was commissioned by someone with a fetish for having sex with narcoleptics.'

Dylan, taken aback by the revelation, was beginning to tire.

'Look, Inspector, I've told you that I don't know the girl I'm looking for, and I certainly don't remember having had sex with her – despite the evidence. I was at De Vere's house on the night in question because I was trying to get some evidence against him in an insurance fraud case that I'm working on. And yes, I did break the law by entering his house uninvited, and maybe I didn't tell anybody that I'd found two... well, it appears that it's one dead body. So charge me with that if you're going to. But I suspect that nobody is actually pressing charges against me for that one. I didn't kill De Vere, and I don't know who did. I was just in the wrong place at

163

the wrong time. So, ask me any other questions that you have to and let me go, 'cos if I have to spend much more time here I will ask for my solicitor to be present... once I find one.'

Cranshaw knew that Dylan's cooperation was almost at an end and decided to end his misery.

'Okay, Mr Morgan. Now, assuming that you are not going to give me the name of your client...?' His words tailed off into a question, to which Dylan said nothing, merely offering a shake of the head, '...Then I have no further questions for the moment. You are free to leave. But please don't leave the country, just in case we need to ask you some more questions.'

Dylan got up and walked towards the door and was about to leave when Cranshaw stopped him.

'A last piece of off-the-record advice for you, Mr Morgan. I'd be very careful, because those pictures over there on the table, the camera footage we have of the murder scene, and the photographs of Gerald De Vere at the beach that were sent to the newspapers, were all taken off of the SD card that we found in your phone when you were brought in here today. I think that you're getting dragged into a swamp here, Mr Morgan.' There seemed to be an almost sympathetic tone to his voice now. 'So, whatever it is that you're investigating, just don't get mixed up in ours or I will be forced to come down on you harder than my conscience is telling me to.'

SEVENTEEN

'Penso che sara una giornata impegnativa.' Dylan called across the office to his colleague who was absorbed in the newspaper.

'Yes, boss,' came the reply.

Instantly, Dylan looked up from the screen of his laptop and over towards where Tony was sitting.

'What did you say?' he asked, excitedly.

Tony again mumbled the words, 'Yes, boss,' without looking up.

'So you understood what I said just then?'

Tony had not been listening to what Dylan had said, far less understood it. He looked up from his newspaper.

'Ah, sorry boss, what did you say?'

'I asked if you understood what I said just then.'

'When, boss?'

'When I said: Penso che sara una giornata impegnativa, and you said yes.'

'Oh, I didn't really hear you, boss, I was reading something in the newspaper.'

'Why did you say yes then?'

'Well, to be honest... some of the time I do not hear what people say. So, I just say yes.'

Dylan looked defeated.

'So, you didn't understand what I said then?'

'No, boss. I told you, I don't speak or understand any Italian. I wish I did, but no.'

Dylan wasn't good in the mornings. Whatever time he got out of bed was irrelevant to his actually being fully awake and aware of what was going on around him. His walk to work in the mornings could best be described as more of a stuporous saunter. His only aim was to get to the kettle in the office and make that first cup of tea, even though the effect was to further enervate his senses. He would seldom have his first tea of the day on waking, back at the flat, because he knew full well that its effect would dull his inclination to venture out to the office at all - it would have been all too easy for Dylan just to stay at home. The motivation of working in order to fulfil obligations and responsibilities was not there for him. Neither was the burden of requiring a steady wage to ensure bills were paid. They would be paid regardless.

He didn't really need Tony as an assistant – Victoria and his friends had already told him as much. But the extra expense was hardly noticeable and, in all honesty, it was more for the companionship than anything else. Even though the workload had been non-existent when he had taken Tony on, it had increased since and his new assistant, accompanied by an inventory of family contacts, was sure to come in handy.

The agency was merely his latest indulgence, but he was determined to make it work because he didn't want to be a victim of his own wealth - to be thought of as a waster. He had no wish to be sheltered from the humbling realities of life, the things that give us humanity and make us worthy of the attention of others, by the shield of

166

prosperity. He wanted to contribute. But in truth, work, and the investigation business, was all a bit of a game for Dylan, something for him to enjoy, and if it didn't go the way he wanted there was no great harm done, he would simply move onto something else. He just wasn't very good in the mornings was all.

'So, what's this summons then, Tony?' he called across to his possibly superfluous, but nonetheless welcome, assistant.

'It's done, boss. I do it yesterday.'

'When yesterday?'

'While you are messing about in the police station I go and do the job. It is not difficult. I find out where he drinks in East London and I wait for him. I find out his name. We make some conversation. I slowly get him drunk and in the end he almost bite my hand off for the envelope. Finish. I go home.'

'Good. So no problems then?'

'Yes. Bloody train break down - again. So I got home very late and my wife, she had to heat up my Linguine Amatriciana in the microwave. Ergggh!' He emphasized his disgust with a wild hand gesture. 'Still, I eat and tell her it is lovely because I know that when she first cook it, it was. That is why we are married for more than thirty years.'

Dylan smiled.

Over the course of the next couple of days Dylan and Tony spent most of the time out of the office. Between them they served another summons, accumulated enough evidence against two parties that had made fraudulent insurance claims, and began the investigation into the adultery case. Tony was to carry on investigating the woman suspected by her husband of having an affair with her cousin's husband and Dylan would drive over to speak to the father of the teenage boy that had gone missing.

*

The father of the missing boy lived south of the river. Dylan wasn't familiar with South London, even joking with Tony that he may need a passport to get there. Never before having had cause to venture across to the other side of the Thames, he was sure that the journey to Blackheath would be an interesting one.

London's skyscrapers had always fascinated him. Seeing them from a distance, as he had done on many occasions from the lofty perspective of Hampstead Heath, recalled memories of the mountains of Snowdonia, the scene he had looked upon as a boy from the window of his bedroom in Porthmadog - the vistas of his youth. However, he had never seen the buildings of Docklands so close-up. Dylan drove with one eye on the road ahead and one eye looking up at the tops of the buildings, reaching for the skies.

He arrived at the house and was greeted by Professor Braddock, a lecturer in Maritime History at the Institute in nearby Greenwich. The first thing Dylan noticed was how very neatly combed his hair was. He was envious of men with moulded hair as his own had a kink that ensured it always looked untidy. Not one grey hair on the

168

professor's head was out of place. In contrast, he wore a white shirt that looked as if it had never even glimpsed an iron, much less been pressed by one, and carpet slippers and a cardigan that looked as if it had stretched in the wash. He was wearing Harry Palmer-style glasses and when Dylan introduced himself he had to fight the urge to say 'My name is...' in a Michael Caine idiom.

The professor explained how he had lost his wife to cancer some years back and since then had struggled to bring up his son, James, alone. He'd wanted James to go to university, but in the last year of school he had let his grades slip so university was not an option in the end. He had managed, however, to persuade him to attend the local college to pursue his interest in fashion, and although this had started well, it seemed that pretty soon his mind was being distracted by something that he would not, or could not, talk to his father about. One morning he left for college and didn't return.

'Can I just ask, Professor Braddock, what made you seek the help of a private detective instead of leaving it to the police? And why Beaumaris Investigations?'

It had been niggling at Dylan ever since Tony showed him the envelope, one of the only ones that looked as if it were genuine; the address was in South London but he did not remember advertising in any of the publications that far afield.

'Well, to tell you the truth, Mr Beaumaris, I was getting a little impatient with the police. You see, if a person is over a certain age they don't

169

seem to be that concerned unless it becomes a murder enquiry. I told them all about my son's behaviour in the months leading up to his disappearance and they made up their minds that he had left home to pursue... an alternative lifestyle, as they called it. They said that they would put a few posters up in police stations, but they didn't think there was much they could do if he didn't want to be found. To be honest, I can't blame them for their attitude, after all there are worse things going on in this world of ours than an eighteen year old who no longer wishes to live at home with his square father. We had him quite late on in life, well my life at least. You see my wife was quite a bit younger than myself, but that dreadful disease is no discriminator of age, and she was still young when it took her.'

The professor's eyes welled up as he spoke.

'Anyway, one day I happened to chance upon a copy of the Ham & High newspaper. Someone had left it in our staffroom, and I saw your advertisement. I suppose that the idea was planted in my mind at that moment.'

'The Ham & High is a local newspaper in North London. What was it doing down here, south of the river?' asked Dylan.

'It isn't unusual. We have staff commuting in from all parts of London. We have one or two from your neck of the woods. I can only assume that one of them had brought it in and left it there. We have quite an eclectic selection of staff. On any given day you may find a glossy French fashion magazine laying next to a Chinese newspaper and an Icelandic trade publication.'

170

Dylan thought this feasible, and his initial suspicion the idea may have been planted in the professor's mind by a third party dissipated.

'Would you mind if I had a look in your son's room, Professor?'

'No, not at all. Hopefully you'll find some clues in there to help with your investigation.' At this point the professor became a little sorrowful again. 'I'm afraid that it's never been my wont to venture into my son's room. When he was here I tried to afford him as much privacy as I consider a young person of his age needs in order to develop. And since he has gone I have found it difficult to go in there. I have peeked in there from time to time but the room has remained untouched. It is just as he left it. Ready for the day he returns home.'

The welling in the eyes returned as the professor turned away from Dylan and began walking towards a small drinks trolley standing in a far corner of the room. He poured himself a brandy from a crystal decanter, and offered one to Dylan, which he refused. Sensing the man's anguish, Dylan tried to assure him that he would do his utmost to find his son, but he had to be prepared to accept that the boy, if found, possibly may not want to return home. The professor looked up from the glass of brandy that he had been staring into and nodded half-heartedly.

EIGHTEEN

A search of James Braddock's room led Dylan to
the comfortable conclusion that the boy was gay.
From publications he found hidden away in one of
his drawers this was evident. Furthermore, the
probability was that he was also a cross-dresser,
having found a few items of female clothing,
including undergarments; these items, in
themselves not conclusive evidence as they could
have been left by a girlfriend, were accompanied
by a ladies compact, two different shades of
lipstick and a card advertising Oscar's, a club in
Soho that Dylan knew from experience was
patronised by the gay and transsexual contingent
of London. This expelled any doubt from Dylan's
mind.

Memories of a night crawling around the clubs
and bars of the West End many years ago came
flooding back. Dylan and a few friends, amongst
them two girls working as escorts in the Soho
area at the time, spent a night touring the London
Night spots. Dylan was nineteen and retained a
naivety nurtured in a quieter North Wales. He
remembered how the girls would disappear off
into a back room with the manager at each new
club they visited only to reappear a while later
waving bottles of champagne, trays of food, and
sporting a "bills been taken care of" expression
on their faces.

Oscar's was amongst the clubs they had visited
and the club he and his friends had enjoyed the

most. He remembered the waitress, an extremely tall transsexual blonde, whose height was accentuated more so by the the roller-skates she was wearing. He remembered the large, white grand piano around which everybody gathered to sing. He remembered his awkwardness when slow-dancing with the girls, and his lack of coordination. He remembered, whilst dancing, how one of the girls had whispered in his ear that some of the male onlookers were watching them with envy - not of him, but of her. This had unnerved the young Dylan a little, but not enough that he hadn't enjoyed the evening.

*

Soho was as Dylan had remembered it, nothing much ever changed in Soho. Walking around he was soon accosted by one of the working girls. As he passed she called out to him from a shop doorway.

'D'ya wanna do some business, darlin'?'

'Yes, of course, my love,' replied Dylan, not missing a step. 'I'll pop round in the morning to give you a quote for your gutters and fascias.'

They both laughed and Dylan continued on his way.

Oscar's was also pretty much as he had remembered it from all those years back. The piano and the bar were still where they had been although there had been a change of décor and there was no six-foot plus roller-skating waitress - probably a banker in the City by now, thought Dylan. Even after all this time it had retained the easy atmosphere. He did feel a little awkward when having to sidestep the occasional bit of attention, but he felt quite flattered.

Sitting at the bar Dylan asked anyone and everyone that queued for a drink if they knew James Braddock. Subsequently, almost everyone in the club did - most of the clientèle it seemed were regulars. He was surprised, however, at the ease with which the people he spoke to gave him the information he wanted - he had not made a secret of the fact that he was a private investigator. The people Dylan spoke to just seemed happy that someone was actually trying to find James. A few said that on his last few visits to the club, James had been quite subdued. They mentioned that he had recently been spending a lot of time with a girl that, though they had never met her, they felt was having a negative influence on him, but nobody knew the girl's name. He was told that James's best friend, Dominic, would be the person to speak to.

Dominic was sitting on a brown leather sofa in a corner of the room where the lighting was considerably more subdued. Sitting next to him, and being outwardly intimate, a man whose face looked to be held together by a series of chains. Dylan found this a little intimidating and approached the couple warily. As he approached they both looked up. The older man with the chains moved his hand, which up till then had been resting on the younger man's knee, and gripped the inside of his thigh close to the crotch, stamping his possession. He shifted himself uneasily on the sofa, chinking as he did so.

174

'Fuck off,' he said to Dylan in a gruff Glaswegian brogue. 'Can't you see we're busy here,'

Dylan tried to compose himself. He wasn't going to be dismissed quite so easily.

'I'm really sorry to disturb you gents, but could I just have a few moments of Dominic's time? I'm looking for a friend of his, see. And I just need to ask him a few questions.'

'What friend is that then, pal?' asked the chains.

'James Braddock.' Dylan was talking to the chains, but looking at Dominic.

Chains looked across at Dominic.

'What do you think? You okay with this?' He looked back up at Dylan. 'Are you police?'

'No. I'm a private investigator. I've been hired by James's father Professor Braddock, to find his son.'

Chains looked back at Dominic.

'It's up to you, Dom. You want to speak to this guy?'

'You can stay too if you want,' said Dylan, in an attempt to appease the older man.

'No, it's alright,' he said, glancing once again across to Dominic. 'I'll get us another couple of drinks and wait by the bar 'til you're finished.'

As he got up he glared at Dylan menacingly and, speaking to Dominic, said:

'I'll be back over when he's finished.'

And with that he rattled off towards the bar.

*

Dylan headed along the A23 towards Brighton recalling what Dominic had told him. At first a little reluctant to talk, he eventually opened up and revealed that James had indeed got himself involved with a girl who he felt, from the little that James had told him, was quite a divisive character.

'He hadn't known her long. I know it wasn't a sexual relationship.'

'What do you know about her?'

'To be honest not a lot. All I can tell you with true conviction is that she was a brunette, and she knew her way around the sex clubs of Soho.'

'So you don't know her name?' Dylan asked him.

'No. James only referred to her as his girlfriend, you know girl-friend. I followed James out of here one night, just after he'd got a text, and she was waiting for him outside. I followed them for a couple of blocks, but I only glimpsed her from behind. Then they went into a club on Berwick Street. I didn't go in, it would have been too obvious I'd been following them. I didn't want him to think I was interfering.

'What kind of relationship do you think James and this girl had?'

'I'm not sure, but I don't think it was healthy.'

'Why do you say that?'

'I just felt she was using him for some reason.'

'What do you mean by that?'

'I just think she was manipulating James. I mean, she even persuaded him that he was a transvestite in denial. Can you believe that? He'd never shown any inclination towards transvestism before that. He started to believe it was true, that he felt more comfortable in women's clothing. He could quite easily pass himself off as a girl, he's a bit of a pretty boy. She played him. Convinced him. She had some kind of strange power over him.'

'You think so?'

'Oh yeah. She was introducing him to what he called "interesting new people". That's when I became concerned. James brushed it off saying everything was alright, and that he was having more fun than he'd ever had before. He wouldn't listen to me.'

'So he was still a regular in here then?'

'I wouldn't say regular anymore. It became just once in a while. Then one day he told me that he'd met someone special, and that this someone was going to set him up in a flat of his own. He said he couldn't stick around here anymore. And the thing I remember most is when he told me that he felt he was getting further and further away from what his father would expect of him.'

'What do you think he meant by that?'

'I don't know. I've never met his mum or dad.'

'He lost his mother some time ago,' Dylan told him.

'Well there you go. He never really spoke about them, except for that one time, and that was the last time I saw him. The next day he was gone. He sent me a text saying that he was headed for Brighton, and that James was no more. From now on he wanted to be known as Lola.'

*

177

The gay club scene in Brighton was not difficult to find. Finding information on James Braddock, however, was a whole lot more so. Dylan visited several pubs and clubs in the gay quarter of Kemp Town, and spoke to numerous people before he finally found somebody who actually knew James.

The barman at The Revelry Club, Todd, didn't recognise the name James Braddock, but when Dylan mentioned the name Lola he acknowledged it immediately.

'You're not a bloody journalist are you?'

Dylan could only just hear him over the loud music which was blasting out from the P.A. system. He thought the question a little strange but didn't press him on it.

'Lola's a newby on the scene. I'm not surprised nobody knew her.'

Dylan's first instinct had been to correct him but he reigned himself in, realising transvestites were referred to as her or she.

'Even if anybody did know her the chances are that they wouldn't have let on to somebody... no offence, but... as straight looking as you.'

'What do you mean by that?' Dylan asked him.

'You look too much like someone a gay guy who's running away from something wouldn't want to talk to.'

Dylan's looks had never before come into question. He wasn't quite sure whether to be offended or not. He looked up and down at his clothing: light blue jeans, white shirt, dark brown linen jacket and tan coloured desert boots. He looked past Todd to examine his image in the

178

mirror behind the bar. His hair was lobe length and maybe a little unkempt, and he hadn't shaved for a few days. The watching barman smiled and made an attempt at reassuring him.

'I hope you're not upset by what I've just said. I didn't mean to.... It's just that... it's not even really your clothing. It's just that you look straighter than the majority of the people in here. I don't know what it is, but some people you can tell right away, some people you can't. You don't always get it right. I mean, if you're drinking with your mates down your local and someone walks in and is really camping it up you'd probably draw the conclusion, rightly or wrongly, that he's gay. Am I right?'

Dylan nodded in agreement.

'And so it's the same with a straight guy in a gay club. As I say, you don't always get it right,' he said, shrugging his shoulders. 'I mean look at me, my barman's shirt and bow tie don't give much away, but with my moustache I could go either way. As it happens I'm straight, but any of them that don't know me, don't know that. I get to sell more drinks if they think they're going to get somewhere.'

As he spoke he mopped up a bit of spillage on the bar with a once white cloth he pulled out from underneath the counter.

'So, you walk into a bar looking like you do, asking questions about one of the gay community and, irrelevant of whether or not they know the person you're asking about, it's easier for them to say no. Chances are that if someone's being looked for they don't want to be found. They're

179

just protecting their own.'

Dylan begrudgingly accepted this. He ordered a Manhattan Dry and offered Todd a drink as reward for his sincerity.

'When was Lola last in here?'

'She was in here the night before last.'

Todd's shouting bounced off the mirror behind the bar, barely audible over the noise of the music, which was considerably louder than at Oscar's the night before.

'Was she alone?' Dylan bellowed in an attempt to be heard.

Todd placed a doily and the cocktail on the bar.

'No. She was with a couple of friends, as usual.'

'Has she ever been in here with a female friend?'

'Well, now you're asking,' the barman replied. 'I've worked here for three years now, and I still can't be one hundred percent sure which are the real girls and which aren't. Some of them really are that good - Lola herself for example. She's obviously fooled a lot of people. I've been over to Thailand and I can tell you that I got fooled a few times by the lady boys over there. So, in answer to your question - no, I can't say for definite that I've seen her with a girl.'

'Do you know where I might be able to find him... her?' Dylan asked, sipping his drink.

'Not really. She could be in any of the clubs around here.'

'What about where she's living. Any idea?'

'Ah well, now there I might be able to help you

out. I've heard that she's got an apartment in one of them big seafront properties on the Royal Crescent. They're a pretty penny, I can tell you. It doesn't belong to her though, it belongs to someone else. She's just a permanent guest, getting everything paid for her.'

Distracted by customers Todd moved along the bar to serve them, returning a couple of minutes later.

'Why did you ask me earlier if I was a journalist?' Dylan asked him.

'Because of the photos in the paper last week... of the art dealer they found dead. You must've seen them. He was walking along the beach with a mystery girl. I know that not everybody reads those dodgy tabloids, but let's face it, everybody has a snide glance at the front page when they're buying their Times or Guardian or whatever - even if they won't admit it.'

'What of it? The pictures, I mean.'

'Well that was the stretch of beach along Marine Parade. And the girl... well, the story round here is that it's Lola, and that it's the art dealer that set her up in the flat.'

NINETEEN

The early morning sky was still a few shades adrift of the azure blue that had been predicted by the weather girl on the 24 hour news channel, but Dylan could see that the day was destined to be a beautiful one. Distant wisps of fine cloud illuminated by the imminent sun. The stones underfoot were wet and uneven as he strolled along the beach that ran parallel to Marine Parade. He had been unable to sleep when he returned to his hotel room after leaving the Revelry Club. Todd had told him that Lola mentioned she jogged along the beach every morning around six o'clock, so if Dylan was going to find her this would be as good a time as any. He was there a little too early; it was a Friday - before long the everyday commerce of the town would start humming into life. For the moment though it was still relatively quiet.

Dylan's hotel on Marine Parade was just along from the Royal Crescent. The photographs published in the tabloid newspaper had been taken along that particular stretch of beach. He stepped out onto the stones and headed west towards the pier, if for no other reason than it looked more interesting than heading east.

As he walked along in the half-light there was one thought that he could not get out of his mind: what would James/Lola be wearing? In all the pictures that Professor Braddock had shown him, James had looked like a normal boy wearing normal boys' clothing. Dylan harboured, in his occasionally ingenuous mind, an image of James running towards him in a full-length, flowing dress and high heels. A ludicrous thought, he knew, but what was it that a transvestite would wear for a morning's jog on the beach?

Another thought that had crossed Dylan's mind was that in the newspaper photograph of Gerald De Vere and Lola he'd not noticed any tell-tale bikini bulge when he checked for the tattoo. What did this mean? Was it James in the picture? Had he had, what was referred to nowadays as, a gender reassignment? Or was it really Victoria's Lola? And if it was the real Lola, and Victoria was right, then what was De Vere playing at?

As Dylan made his way along the beach he passed a few of Brighton's homeless sheltered in the recesses beneath the promenade, deep within sleeping bags or beneath layers of cardboard and paper. Some were fast asleep, others stirred at the sound of stones crunching under Dylan's shoes as he approached.

'Any chance of a few pence for a morning cuppa?' one voice cried out.

Dylan looked at the man snuggled in the filthy, stained, green sleeping bag. His only possessions the padded fabric he slept in and the contents of a large Tesco Bag for Life filled with a few meagre items of spare clothing. Dylan immediately reached into his pocket for some loose change, and thought he'd take the opportunity in asking if the man knew Lola.

'Lola? Yeah, of course I know Lola. She's always around these parts.'

183

The insincerity in his voice made it clear to Dylan that giving any credence to his answer would be foolish.

Dylan dangled two pound coins in front of him.

'So? What does Lola look like then?'

'Look like? You know what she looks like, man. Blonde, big tits. That's Lola.'

Dylan dropped the coins in the man's open palm.

'Yep. That just about sounds like her.' Dylan walked off, smiling. 'Thanks.'

The man called out after him.

'Cheers, man. You need to come back tonight for Lola though. She's never up this time of the morning. She's probably fast asleep now.'

Another smile crossed Dylan's face.

The next man Dylan came to had a small Jack Russell dog laying by his side.

'Excuse me. Any chance of some spare change, mate?' he called out to Dylan.

'I suppose it's for your dog, is it?'

Dylan immediately felt a tinge of guilt at his jibe. Reaching into his pocket he took out some coins to repair the situation, feeling uneasy with any sort of confrontation. The man watched Dylan retrieve the coins and drop them into his gloved palm as his fingers closed in to secure them.

He was possibly only in his mid-twenties, but the wear and tear on his face made it difficult to tell for certain. He continued staring up at Dylan. Years of hardship had honed in him a sixth sense, and he considered himself a very good judge of character. Whether it was in the mannerisms, or something in a person's eyes, he rarely judged people wrong and in Dylan he saw something intrinsically good, despite the briefest of acquaintances; an opinion not provoked merely by Dylan's beneficence (even though this may have been borne of an attempt to make amends for the stereotypical assumption Dylan had made).

'I wouldn't have said the money was for my dog,' the man said, softly. 'Because it isn't.'

'Well, it doesn't matter anyway,' Dylan mumbled, embarrassed. 'You've got some now and you can do whatever you need with it. I'm sure you'll get the dog something with it though, won't you?'

'Are you joking?' He sensed Dylan's discomfort. 'This mutt here eats far better than I do. All day long he's up and down this beach scavenging for stuff and getting titbits from the cafés and the passers by. I just about get by, myself.'

'Oh well, as long as you're both okay.'

The man thanked him for the money and Dylan went to walk off, then stopped.

'Actually, you may have seen the person that I'm looking for.'

'Go ahead,' invited the man. 'Who're you after?'

Dylan took out the photograph of James Braddock and showed it to him.

'Trouble is, I don't know if he would have looked like this jogging around here, as I'm told he does most mornings. I'm told he's usually wearing women's clothing. He's a transvestite... or transgender, I don't really know what they call it....'

Sensing Dylan's awkwardness the man on the ground thought the opportunity for having a friendly laugh too good to miss, and lifted himself up into a sitting position.

'Of course I've seen him. He runs past here every morning wearing a lovely little off-the-shoulder Alexander McQueen number and matching Jimmy Choos.'

Dylan couldn't help but smile.

'Bloody piss taker, you are – but you're okay.'

'Oh yeah! Well give me some more money then.'

Dylan's hand reached into his jacket pocket and after a little fiddling about emerged holding a note. He handed it to the man.

'There you go. Fill your boots.'

Astounded, the man took the ten pound note and started unzipping his sleeping bag. He stood up to his full height. He wasn't a tall man; Dylan was an inch or so shy of six foot, but this man had to crane his neck in order to look him in the eye.

'I knew there was something about you when I first saw you,' he said. 'It's not often someone gives us money like this. Eh, girl?'

He clutched the ten pound note in a tight fist and shook it in the direction of the dog, now awake and sniffing at stones a few feet away.

'Let me have another look at that photograph. What did you say his name was?'

Dylan hadn't mentioned any names but he confirmed that although the boy's name was James, he was calling himself Lola.

'No.' He shook his head. 'The only Lola I know

is blonde with big tits and is a friend of Geoffrey's over there.'

He looked back along the beach at the scene of Dylan's previous encounter. Both men laughed.

'Seriously though,' he continued, 'I can't say I've seen him, either like that or dressed up as a Lola. I can't be sure though, as I imagine he'd look a bit different.'

'Never mind,' conceded Dylan. 'I'm sure that I'll track him down soon.'

'I hope you do, my friend. I hope you do.'

'Hold on a minute, though.' Something had suddenly occurred to Dylan and he reached into his jacket pocket, taking out the photo of Lola that Victoria had given him. 'It's not a great picture, but this is what he may look like now.'

'Now you're talking,' he said, looking at the photograph. 'Yeah, I've seen her - but not for a couple of days. She's been taking morning runs on the beach for the past few weeks.' He looked carefully at the photograph. 'Yeah... I couldn't swear to it, but I'm pretty sure it's her.'

As Dylan walked away he wondered about the number of people he had met in his life that had the potential to be good friends if the circumstances of their meeting had been different. He felt that this man would almost surely have fallen into that category. There was a certain ease felt in the company of some people, and an empathy that was the basis of any good and lasting friendship. It was friends such as this that he had had difficulty in finding in later life, and why he so valued the handful of friends that he did have.

Dylan walked past a number of upturned boats that lay on the stones like a herd of beached whales. Barnacled and rotting, many looked as if they had lost the capacity to fulfil the purpose for which they'd been built.

Passing under Brighton Pier he approached a groyne not far beyond. It jutted out like a callused arm grabbing for the gloomy sea in an attempt to pull in the distant horizon. He saw that at the end there were still a few men that had been fishing the night tide. Most had already begun packing away to leave, but one or two chatted quietly as they allowed for an extra few minutes in the hope that they would feel a last pull on their lines.

As he walked past the first groyne Dylan could see beyond it a second groyne, the wall of which effectively cut off that section of beach. The wall was neither too high to dissuade Dylan from climbing it, nor low enough so as not to cause him some problem in doing so. On the other side of this wall was a beach bar, which at that time of the morning was still closed and dark. Dylan struggled to climb over the wall, but he did it with the aid of a drinks crate that somebody had thrown over the wall from the bar.

Visible near the tip of the groyne was a sculpture that looked like a huge green doughnut. Dylan approached it. Made possibly of copper, or bronze, it was covered with verdigris. He smelt the early morning stench of late night urine and lifted a hand to cover his nostrils. The previous evening's revellers had obviously been using it as a public convenience, possibly only a few hours ago judging by the intensity of the ammonia smell. With a whole wide sea in which to relieve themselves, thought Dylan, why do it on a sculpture that quite obviously represented something? Although, after several seconds of deep thought, he failed to come to any conclusion as to what a huge copper doughnut could possibly represent - unless it had been commissioned by a local bakery.

Just at that moment, as he stood looking at the oversized curio, one of those awkward unscheduled moments in life which every now and again happen, happened. Psychosomatically triggered, a sudden and desperate urge to empty his bladder came upon him, like a dog that smells another dog's urine and is then compelled to urinate also. He looked around. He knew there was no way he could make it back to his hotel - he wasn't even sure if he could make it back to the mouth of the groyne and the steps which led up to the promenade. Looking for anything that could be used as a makeshift toilet, an empty bottle or a carton, he could see nothing. The nearby cafés were not yet open, and even if they had been, getting to the nearest of those would've meant straining his bladder to its limit. The pressure building up within him was screaming for a quick release. He went right to the end of the groyne and stood facing out to sea. Although the wall around the edge was only three feet or so high, looking down, he saw that there was a further concreted section at the base which jutted out another few feet into the water. If he relieved himself there it would not have been into the sea but onto the lower platform on which there were

189

several birds resting. He rushed quickly to the side, but one or two early morning walkers were strolling the beach, possibly able to see him. Also to consider was the hint of a breeze blowing in off the English Channel. It was only light, but possibly enough to have caused a little unwanted splash-back were he to attempt a urinary aim over the wall and out to sea.

There was no-one else on the groyne yet. There was nothing else for it; he couldn't believe how quickly it had crept up on him. The pain of trying to keep it in was now almost unbearable. Standing behind the huge green doughnut he answered the call of nature with a tremendous sense of relief. The stream was seemingly endless. Each time he thought it had stopped was a mere moment of respite before it started to flow again. Three or four times this happened before Dylan felt confident enough to put things back where they belonged, and even then he wasn't sure that he hadn't tidied away a mite prematurely.

Having concluded his business, and with another quick glance around to make sure that nobody had observed his little indiscretion, he walked off and away from the groyne accompanied by a niggling sense of shame, tinged with more than a small helping of hypocrisy.

There was an opening in the wall allowing access to the next bit of beach but Dylan decided that he didn't want to walk any further west. He could see the remains of the old burnt out pier lying dark and brooding, an abandoned wreck at sea, and it didn't look very inviting. There was something about seeing the ghost of something inanimate that spooked Dylan, and so he chose instead to head back in the direction from which he had come. He found it much easier over the wall on the return journey.

There were a few more signs of life now than when he had started out on his journey, and the sun was rising steadily. He was not sure how much time had passed since he had first walked past the main pier and the first groyne, but he noticed that the fishermen that had been there earlier were now gone. As he rounded the mouth of the smaller groyne he looked out onto the small stretch of beach that lay between it and the base of the pier - a stretch that took in a mere few hundred square feet before giving way to the sea. Dylan stood still and watched the tide lapping benignly onto the shore. As he stared, he thought that he could just make out a small dark shape lying on the stones by the water's edge. He started to walk towards it. The nearer he got, the more he became enveloped by a powerful sense of foreboding. Something in his head at that moment screamed at him to *Turn around now!* But something else had already taken him and was carrying him onwards, towards whatever it was that lay there.

Dylan knew exactly what it was that he was faced with, many moments before the shape on the ground was clearly defined in the subdued light. The question was: Had his luck gone from bad to worse, and was this the person that he had come down to Brighton looking for?

...It was.

There was a familiarity in the pallid, inert

191

features that Dylan cross-referenced in his mind with photographs he'd seen in recent days.

He didn't have too much time to ponder. Just as he reached the lifeless body of James Braddock a mobile phone went off in the pocket of the diamanté studded jeans that the boy was still wearing. Dylan panicked. The ringtone had been turned up to full level and its sound could surely be heard from some distance at that time of the morning.

Dylan's heart pounded and his tousled head swivelled from side to side as he looked around frantically for anybody else that may have been witness to what was happening. He couldn't see anyone at first, but after a few seconds he noticed a middle-aged couple emerging from beyond the pier supports. The woman let out a scream. The man rushed to where Dylan was standing.

'What's happened?' asked the sombre looking man.

He was wearing an overcoat under which Dylan caught a glimpse of what could possibly have been a uniform that carried with it some authority.

'I don't know,' answered Dylan, nervously. 'I've just been walking along the beach and I looked down here and saw him... just lying there.'

'Him?' the man exclaimed, looking at the figure on the floor dressed in female clothing. 'Oh... I suppose I should be used to it by now. Is he dead?'

Dylan hadn't really had time to check whether he was dead or not, he just assumed that he was. For all he knew the boy may have just collapsed and his heart was still happily beating away beneath the cream coloured blouse that clung to his body.

'I don't know. I've only just this second found him. I didn't get a chance to check before his phone started ringing.'

'Damn and blast the bloody phone, man. Get out of the way and I'll check.'

The man slumped to his knees by the side of the body as he tried to find signs of life. He was getting extremely annoyed with the distraction of the phone and reached into the pocket of the jeans, which took some effort as they were extremely tight - and clung even more so due to being wet. He pulled the phone out and threw it over to Dylan who failed to catch it, watching helplessly as it fell onto the stones by his feet.

'Pick it up and answer it will you. It's getting on my bloody nerves.'

Dylan looked at the screen but there was no caller-ID showing. A withheld number. Accepting the call he lifted the phone to his ear, but as he did so the call was terminated.

'Is he dead?' Dylan asked the man, who had given up on his search for a pulse.

'I'm afraid so. Look... sorry that I was a bit short with you just then. No offence or anything, son, but in these situations you have to act fast.'

If he was looking for a response from Dylan he didn't get one.

'I can't see any obvious signs of how he died. It would be too easy just to say he drowned, but in actual fact he isn't even that wet - just wet enough to dampen his clothing, and that's probably only because he's so close to the edge of the water and got caught in the tide. He looks young. Late teens, early twenties.'

The man's wife was watching from the base of a pier support. He motioned for her not to come any closer.

Dylan hesitated. 'He's eighteen... and his name's James Braddock.'

'You mean you know this lad?' he said, getting to his feet.

'Yes, I'm afraid I do. He's the reason I'm down here. I'm a private investigator and I've been looking for him. I didn't think that I would find him like this though.'

'So, let me get this straight... You come down here looking for this boy and coincidently you're the one that accidentally finds his body? Doesn't look very good, does it, son? What's to stop me from thinking you're responsible for this?'

'With all due respect, sir, any questions I have to answer about my relationship to the dead boy I'll answer to the police when they turn up. I'm not running away.'

The man raised his eyebrows as a precursor to his next statement. 'They're already here, son,' he announced.

'My husband is the Chief Constable of the Sussex Police, young man,' his wife added from a distance.

The man, almost for effect it seemed, took off his overcoat and laid it over James Braddock's still body, revealing the uniform of authority that Dylan had glimpsed a few moments earlier.

The   Dead   Transvestite,   The   Private

Investigator, The Chief Constable, and His Wife.

Great, thought Dylan, just great. He'd wandered into a Peter Greenaway film - and it was him that was slowly being eaten.

TWENTY

The police station to which Dylan was taken seemed unusually quiet. He knew Brighton, by reputation at least, to be a town that never slept and assumed that this would include Thursday nights. So where were they? Where were Brighton's broken and ravaged masses?

He sat on one of a line of blue padded chairs facing the front desk and waited for someone to collect him and take him to the room in which he was to be questioned. Unlike his interview with Detective Inspector Cranshaw he was ready for them this time.

He watched the female police officer who was manning the desk as she furiously scribbled away on sheets of paper. She looked up suddenly and caught him staring at her. Her expression in that moment was quite a stern one, but Dylan thought her attractive nonetheless - certainly her uniform did nothing to detract from her appeal, he thought. He smiled at her, but she didn't reciprocate. She just carried on with whatever it was that she had been writing.

Dylan turned his attention instead to the posters on the walls. DIAL 101 TO CONTACT THE POLICE instructed one. HAVE YOU SEEN THIS MAN? enquired another underneath a photograph of the person in question, a man with a face that could surely only have been wanted by the police. MISSING declared another couple of posters, also accompanied by photographs of

196

those that were no longer where they should have been. However, James Braddock was not among them. RAPIST was the legend on another and beneath a photo-fit picture of the man that they were looking for. That's Kryten from Red Dwarf, thought Dylan, they'll never catch him, he's already three million light years away. Finally, one provocative poster asked: WHAT DO YOU CALL A BLACK MAN IN A BMW? A POLICE SERGEANT ON PATROL.

A door to the left of the desk swung open and out walked a man in a dark suit and loosened tie. The suit looked as if it needed a good dry clean and his hair a good comb. He introduced himself as Detective Inspector Dooley.

'You're free to go, Mr Morgan.'

'What?!' exclaimed Dylan in his surprise.

'Yes, you can go. I've just spoken to Chief Constable Barry, the gentleman you met earlier with his wife, on the beach, and he says that you're to be allowed to leave.'

'Really?'

'Yes, really. However, it has been requested that on your return to London you report to my colleague in the Met, Detective Inspector Cranshaw. I believe you know him?'

Dylan's anxiety rose just as quickly as it had fallen moments before.

'Now, we can trust you to do that, can't we, Mr Morgan? It seems that my colleague in the smoke does... trust you, that is.'

'Yes, of course. I've already said to your Chief Constable that I'm not going to run away. But look, I haven't had any sleep since yesterday morning and I'm really tired. Could I at least get some rest today and drive back to London tonight? I'll report to DI Cranshaw first thing tomorrow morning.'

'I'm sure that'll be okay. I'll let him know that's what you're doing. We wouldn't want him to worry now, would we?' He turned to the officer on the desk. 'Maggie, can you please sign Mr Morgan out and make sure we've got all his details, and that he's got everything he came in with. Then he's good to go.'

She nodded in acknowledgement.

'Hold on though, Inspector. What about the boy's father? The man I'm working for. He has to be notified of his son's death.'

'Oh, don't you worry yourself about that, Mr Morgan. We'll have the Met boys send a couple of extra-sensitive uniformed officers to see him. But obviously, when you get back I'm sure that you'll fulfil your obligation to your client in your own way.'

Dylan, feeling protective of Professor Braddock, didn't appreciate Dooley's tone.

Wishing him a safe journey back to London, Dooley disappeared back through the doorway from which he had emerged a minute earlier, leaving Dylan staring at wood. He turned towards the desk and watched WPC Maggie as she prepared the papers for his departure. He noticed that she wasn't wearing a ring on her left hand. He looked up into her face and thought it even more attractive than when he had studied it earlier - and, he was now looking at her with eyes that she knew were innocent. Surely it would make all the difference. At least that was Dylan's theory. And also, they were on first name terms... well, they now knew each other's first names at least. Again she looked up and caught him staring at her, but this time her face displayed the hint of a smile. His theory proved.

'You seem to have something of a guardian angel watching over you,' she said, with a seductive Mariella Frostrup huskiness in her voice.

This was it, he thought. He would seize his opportunity and try at least to end up with something good out of a bad situation.

'Listen... I don't suppose you'd...' he stuttered in his attempt at a chat-up line. It lacked any trace of conviction and was cut short before he could finish.

'You suppose right, Mr Morgan,' she replied without so much as a hint of empathy as she handed him back the few possessions they had taken from him on his arrival. Then, almost dismissively, she too wished him a safe journey back to London.

*

When Dylan returned to London it was the middle of the night and so he went straight to his flat. Entering the building as quietly as he could, he made his way up the staircase. He tried to be particularly quiet making his way around the landing on the first-floor as he knew Mrs Sumner to be a light sleeper - oh, the number of times she had informed him of this fact. The very last thing

199

that he wanted was to arouse any attention from Mrs Sumner, bless her. Especially at three o'clock in the morning.

Since the break-in a few days ago, each time he had entered his apartment it was with a degree of caution, reaching in first to turn the hall light on before venturing any further. He then had to check each room in turn and make sure that they were all free of any intruders before he could relax.

Despite being a little tired still he decided he wasn't going to try and get any more sleep. He feared that if he did he may not have been able to wake up in time in order to meet with DI Cranshaw early enough to suit - thus forcing the good inspector into sending a couple of officers banging on his door for fear he may have absconded.

Instead, Dylan went into the living room, lit a lamp and a few candles, poured out a single malt that was simply crying out for attention, and selected an especially soulful Chet Baker album on the MP3 player with which to contemplate the previous days' events. Thoughts of preparing the hookah flashed though his mind, but only briefly as he was too tired to put together the bits and pieces. He fell back instead onto the sofa clutching his glass of Laphroaig and humming My Funny Valentine in low tones.

'Oh, hello there,' said Dylan on opening his eyes and seeing the aged Indian gentleman sitting in the chair opposite him. 'It's you again.'

He caught a scent of fine incense in the air,

assuming it to come from one of the candles.

'I have already mentioned, young man, about how things may seem and how they really may be. Do you remember?'

'Yes, I remember... Ravi.'

The aged Indian gentleman looked deep into Dylan's eyes with a serene expression.

'Why is it,' he asked, 'that you are referring to me as Ravi?'

'Ravi! Ravi Shankar!'

'I do not know who this Ravi Shankar is. If it is the name you have chosen for me, then I will accept it with humble gratitude, as all gifts should be.' He bowed his head. 'The gifts that *you* have received, and those which you are *still* to receive, you also will one day be most grateful for. Of this I am quite sure. But you must learn to recognise which are gifts and which are not. For you will find that the gifts of a false benefactor can also be of considerable hindrance.'

'What gifts are you talking about?'

'Oh, you will find out soon enough, young man. And find out you must in order to determine your exit from this dark maze that you have ventured into.'

As he spoke his voice trailed off and his body slowly merged with the air around him, leaving only the chair that he had been sitting in.

Dylan closed his eyes, pressing the lids tightly together then opened them again. He looked at the empty glass and wondered whether to have another. As he had the drive to the police station in a few hours time, he decided perhaps it was best not. When had he turned the corner into

201

Sensibility Street, he wondered?

Chet was still blowing. Dylan assumed at first that it must have been the same play of the album. Then he noticed that it was now light outside, and the album must therefore have gone round in a loop. He went round the room extinguishing all the candles he had lit earlier. He looked at his watch: seven forty-nine. He would have a shower and get ready for the day. That's what he would do. Maybe today he would begin his search for these gifts that he couldn't remember ever receiving.

TWENTY ONE

Whilst Dylan had been combing the gay clubs of London and Brighton, finding dead bodies on the beach, getting himself arrested, then mysteriously released from police custody, Tony Spinetti had not been sitting idle. He had been traipsing around London, mainly its shopping centres it's got to be said, in an attempt to prove that Mrs Alison Puckett had been having an affair with her cousin's husband. Beaumaris Investigations had been hired to obtain evidence to this effect by her husband, Gary - a client thought to be one of those passed on by Mr Stone.

Needless to say, this was not *the* Gary Puckett of Union Gap fame, who was probably thousands of miles away, lounging in the warmth of the Florida sunshine. And, whilst Tony was chugging along the North Circular Road in pursuit of Mrs Puckett's yellow two-seater sports car, heading for the wilds of the Brent Cross Shopping Centre, chances were that the erstwhile singer of the classic pop ballad Young Girl was probably somewhere considerably more glamorous, sipping Pina Coladas around a pool. However, as Tony had very little interest in the purveyors of sixties popular music the coincidence didn't bear very heavily on his mind.

Tony didn't possess a motor car, but he could drive. Dylan had promised him that as soon as they found time enough to search for one he would buy Tony a discreet little run-around, just like his own. But Tony, as usual, had a cousin for the job, or in this instance a cousin's son, and at that moment he was being transported around London, in his pursuit of Mrs Puckett, on the back of a 125cc red, white and green coloured scooter.

His cousin Carlo's son, Gabriele, had offered to take Tony wherever he wanted, deeming it an honour to help out his Uncle Antonio. And so, subsequently, as they powered along the A406 trying to catch the little yellow sports car that had left them standing at the previous set of lights, Tony was clutching hold of the leather jacket that covered Gabriele's hefty frame for dear life.

Tony thought a scooter quite handy for pursuits around London; however far ahead the pursued car managed to get, it was pretty certain that the good old London traffic would sooner or later do what it did best and slow it down enough to enable the scooter to catch up. It was also good for weaving in and around slow or inert traffic in order to get to the best possible position in a surveillance situation. Yes indeed, very handy, thought Tony. He would ask Dylan to purchase a scooter instead of a motor car. Certainly cheaper to run than a motor car - not that economy seemed to be a major issue with Dylan - and much more fun, he remembered. He had owned one in his younger days, in Italy. He was not too old to have a little fun still.

The little scooter maintained a four car distance as Alison Puckett waited in line to get into the car park of the Brent Cross Shopping Centre. A bright yellow sports car was difficult to miss so even if it took them an extra minute or so to enter the car park, it didn't matter as they would soon be able to find her.

This was the third shopping centre that she had visited so far, departing the first two carrying at least half a dozen bags each time. Surely there can't be that much room left in that small car of hers, thought Tony. After all, the boot couldn't be all that big, and apart from that she only had one seat and a footwell to fill, and most of the bags were not small. He watched her go into one shop after another until she had exhausted every retail establishment the centre had to offer, then he watched as she made her way back to her car with yet more bags. But not once had he seen her come into contact with anyone that wasn't a shop assistant. He hadn't even witnessed her using a mobile phone to speak to anyone.

Mrs Puckett was like a shopping machine with but one purpose: driven to shop until she dropped, which didn't look like it would be any time soon.

They followed her for the final time that day as she returned to her Wanstead home, at which point Tony decided it was late enough and that they should call it a day.

From beneath the branches of a vibrant horse chestnut tree on the opposite side of the road he watched as she entered the house and turned on the light in the living room. He watched as she dropped the bags, removed her coat and threw it onto a chair. And he watched as she poured herself a drink and collapsed into a chair beneath the level of the window, no longer visible. At this point it was evident to Tony that she was in for the night, and any potential secret assignations, if they were to occur, were being deferred to another day.

*

Tony's surveillance of Alison Puckett carried on the next day. There was more shopping and more sitting in cafés, either on her own or, this time, accompanied by a girlfriend.

At one point she and her friend paid a visit to a place that Tony found most intriguing. From outside a men's clothing store on the other side of the concourse Tony observed as they, and several other women, sat with their legs dangling in fish tanks whilst the fish sucked and nibbled at the skin on their feet. The more Tony watched, the more he came to the conclusion that the world was moving in new and decidedly strange directions to the one in which had been brought up.

The places Mrs Puckett visited were all pretty innocuous. There was no hint of anything extraneous to, or contravening of, the marriage vows that her husband should have been worried about. However, Beaumaris Investigations was being paid by Mr Puckett to keep surveillance on his wife and this was exactly what Tony would do until he was told otherwise. If this was a wasted venture, and suspicions proved to be unfounded, then that was the husband's problem and not theirs.

Tony called Dylan in order to keep him updated, and thought his voice strained. Dylan told him he was just very tired and getting a little rest after a hectic day. He would be driving back to London overnight and would call him the next day, after his appointment with D.I. Cranshaw, and let him know everything that had happened. He said things were getting even more complicated, but wouldn't be pressed on the issue any further than that. Tony told him he was starting to get the distinct impression that the jobs he'd been working on were merely decoy work. Dylan agreed. That was a distinct possibility, but Tony was to carry on with the investigation of Mrs Puckett regardless.

*

'You appear to have done it again, Mr Morgan.'

DI Cranshaw paced around the table.

'You seem to have got yourself involved in our murder enquiry, again. Only now, between us and our colleagues down on the south coast, we have two murder enquiries which are inter-linked that you appear to be involved in.'

DI Cranshaw stopped pacing and stood directly behind him so that Dylan had to swivel his neck.

'You've not been in the private investigation business very long, have you, Mr Morgan?'

'About three weeks, Inspector,' murmured Dylan.

'About three weeks,' repeated Cranshaw. 'And in those three short weeks you appear to have got yourself into far more trouble than I suspect any of your clients are in. Not a *very* good start is it? Perhaps you can tell me what you were doing down in Brighton.'

'You know what I do, Inspector. I was on a case.'

'Can you tell me who it is that you're working for this time, or is this one a state secret too?'

'I already told the police in Brighton that I was working for the boy's father, a Professor Braddock.'

'Ah, yes. Professor Braddock. Well, I can tell you that a couple of officers went to see the good Professor at the address that you gave in Blackheath. Would you be surprised to hear that nobody at the house, student digs, or at the institute in Greenwich has ever heard of him?'

'What?' Dylan turned a hundred and eighty degrees in his chair to face the inspector. 'What do you mean nobody has heard of him?' The blood drained from his face. 'He seemed such a genuine man. I felt so sorry for him when he told me about his wife passing away and how he was having problems with bringing up his son... and, well... he just seemed so bloody genuine.'

'Maybe, Mr Morgan. But what I *can* tell you is that the real Professor Braddock is living somewhere out near Cambridge with his very much alive wife. We managed to track them down to an address, which is nowhere near Blackheath. They're both university lecturers up there. Needless to say, he claims never to have set eyes on you. They're being taken down to the south coast to make a formal identification. So, at the end of the day, we only have your word for it that this other Professor Braddock even existed.'

'Of course he existed. I'm not making it up. Why would I?'

'Well, where do I start?' Cranshaw smirked, a precursor to another big speech. 'I know it's only been a couple of days since we last had the pleasure of your company, but let's just recap on all the facts shall we?'

Cranshaw made his way around the table and stood in front of Dylan.

'First of all we have the prominent murder of a gentleman who was quite high up in social circles and had a taste for something a little kinky.' He walked towards the two-way mirror that covered quite a lot of the wall to Dylan's left. 'You then appear on our radar for the first time a couple of days later, after it emerges that you broke into... sorry, trespassed on, the said gentleman's property. Supposedly investigating an alleged false insurance claim, you were photographed in his bedroom standing next to his dead body...'

Cranshaw looked into the mirror and flattened a tuft of hair that was sticking up.

'... one which, I may add, was still obviously undiscovered by the authorities at that point, but which you failed to notify anyone of.'

He turned around again to face Dylan.

'Next to his dead body was what appeared to be a naked woman chained to the bed, but actually turned out to be a rubber sex-doll. And this doll just happened to bear a remarkable resemblance to the person that he had been photographed with on the beach.'

Dylan tried to interrupt the inspector's flow. 'But, Inspector, I've already told you that...,'

Cranshaw cut him short with a forefinger pointed to the skies.

'Then we come into possession of more photographs, this time showing our friendly neighbourhood private eye in a compromising position with somebody who, albeit only visible from behind, could very well be the young lady on the beach who had been getting fruity with our murder victim. And could also be the person that the silicone doll, found alongside our murder victim, was made up to look like.'

The inspector lay his palms flat on the table to support himself as he leaned over until his face was level with Dylan's, and stared straight into his eyes.

'Then, to top it all, you are discovered early yesterday morning, at a time when even the birds are still sleeping, standing next to the body of a young man who is done up like a lady who, surprise surprise, bears an uncanny resemblance to all the other young ladies, real or otherwise, that I have just mentioned. And you are discovered in this most compromising of positions not just by anyone, but by the Chief Constable of the Sussex Police and his good lady wife out on an early morning stroll after a late-night bash.'

Pulling out a chair he sat opposite Dylan.

'Yes, well,' Dylan mused, 'I was thinking that it was strange that he should be the first person at the scene when I found the body.'

'Congratulations,' said Cranshaw, sarcastically.

For the next few seconds they sat looking at one another in silence. Dylan allowed time for all the facts to once again sink in, as if they had not already been indelibly etched into his mind over the past few days.

'It's not looking good, is it?' he said, quietly.

'No, Mr Morgan. Good is something that it most certainly is not.'

'Okay then, Inspector, but what I really don't understand is, considering everything you've just mentioned, why I keep getting released. I mean, short of being found with the proverbial smoking gun, even I've gotta admit that the odds seem to be stacked pretty heavily against me.'

'I was wondering when you were going to ask that question, Mr Morgan. And so I'll tell you why that is. You see, there appears to be a bigger picture here. I can't say too much as we don't know yet exactly who it is that's involved. And the thing is, we're having to change our position a little here because, contrary to what I may have said to you before, we'd actually quite like for you to carry on with your investigations to help us flush out the people who are behind it all.'

'What!'

'You will of course be afforded a certain amount of immunity, but only as long as you don't push it.'

This new and sudden change in stance confused Dylan.

'So, what you're saying, Inspector, is, that I should allow myself to continue to be used as bait for your trap?'

'Pretty much, Mr Morgan, yes.'

TWENTY TWO

When Dylan left the police station he went straight to the office. It was unmanned as Tony was still out on the Puckett investigation. That was good though, because Dylan needed time to think.

Cranshaw had given him the bigger picture as he felt that it would have been unfair not to have done. And the bigger picture was that the whole scenario revolved around some big oil deal the British government were negotiating with the Canadians. Crucial to the deal going through was the retrieval of paintings stolen many years ago from an art gallery in Montreal, which they suspected were being held somewhere in the UK. Extraneous to this was the death of Gerald De Vere, an art dealer recruited to help find the missing art through his known connections with the criminal underworld. Not wanting the paintings found, somebody had tried to tarnish his reputation and then had had him killed. This was as much as Cranshaw had told him.

Dylan suspected that in order to hide their tracks, the criminals had found someone to frame for the murder and he thought that this someone was probably Lola. Unfortunately for them, Lola had managed to escape the murder scene. The home security system recordings had gone missing, presumably in the hands of the murderers. These recordings would have proved that Lola had not murdered De Vere, even though she was there at the time. Of course the police would find fingerprints but De Vere was well known for entertaining company so finding her fingerprints in the house would not, in itself, be cause for suspicion.

This then left the murderers with another patsy to find, and that person was Dylan. He was unsure as to the reason but suspected that he may have been chosen after his visit to De Vere's house. Perhaps he had been watched whilst there, and had then become the perfect picture for the frame. Fortunately for him, the frame didn't seem to fit.

Things were bothering Dylan and they were beginning to mount up; what was Victoria's role in all this and was she being one hundred percent truthful? Just who was Lola? Was she the girl in the beach photographs with De Vere? Was she the girl in the photographs with Dylan that he had no recollection of? Was she the girl that James Braddock was spending time with shortly before he left for Brighton? Had James been used just as Dylan was being now, and if James was murdered, how long would it be before Dylan was too? And, who was the mysterious Mr Stone, and was he the cause of everything that had happened to Dylan?

He needed to speak to Victoria, she was the link in all of this. He hated the thought that she may be involved more than she had let on, and that his trust may have been misplaced.

*

'Hello.' Victoria's voice sounded distant and

weary.

'Victoria? Where the bloody hell are you?'

'Dylan? I was going to call you later. I'm in Rome.'

'What are you doing in Rome?'

'The client I told you about the other day is attending a conference out here and wanted me to accompany him. He's paying big bucks so I couldn't refuse.'

'When will you be back?'

'Probably the day after tomorrow. How are you getting on with finding Lola?'

She came right out with the question with no hint of insincerity in her voice. She's genuine, thought Dylan. She must be. There was no instigation on Dylan's part. She can't be lying about all this. How could he ever think that she was?

'Victoria, I have to ask you a question. Is there anything else you want to tell me about Lola?'

'Like what?' she asked, confused.

'Like... is Lola a girl?'

'Is Lola a girl?' Her tone was strained. 'What do you mean, is she a girl? Of course she's a girl, Dylan. What else would she be?'

'Look, I have to ask, Victoria, 'cos stuff has been happening around here, right. So, Lola's not a young boy who just likes to dress up in women's clothing, or anything like that then?'

'No, Dylan. She's not a transvestite. I'd know if my best friend was really a man in drag.'

She was agitated, and with every passing word coming out of her mouth he was more convinced that she was telling him the truth.

214

'What's this all about?'

'I can't say too much over the phone,' replied Dylan. 'But things are happening around here at great speed. Just one more question though, did Lola ever mention to you a boy called James Braddock?'

There was a few moments silence. When Victoria responded her agitation had subsided.

'Yes... I vaguely remember her mentioning something about a James. I can't remember much about what she said, but I think that she'd met him at some club or other in the West End.'

'Soho?'

'Yes, probably. I really can't remember. Lola's always making new friends. I worry about her, as some of them can be dubious. As for this James... all I remember was that he was quite a young boy. Late teens, I think. That's all I know. She really didn't tell me much.'

'Okay, thanks. So you think you'll be back in a couple of days?'

'Yes. But to tell you the truth, I shouldn't have taken on this job. I thought that it was just going to be the usual one nighter, but I couldn't say no when he asked me to stay on. To tell the truth I could do with being at home because it's the anniversary of my parent's death tomorrow. Every year, at exactly the time that they died, I lay flowers on their grave. It's just a ritual I've followed over the years.' A few seconds pause. 'I'm sure that they'll forgive me... just this once...' Her voice trailed off and Dylan thought that he could hear her filling up over the phone.

'Do you want me to go for you?' said Dylan.

215

'Just tell me where and I'll go and put some flowers down.'

'No, no, no. I couldn't ask you to do that. It's my ritual. I'd really much rather that you concentrate your efforts on finding Lola. I'm not sure how much longer I can afford to pay you, even at the special friends rate.'

'Well, you know how I feel about that, Victoria.'

'Anyway it wouldn't be the same. My parent's would expect me to go.'

'Nonsense. I'm sure they'd understand. I'll smooth it over with them, don't worry. You just leave it to me.'

'I'm not sure that they would understand, I think that I've told you before that they didn't know about what I did. This is kind of my way of trying to make it up to them for having hidden the truth from them for so long. I know I'm being silly, but I'll just go when I get back.'

What Dylan wanted to say to her was that her parents were dead and so there was probably very little chance that they would be concerning themselves with anything that she got up to any more, but knew that this would be extremely insensitive.

'It's sorted then. I'll go.'

'I really appreciate it, thanks. I owe you one, and when I get back I'll come see you straight away.'

After she'd rung off, Dylan sat looking at her photo on his phone for some time before finally placing it down on the green leather-topped desk. It was only fairly recently that Victoria had told him that her parents had died in a road accident when she was in her early twenties. She was already involved in the escort business, had been for a couple of years by then. After their deaths, because of her friendship with Lola, she had come to look upon Lola's parents as her own, and they had come to accept her as a second daughter and had helped her through her grief. And that, he reasoned, was why it was even more important to her to find out what was happening to her best friend. Not only for Lola's sake, but also for Lola's parents, even though, according to Victoria, they appeared oblivious of the fact that anything at all was happening.

*

The warmest April for a great many years had continued, and on this particular Sunday morning the pleasant weather ensured that the cemetery was busy with people laying flowers in remembrance of loved ones.

With the instructions that Victoria had given him of the whereabouts of her parents' plot, Dylan negotiated the pathway that cut through the lines of graves. At intervals the path branched off to stretch towards the various sections of the cemetery. This was the first time that he had visited a cemetery since the internment of his mother. It wasn't so much that grief was alien to him, it was just that he wasn't quite sure how to react when he encountered it. He had been unable to grieve for the only person he had lost in his life so far, so understanding other people's grief came difficult to him. Even the speech that he had given at his mother's funeral was emotive rather than emotional. But, as Angharad had systematically alienated herself from just about everyone present at her funeral (most were there to support Dylan, feeling he may need it), the blame for his lack of emotion was laid firmly at her door and not necessarily seen as uncaring indifference on his part.

As he walked through the cemetery, he studied closely the behaviour of people at gravesides. It was not so much fascination that made him stare, it was instruction. He had promised to do this for Victoria, and he wanted to do it, as he was sure she would have, with propriety and due respect.

When he located the joint grave of Reginald and Margaret Henson, and the time was exactly right, he separated the flowers and placed them carefully through the holes in the two pots at the foot of the granite headstone. He stood up and took a few steps back in order to take in his handiwork. He thought that maybe he should offer up a small prayer; he was sure that this was what Victoria would have done. But Dylan wasn't one for prayer. He wasn't a great believer in anybody being there to listen to them. He stood at the foot of the grave looking at the two names, four dates and seven words of remembrance that were carved into the stone. After a few moments of contemplation the only thing he could think to say was 'Amen.' He felt awkward and looked around him to see if anyone had seen or heard, but there was nobody within distance that he could see.

Having fulfilled his duty to Victoria he began

making his way back to his car. As he walked he felt conspicuous, constantly checking behind to see if anyone was in tow. Pretty soon it began to occur to him that he had followed a different path back as he'd found himself in a whole new section of the cemetery that he hadn't remembered seeing on his way in, an area of the cemetery which was both secluded and had a tranquillity disturbed only by birdsong. The trees and shrubs around the area had been neglected and left to overgrow. Creeping ivy clung to the gnarled trunks of trees and unrestrained bushes, choking everything around and creating a natural barrier. Dylan could see, through a small section that had been cut back for access, a terrace of ten family crypts which looked to have been standing since Victorian times. He moved in closer for a better look. He hadn't considered finding anything like this here. Crypts, he thought, were usually only found in big city cemeteries such as Highgate, not out here in Hertfordshire.

As he made his way gingerly through the gap towards the crypts he read the family names of those laid to rest within. Moving along at a snail's pace, the ground underfoot being quite uneven, he came to a sudden halt in front of one of the crypts. Chiselled into the stone above the entrance was the name Devere. Could it be, Dylan wondered? Could it possibly be the family of the same De Vere that had been drawing him into his story. The name was slightly altered but he knew that there were those that, for various reasons, did alter the spelling of their family name.

Dylan thought about the coincidence of Gerald

De Vere's family lying in the same cemetery as the remains of Victoria's parents. However, he was aware that both Victoria and Gerald had originated from Hertfordshire and so, as this was one of the main cemeteries in the county, maybe it wouldn't have been that much of a coincidence after all. Victoria could have no idea that the Devere family crypt stood a mere few hundred yards from her parents' grave. He'd only found the crypt himself by getting lost.

Just then a shuffling sound came from within the crypt. Probably rats, thought Dylan, but it spooked him enough that he started to head back.

Arriving back at the car he chose not to drive straight off and sat instead enjoying the peace and serenity of the cemetery. There was very little human noise to be heard except the distant squeal of children playing excitedly in the surrounding streets. He listened closely to the chirping of the birds and lay his head back on the headrest and closed his eyes, taking it all in. When he opened them again he was startled by what he saw - someone he had encountered just recently, many miles from where he was now. He watched fascinated, as the man with the chains from Oscars walked into the car park, got into a silver BMW saloon car, and drove off. Another coincidence? thought Dylan. He decided to follow him.

Dylan was sure that Chains hadn't seen him sitting in the car, but thought to leave it a moment before he drove after him. As long as he could see which way the BMW turned once it got outside of the cemetery gates it wouldn't be difficult to catch him up. The surrounding countryside was pretty open and the roads tended to go on for long stretches without any major turnings off.

Keeping his distance he remained undetected. The BMW eventually came to a stop outside a house in Edmonton, North London. Dylan parked along the road a little. He watched as Chains got out of his car and called out to a group of children that were playing across the road, but Dylan couldn't quite make out what it was he'd shouted. Chains then entered a house with a bright red front door.

Dylan got out of the car and began walking towards the group of children. As he approached he called out, just loud enough to attract their attention, and they all stopped the game they were playing and looked up.

'Yeah? What d'ya want?' asked one of the older boys, looking to take courage from his friends before turning back towards Dylan. 'You're not a paedo are ya mate?'

He evidently thought this funny and laughed wildly. One or two of the other children accompanied him in his laughter.

'Cos I only live over there,' he said, pointing towards a house a few doors along from the one that Chains had just disappeared into, 'and mi dad can be out here in ten seconds flat to kick shit out of ya. He don't get up much, but he's fast when he does.'

All the others that hadn't previously joined in now started to laugh too.

'Yeah, fuck off if you're a paedo,' shouted one of the others. 'We all live along here and all our dads, except for him and him, are at home.'

He pointed at two boys whose fathers were obviously absent from the nest.

'Yeah, and they all hate fucking paedos.'

'Yeah. So fuck off if you're one of 'em.'

Dylan looked down at the cream of future British society before him, and despaired.

'Look boys, I'm not a paedo, or anything like that. I just want to know who that bloke was that just went into that house over there. The one that spoke to you.'

'Who's asking?'

'I am. I just want to know who he is. There's something in it for all of you if you tell me.'

'Yeah, like what?'

'If you tell me I'll give you a quid each.'

'Fuck off mate. It's gotta be worth at least two each.'

Dylan did a quick head count.

'But there's eight of you. That's sixteen quid.'

'Yeah, and? I tell you what, make it a round twenty and we'll split it between us.'

There was a resounding chorus of 'Yeah, twenty' from the others.

'Twenty bloody notes? And how do I even know that you're going to tell me the truth?'

The boy looked around at all the others and laughed again in anticipation of what he was about to say.

'Well, you know where we live, don't ya?'

They all laughed in unison. Even Dylan laughed.

'Okay, there you go,' he said, taking a twenty pound note from his wallet and handing it over.

'Ta, mate,' the boy said, virtually snatching it from Dylan's hand.

'Well? What's his name then?'

'That's Chas, that is. He pays us to mind his car for him.'

'Chas? What's his surname?'

'What's a surname?' asked one boy.

'His second name, stupid,' answered one of his friends.

'His second name?' said the first boy. 'No idea, mate.' He broke out into laughter again. 'That one over there,' he said, pointing towards one of the smaller boys whose forefinger looked in need of surgical extraction from up his nose, 'he doesn't even know his own surname.'

They all fell into wild fits of laughter at this and then set off, running down the road arguing over who was going to hold the twenty pound note. As they ran, one of the smaller boys looked back at Dylan.

'Fucking paedo!' he shouted at the top of his voice, and his friends all joined in, singing 'Paedo! Paedo!' as if it were a football chant.

Dylan stood watching as they disappeared around the first corner. Shaking his head he smiled. He had bigger issues than broken Britain to think about for the moment.

Chas? Wasn't that what Victoria's boss's name?

TWENTY THREE

At 6:49pm the red door to number 57 opened and Chas left the house to get back into the silver BMW. Dylan had been waiting patiently, assuming he would be leaving the house at some point that evening. If he was Victoria's boss there would of course be an escort agency to run. Dylan had moved the car further down the road so as not to attract any more attention from the children, but close enough to keep an eye on Chas's house and car.

If this was the same Chas, and the way things were going recently there was every chance that it was, he assumed that he would be following him to an address somewhere in Enfield. He remembered Victoria telling him that the agency was located there. After fifteen minutes of covert pursuit, combined with tricky traffic negotiation, he watched the silver saloon come to a halt outside a parade of shops in one of Enfield's main drags. Dylan's memory had served him well.

He watched as Chas unlocked and went through a white door that stood in between a small newsagents and a shop selling kitchen equipment. The street didn't look like one safe enough to park on, even on a Sunday evening, without risking the contravention of a few road traffic laws. This hadn't deterred Chas however, and Dylan imagined him to be one of those people who drove around with their back seats covered in unpaid parking tickets.

Dylan noticed a small sign indicating a car park down a nearby road and decided to head there. Once parked, he walked back along the main road towards the white door but, unsure of what his next move would be, he decided to go into the newsagent. This would give him a few extra valuable minutes to come up with some sort of plan.

He picked up one of the Sunday newspapers. There were only one or two left this late on a Sunday so he picked up the only newspaper that didn't have a sensationalist headline about the footballer who had had sex with his team mate's under age daughter, or a girl juggling her Double D size breasts in the name of sport.

As he was paying for the newspaper he thought he would ask the young girl behind the counter who it was that rented the office upstairs. In her late teens, she had neatly brushed long, dark brown hair which she was trying to separate into strands. She would then delicately run the strands in between her fingers before letting them fall back into place again.

The other thing Dylan noticed, when the girl had first looked up to serve him, was how very lucent her eyes were. Light brown in colour, they shone with faint flecks of green.

'My father rents that out to a man. He told me that I mustn't concern myself with him or talk to him, unless he comes in to buy something, of course.'

She smiled at Dylan.

'So you don't know his name then? Or what his business is?'

'I only know his name, Charles, because I hear my father call him that, but as for his business, I'm not sure. I heard my father tell my mother once that he's in the hospitality business, but quite what kind of hospitality it is with all those chains, I don't know.'

She made a dismissive gesture with a wave of her hand and a facial expression to match.

'Do you ever see anybody else go up there?' asked Dylan.

'Well occasionally there are people, yes, but I'm not here all the time. I only help out at weekends when I'm not at college so I don't know how often.'

'Any women?'

'Yes, I have seen a few women - but mostly men.'

'The women that you've seen, did they strike you as being any particular type of women?'

'What do you mean? What type of women?'

'No, I'm just saying... did they just look like normal business women, or...?'

'Sorry, but I'm not quite sure what you mean. The women are always very nicely dressed but I don't remember there being anything particularly strange about any of them, or the men - only him.' She passed her hand over her face as a demonstration of the facial trimmings she was alluding to. 'Do you think that there might be something funny going on up there then?' she said, excitedly.

'No, no, not at all, sweetheart,' Dylan was quick to quell her suspicion. 'I'm just trying to find out who he is. I work for the local newspaper, see...'

'You're a journo?' the girl screeched.

'Yes. And we do weekly features on some of the local characters. I saw your man upstairs as I was walking along and thought he looked interesting and that he may be a good candidate for one of our future articles.'

Phew, thought Dylan, that was quite good. I could almost believe that myself.

'Don't bullshit me. And don't call me sweetheart. Why are you really asking these questions? You're not a journalist. Who are you really?'

'You don't believe what I just told you?'

'No, course I don't. Now, are you going to tell me the truth?'

She was a determined young lady with no real connection to Chas, as far as Dylan could tell, so maybe the truth wouldn't do any harm. Just then another customer came in and, after a quick glance towards them, walked to the magazine rack. He stood looking at the section of the shelf containing the sporting and leisure publications and eventually took down a fishing magazine. Walking over to the counter he asked for a packet of his usual cigarettes. He paid the girl for the two items and left. They both watched him leave then the girl looked back at Dylan.

'Well?'

'Well... okay, I'll tell you, but really I'm trusting you here, so you don't say anything to anyone. Especially not your dad. Okay?'

'Okay, okay. So, what is it?'

'I'm a private investigator. I'm looking for

someone...'

He didn't finish his sentence before she interrupted him.

'A private detective? What, and you think that this person is being held up there?'

Enthusiastically she pointed towards the ceiling.

'No, hold on, let me finish. I just think that the guy upstairs might know where I can find this person.'

'Piss off!' she exclaimed. 'If you think he knows where this person is then why aren't you upstairs asking him? Why are down here asking me *about* him?'

'Cos I'm trying to find out what kind of man he is first. He may not be the sort of guy that wants to help me. And let's face it, I know that looks can be deceiving but he looks quite intimidating and I'm not into violence.'

'Fair enough,' she conceded. 'But I'm not sure how much better off you are. I can't tell you anything else. Leave me your phone number though and if I see anything suspicious I'll give you a call. I promise.'

'Okay, thanks, I appreciate that. And remember that mum's the word, so don't tell dad.'

Having written his details on a piece of paper he turned to leave.

'Oh and you've got gorgeous eyes, by the way,' he called over his shoulder.

'I know,' she replied. And she smiled, but Dylan didn't see.

Dylan considered what to do next. If this was the

office for an escort business, chances were that Chas wouldn't be leaving any time soon. He had two choices. The first was to leave now, get in his car and drive away and go back to Chas's house in Edmonton tomorrow, on the off chance that he may lead him somewhere else. The second choice was to bite the bullet and go up there on the pretext of business to see what he could find out.

He couldn't stand just outside the doorway of the newsagents any longer without raising suspicion. He sensed the girl watching him. He could feel the prickle on the back of his neck. He didn't want to give her the impression, especially after his parting compliment, that he had any kind of untoward intentions so he turned around and called into the shop.

'Look, I've decided that I'm going in. If I'm not out in an hour, or you hear anything suspicious up there, you call the police. Okay?'

A huge grin formed on the girl's oval face and she stopped playing with her hair long enough to give him two excited thumbs up. Dylan braced himself for a few seconds then went through the white door that Chas had gone through ten minutes earlier.

TWENTY FOUR

The climb up the long dark stairwell proved tougher than Dylan would have liked. Not because they were steep and dark, but because during the slow and laboured ascent he had been trying desperately to come up with a plan of action. With a few steps to go before he reached the top he could see the reflection of a soft light on the wall in front of him and hear the tinny sound of a radio, but still he had no plan formulated in his mind. Stopping one step from the top, the back of his throat felt dry and tight. He swallowed hard.

If Chas recognised him he would have to come straight out with the questions that needed asking and hope that he got the required responses. If he wasn't recognised, and he didn't realistically think that this would be the case, then he would bluff his way through. After all, as far as he was aware, Chas only associated him with the search for James Braddock, and so he could say that he was there on the pretext of that investigation.

He moved hesitantly onto the top step and turned his head towards the orange glow and the music - Smoke On The Water by Deep Purple. When he reached the room he paused in the doorway and looked cautiously inside. Chas was slumped over a desk, head down, face in hands. As Dylan leaned in to see if anybody else was in the room he shifted his foot to stabilise himself and stepped on a loose floorboard. There was a loud crack, and Chas lifted his heavy head off of the desk, accompanied by the sound of chinking chains, to see Dylan standing in the doorway.

'What the fuck do you want?' he croaked.

His eyes were red and a little puffy as if he'd been crying.

'Wait a minute, don't I know you?' His eyes narrowed to a squint. 'Yeah, it is you. You were the one in the club the other night asking all the questions about James. What are you doing here? What do you want?'

Dylan remained silent. Entering the room he grabbed one of the chairs lined up against the far wall and sat down, defiant attitude and all, opposite Chas. This was it. He had legislated for being recognised, so he should have been prepared, but his posture really didn't reflect it. Chas was a bit of an unknown quantity. Victoria said that he had helped her out on occasions, but that he was also prone to the odd bout of violence if life wasn't going his way. Ernst Stavro Blofeld stroking his fluffy white cat whilst planning world domination may have revealed a softer side to his character, but Chas didn't look like he had a soft spot for kittens. Then again looks could be deceiving, and to catch him crying like he obviously had been...

'I asked you a question, pal.'

Dylan assessed the situation in his head. Essentially he had to ask possibly provocative questions to a man with probable psychotic tendencies who seemed to be suffering from some degree of emotional disturbance. Upon reflection, a few more minutes in the newsagents downstairs preparing a decent plan may have been favourable. Too late now. He was already in the lion's den.

'Yes, that was me.' Dylan finally replied.

'Was it you that killed him?' Chas asked, dispassionately.

Dylan assumed by Chas's tone that he wasn't unduly concerned about James Braddock's death.

'No. It wasn't me that killed him. But I'm not going to lie to you, I was the one that found his body on the beach.'

Dylan hoped a little honesty may buy him some trust.

'How did he die? Was it accidental drowning or... was he murdered?'

Again his tone was blasé at best.

'I think he was murdered. The chief constable of Sussex was there with his wife when I found the body. He said he didn't think it was a drowning, despite the circumstances.'

'The chief constable, eh? That must've been nice for you. Anyway, Dominic's really cut up about it. Under the circumstances I suppose that he would be though.'

'And you? Are you cut up about it?' asked Dylan.

Chas's response took him a little by surprise.

'Well, I'm no gonna lie to you either. I'm no all that gutted.'

Well well, maybe the honesty for trust policy was working.

'Sure, I didn't want the fella dead but, to be honest, me and him never really got on. I suppose we were both fighting for Dominic's attention. In the end I guess I won, by default.'

Chas scratched at one of the few free spaces left on his face, and all Dylan could think of was how long it took him to remove the chains each time he shaved.

'I think that's possibly why he went off the rails and started getting into new stuff and hanging out with different people.'

'Do you mind me asking, you're obviously not bothered about what's happened so why you were crying when I came in?'

'That's none of your fucking business, pal. Don't go getting beyond yourself.'

Chas stared into the distance. Dylan was staring at the patterns of flowers in the flock wallpaper that shone orange in the glow from the lamp.

'Okay, fair enough. I apologise for asking. None of my business.'

Just as Dylan was thinking things were going much better than expected, he got a sample of Chas's unpredictability.

'Too fucking right, it's none of your business. What is your fucking business anyway, pal? Why are you up here in my office?'

Plan B (just formulated), thought Dylan: shit or bust.

'Okay, I'll get to the point. I'm looking for Lola. I think you may know where she is.'

A puzzled expression fell upon Chas's face.

'Lola? Are you okay, pal? Isn't that what we've just been talking about? Lola was the name that Dominic's friend took when he started wearing women's clobber. Remember?'

The level of aggression in his voice had risen. Dylan knew that if things got physical there would only be one outcome – and it wasn't going to be a good one for him.

'Yes, I know that, but I'm talking about the other Lola.'

'Other Lola? What other Lola? Why would you think that I know anything about any other Lola?'

'The Lola that Victoria's concerned about, maybe?'

Chas knew then that this was not just about James Braddock.

'Victoria? How do you know Vicky?'

'Because she's asked me to help her find Lola.'

In that moment Chas's whole posture changed. With arms stretched out in front of him on the desk he sat bolt upright in his chair. Dylan sat back as far as he could in his.

'Oh, you're trying to find Lola for Vicky? That's what you're trying to do, is it? Okay, pal, if you're no out of my fucking office in the next ten seconds...'

With the sudden shift in mood the air grew menacing and Dylan braced himself for the full flesh and metal force of Chas coming at him over the desk. Chas stood up and leaned across the desk. It was obvious to Dylan that the situation was not for turning, and that playtime was definitely over. The only option Dylan now had was to leave as fast as he could. Once he was downstairs he could think about what had just happened and the possible reasons why, from the sanctuary of the street. For now, it was just a case of running.

234

He would look on that moment later and laugh at how childish his retreat from Chas's office must have seemed, but he knew full well that there was no time for graceful sprinting. This was a life or death dash and there was certainly no point in attempting to look cool.

It was fair to say that the stairwell was negotiated considerably faster on his descent than it had been on his ascent. Reaching the bottom he flung the door open and ran out into the lamp-lit street. Pausing for a few moments to catch his breath, and making sure that he could hear no pursuing footsteps on the staircase, he turned towards the newsagent.

He poked his head through the doorway and saw that the girl was still standing behind the counter playing with her hair and reading a magazine. Sensing someone was standing there, she looked up. Dylan gave her a relieved thumbs up, to which she cheerfully reciprocated with two.

'Well, what happened?' she asked him. 'I heard the footsteps on the stairs. Sounded like you left in a bit of a hurry?'

'That's right, sweetheart.' He said, panting. 'I don't think he wanted to talk to me any more. But do me a favour, will you? Call me if you see or hear anything suspicious. And watch yourself with him, won't you? He's not a man you want to go upsetting. Okay?'

'Okay,' she said, flashing him a smile and another thumbs up. 'And I told you before, don't call me sweetheart.'

*

Dylan drove home, his mind in confusion. Questions, different ones now, were doing circuits round his head. Why had Chas reacted like he had? Why had his attitude changed so suddenly when he realised who Dylan was? He didn't seem to be too worried about the death of James Braddock - he said so himself that they weren't the best of friends, and he gave no indication that he may have had anything to do with his murder. But it was his reaction, when he found out that Dylan was helping Victoria look for Lola, that came across as highly dubious. He had used the name Lola himself quite comfortably when referring to James Braddock's female pseudonym, so why had his mood changed as soon as he mentioned the other Lola? Especially being as Lola was one of his girls? One thing was for sure, Dylan hadn't given up on his pursuit of Chas. He wouldn't be scared off, although he would have to admit to being quite scared. He would carry on the pursuit tomorrow, only now, with Chas aware of him, he would have to be a lot more careful. If Chas was indeed guarding a secret he now knew who to look out for.

TWENTY FIVE

When Dylan rang that evening, Tony and his family were about to sit down to dinner. He could hear the commotion in the background, and it made him a little envious. All he would be having was the usual combination of takeaway, followed by the hookah and a single malt or two, accompanied by the honeyed sounds of some smooth jazz on the radio. Not a bad evening in Dylan's eyes but that was every evening; now and again he craved a little company too - and Victoria was not even in the country.

Dylan offered to call back but Tony wouldn't hear of it; not a man to turn anybody away, even on the phone. Tony would eat cold linguine before running the risk of upsetting anyone. Sensing his loneliness down the line, Tony invited Dylan to join him and his family for dinner - the journey from Hampstead to Tony's home in Islington was a short one. However, Dylan politely declined the offer citing tiredness and a planned early start in the morning as his reasons.

Tony told Dylan he was now convinced Mrs Puckett was up to nothing more than spending all her husband's money. They agreed again that in all probability the case was just a decoy, but they should give it a full week before reporting back to Mr Puckett. Dylan gave a résumé of his own movements after which Tony settled down to his fresh pasta and meatballs with his very loud family, and Dylan settled down alone to a smoke, a drink and Julie London singing *Cry Me A River*.

*

By 11.53pm, Dylan was tucked up warm and snug in his bed; somewhere between consciousness and unconsciousness, so the buzz of the intercom came as somewhat of an irritation to him. But this was a different Dylan nowadays, a Dylan braced and ready for just about anything. He leapt out of bed and made his way out of the bedroom and down the hallway unconcerned that he was wearing nothing but a pair of boxer shorts.

Any irritation was considerably eased when he got to the intercom, pressed the button, and found out who it was that had disturbed him this close to midnight. Victoria asked to be let in. Without hesitation Dylan pressed the door release button and listened as a pair of high heels, and the wheels of a travel case, made their way along the hallway and up two flights of stairs. He quickly ran back to the bedroom to put on a t-shirt. Why had she returned from Rome early? When he had spoken to her the previous evening she told him that she was due to return in a couple of days, yet here she was, back in London.

Victoria saw Dylan standing in the doorway dressed only in a t-shirt and boxers.

'Oh, sorry,' she said softly. 'Did I wake you up?'

It only took the sound of her voice to make him melt inside.

'No matter,' he murmured.

238

He widened the doorway to make room for her and her case. She leaned over and kissed him on the cheek as she made her way through. He inhaled her sweet odour as she brushed past him.

'I've got a surveillance job tomorrow,' he said, 'and I was thinking of getting an early start, but...'

'Look, you go back to bed. I'll just crash out on your sofa, if that's okay. I'm that tired anyway. I just didn't want to go home tonight.'

She walked into the living room, leaving the case standing just inside the doorway, and slumped onto the sofa.

'I really hope that you don't mind me turning up like this.'

'No, not at all. Really. Anyway, thinking about it, I don't think that the guy I'm watching is going to get a very early start. I imagine he'll be having a late night.'

'Yeah? Who is it?' asked Victoria. 'Anything to do with Lola?'

Dylan had decided not to say anything to Victoria about Chas, until he had a little more evidence at least. He didn't want her thinking he was harassing her boss unnecessarily. But now that Chas was involved in the James Braddock case he felt justified in doing so.

'Actually, Victoria, it's Chas that I'm watching,' he said hesitantly.

'Chas? My boss Chas? Why are you watching him?'

Her hands were clasped firmly together as if in prayer. Dylan saw this as sign of anxiety. Perhaps she was more frightened of Chas than she was letting on.

'I've been working on this other case, see, and I've found quite a few crossovers with Lola's case. And in the course of my investigation I came across Chas.'

'What does he have to do with this other case?'

'I'd been looking for this young boy who had run away from home. Remember I asked you about a James Braddock the other day?'

'Lola's friend?'

'That's right, Lola's friend. Anyway, when I went to check him out at this gay club in Soho I was told he'd gone down to Brighton. So I went down there looking for him and... well... I found him.'

'So, you found him? What did he have to tell you... about Lola?'

'Nothing at all, I'm afraid, Victoria. He was dead. I found his body. Right there on the beach. I was out walking early in the morning and stumbled across the poor bastard.'

'Dead? On the beach?'

'That's right. Just like you were told Lola was found. *Your* Lola.'

'Why do you say "*Your* Lola" like that?'

'Because this young chap was dressing in women's clothing and calling himself Lola as well.'

Victoria was now looking across the room, her gaze upon a jelly bean dispenser that Dylan kept on his mantelpiece, but her thoughts quite obviously somewhere else.

'And Chas?' she asked, so quietly that it was almost inaudible.

'Well, I came across Chas in this gay club, a

place called Oscars in Soho. It turns out that your boss Chas is the boyfriend of James Braddock's best friend. I take it you knew that your boss was gay?'

'Yes, of course I knew. He never hid it. Not from the girls anyway. And I've met his boyfriend, Dominic, a couple of times.' She paused momentarily. 'What he got up to in his own time was his business. We didn't need to know any of that.'

'Do you know much else about him, Victoria?'

'Chas always has a lot of contacts, so we're never short of work. That's all we're really interested in. And he looks after us. We know that he's got a bit of a temper but he's never done anything to any of the girls. We just know that if we have any trouble with a client Chas can usually sort it out. If you've seen him you know that he looks pretty scary, right? Usually he'd only have to show his face and it'd be enough.'

'He scared me alright. I went to see him today and when I asked about Lola, I mean your friend Lola, he threatened me and chased me out of his office. I don't mind admitting I was pretty terrified. I've never run so bloody fast.'

He let out a short nervy laugh.

'So, that's why you asked me on the phone if Lola was a transvestite?'

'That's right. But another thing that connects these two cases is that the young lad was living in Brighton in a flat that belonged to Gerald De Vere.'

'What?'

'Yes. I found out that the mystery girl, in the

241

photographs taken of De Vere on the beach that were published in the newspaper, which you identified as Lola, was in fact this young boy. Well, I'm pretty sure anyway.'

'What?!'

'And you seemed so sure that it was your friend.'

Victoria's gaze cut through him. She had to defend herself.

'Look, Dylan, I remember when we looked at those photographs that I said to you that I was sure it was her, because of the tattoo. Remember? But you have to admit that they weren't very clear pictures so I could have made a mistake.'

Dylan noticed the reddening of her skin as her anger level rose. He attempted throwing water on the fire.

'Okay, sweetheart, okay. I'm not accusing you of anything. I'm just trying to piece everything together.'

'Well....,' she said angrily. Her tone softened once more. '.... I know you are.'

She looked around for a decanter or a bottle of something. There were a couple of bottles sitting on a table on the other side of the room.

'Could I have a drink, please? I could really do with one.'

Dylan poured out two drinks. Victoria patted the space next to her on the sofa.

'I've had a bit of a hard time of it in the last couple of weeks, Victoria. Some bastard seems to have it in for me, and I want to find out who this bastard is.'

Victoria started running her fingers through his

242

hair with one hand and rubbing his upper arm with the other.

'I know, baby, I know.'

'Also, I was told that shortly before James disappeared he had been spending a lot of time with a girl that nobody seemed to know very much about. All they agreed on was that she was a brunette and she'd encouraged him to wear women's clothing, possibly even persuaded him to have a gender reassignment.'

'Oh, Dylan,' murmured Victoria, smiling. 'You don't *persuade* people to have gender reassignments. It's something that's deep rooted within them, a feeling.'

'Well... anyway, it's pretty certain that this girl was the one who introduced him to Gerald De Vere. Ring any bells?'

Victoria leaned back to look him square in the face.

'Are you suggesting that this brunette could be Lola?'

'I don't know, but everything looks to point to that fact, don't you think? The thing with the tattoo is a bit of a coincidence, wouldn't you say? And I assume that it was Lola who introduced you to De Vere?'

'The first time Lola met Gerry he wanted a third. He wanted another brunette but one couldn't be found at such short notice so I stepped in. I don't think he was too disappointed but I got the impression that I wasn't really his type.'

Dylan found it difficult listening to her talk of encounters with other men.

'Was it Lola herself who asked you to go to De

Vere's house that night?'

'No. Actually, it was Chas.' She uncrossed her legs and pulled herself to the edge of the sofa. 'He told me that a client had just called asking for a second girl for a little private party. And that Lola was already there.'

'So Chas knew De Vere?'

'I can't say for certain that they'd actually met. Lola may have made the initial contact with Gerry. I'm not really sure. The girls sometimes find their own clients, in clubs, hotel bars and places like that. As long as we let Chas know, he's alright with it. He still wants his cut, of course. Basically we pay him for protection, whoever finds the actual client. That's how it works.'

'And does Chas work alone or is there anyone backing him?'

'Chas is the only person that we see, but I do know that he's got a few shady associates. I suppose someone could be backing him.'

'Do you know if any of these associates could be into stolen art?'

'Stolen art? No... I mean... I don't know. Gerry was an art dealer though. Why do you ask?'

'Don't worry. Do you think that there's any chance that Lola might have got involved too deeply with Chas and some of the others?'

'What are you implying?'

'Nothing. I'm just exploring all avenues. After all, it was Chas who told you about the phone call supposedly from the police, and the call saying Lola was going away for a while. You only have his word for it that anybody called at all.' He

244

paused for a few seconds. 'Look, Victoria, I'm just trying to find out as much as I can....'

Dylan cut short his sentence - Victoria's head was down and she was on the verge of tears. He reached over and took her in his arms.

'Don't cry. I promised you that I would find your friend and I'm still intent on keeping my promise. Okay?'

'Okay. I'm sorry. I know that I have to be stronger.'

'It's understandable that you're like this, but we really don't know what's happened to Lola. As I've said before, you'll have to prepare yourself for anything.' He got up to pour them both another drink. 'Oh, and another thing. Any idea what business Chas would have being in the cemetery where your parents are buried?'

'What? No. Except, I do remember telling him that I should have been visiting the cemetery this weekend...maybe he decided to go there for me. I didn't ask him to though.'

'Did you know there is a Devere family crypt there?' he asked her matter-of-factly.

'No... I didn't. Why, is it relevant?'

Dylan stood up and reached down for her hand.

'No, probably not. No more questions. Come on. You're not sleeping on any sofa tonight - you're sleeping with me.'

He took her glass and placed it on the coffee table. Pulling her up he led her to the bedroom.

'But definitely no touching though, eh?' he said. 'I'm tired and I've got a bit of a headache.'

Dylan could see Victoria was totally shattered, but as he watched her sliding out of the little red

245

dress and in between the bed sheets he was already regretting those words.

TWENTY SIX

At 8:45 the next morning Dylan was sitting in his car in Edmonton. He had parked far enough from Chas's house so as not to be easily seen, but near enough to keep an eye out for his prey. He'd managed to avoid unwanted attention from the children. He'd watched them head off to school, in dribs and drabs, in the opposite direction.

Whilst waiting, Dylan thought about Victoria. Could she possibly have anything to do with all this, he wondered. Not always the best judge of character, he had been fooled many times by people pretending to be something they were not. By nature he was a person that saw the good in people before contemplating the bad, so he got caught out on occasions. He didn't want his vision of Victoria to be so gilded that he was blind to the real picture but she had seemed so very genuine. The tears flowed at all the right times and the expressions of shock and concern were apparent on her face at just the moments that they should have been. If these indications were anything but genuine she must be a very good actress, he thought.

Dylan had offered for her to stay at the flat for as long as she wanted, but Victoria said she no longer felt safe in London. Certainly not if Chas was involved, and she couldn't be sure after what Dylan had told her that he wasn't. She would go and spend some time with Lola's family at their home in Hertfordshire. On her last visit there a fortnight ago, Prudence Douglas had said she could stay any time, and for as long as she wanted. She would have to tell them the truth this time but felt they'd be able to support each other up until, and beyond, the outcome of whatever it was that was happening, or had happened, to Lola.

By 9:30am everything had quietened down and Dylan sat in his car waiting for the red door to open and Chas to emerge. He desperately wanted to use the little spy camera that he had used on his surveillance of Gerald's house again, however, this time there would have been no benefit to it as there was no pub within walking distance – well, not Dylan-walking distance anyway. Besides which, once Chas left the house he probably wouldn't hang around, so it was best to be ready and waiting to go. And, most importantly, it was only 9:30 - in the morning. In Dylan World the pubs would have been open by now, but in the real world legislation dictated that they remain closed for another couple of hours.

So Dylan just sat and waited, and a short while later he was rewarded for his patience. At 9:53 he watched as Chas came out of his house and got into his vehicle. Pulling away, he drove past the little blue car and on towards the junction with the A10. Dylan, who had ducked down beneath the level of the dashboard, straightened in his seat and started up the car in order to give chase - doing a speedy three-point turn first as he was facing the wrong way. Dylan's note to self: always face your car in the same direction as the car you'll be following.

By the time he got to the intersection with the A10, Chas had gone, and Dylan started to panic. A barrier divided the two directions of traffic. The only way to turn was left towards the Great Cambridge roundabout. He waited for the first opportunity to turn out onto the dual carriageway and head south. As he neared the roundabout he spotted Chas's car through the barrier, heading in the opposite direction. The silver BMW had gone round the roundabout and was now travelling back on itself, north towards the M25, or even possibly Cambridge.

The Great Cambridge roundabout was always busy, and so, difficult to negotiate. This day the fates were kind to him, and he managed to drive straight out onto the roundabout, around it, and back onto the A10 without a problem.

There was one slightly surreal moment, however, when a bright yellow Mercedes sports car was pulling out onto the roundabout from the east, just as he was pulling out himself from the north. Waiting to pull out behind the yellow sports car was a small moped. Resplendent in the tricolours of Italy and ridden by Tony's cousin - once removed. Dylan assumed this as he could see the slightly-built, helmeted figure of Tony sitting behind him hanging on for dear life, with the tell-tale trilby secured to the back of the moped with bungee ropes. As Dylan passed in front of them he watched Tony's helmet swivel in perfect alignment with the movement of the little blue car as it made its way around the roundabout. He then saw the tiny moped in his rearview mirror as it pulled out behind him and then exited west in pursuit of the little yellow motor - the helmet's visor still trained on the little blue car. Dylan was unsure whether he should wave or not. He smiled to himself at the coincidences that life sometimes throws up, but mainly at the caricature image of his trusty assistant and his personal chauffeur in a scene reminiscent of a Jacques Tati film.

Back on the A10, Dylan kept one eye on his speed, wary of speed cameras. The lights too were kind to Dylan and by the third set he could see the BMW a safe distance away in front of him. He was now truly back on Chas's tail, being very careful not to step on it and give himself away.

There were times on the journey north when Dylan suspected Chas must have known he was being followed. Some of the roads, once off of the A10, were single-lane country roads with hardly any other traffic on them. No matter how far behind him he was, there had to be times when Chas looked in his rearview mirror to see the little blue car coming up behind him in the distance. And if Chas had indeed cottoned on to his tail where could he be leading him, Dylan wondered? Surely he would not still be heading for his original destination - unless of course that was the intention in the first place. By going to his office the evening before, Dylan had alerted Chas. Therefore, it was quite feasible that Chas had prepared for this, knowing, or at least suspecting, that Dylan would be following him from then on in.

There was no option now for Dylan, he had to

go the whole hog. It wasn't as if he could just stop the car, do a U-turn and head back home. That's not what happens in the films, he thought. Whatever the potential danger of a job, you never, ever saw the pursuer stop in the middle of a pursuit, turn around and go back home. Well, not in any of the films that he'd seen anyway. He was in this for the long haul. He would see this whole damn Lola saga through to its very end, whatever the conclusion. With everything that had happened it had now become personal.

Dylan slowed down. He could quite clearly see Chas's car in the distance, although it was more of a silver speck, but the undeviating road allowed him license to leave extra space between the two vehicles. This made him feel a little happier and slightly more secure in the knowledge that, if he hadn't already been spotted, he was now less likely to be.

After a further twenty minutes or so of driving they entered the small market town of Tring and the traffic became a little denser than it had been. There were now more turnings that Chas could take and it was all that Dylan could do to keep an eye on him whilst also keeping an eye on what was immediately in front of his own vehicle, or in danger of walking in front of it. This was something that, as a private investigator, he would have to learn to master and execute with a lot more casualness than he was exhibiting. He could feel himself starting to panic. Fearful of losing sight of Chas, his eyes darted about frantically as he monitored everything that moved.

He needn't have worried though, as both human beings and animals managed to stay on the pavement where they belonged and were safe, and one by one the vehicles that were in between him and Chas either pulled into parking spaces or turned off into side roads. Chas was now just two cars and a van in front of him. Perfect, thought Dylan. After another couple of minutes' pursuit the road took a bend to the right and Dylan watched as Chas turned left into a cul-de-sac. The end of the trail, thought Dylan.

Dylan slowed down as he negotiated the bend. At the entrance to the cul-de-sac stood a church on the right-hand side and the Queen's Head public house on the left. He saw the small church car park just around the bend and pulled into it. There was only one other vehicle parked. A pretty quiet part of the town, thought Dylan, as he parked facing the church wall. He got out of the car, walked to the edge of the wall, and looked down the road. Chas had parked at the very end and was getting out of his car. Dylan watched as he went through the open gates towards a building which, except for a couple of sections of roof, was completely obscured from view by an eight foot high white wall and the unbroken line of ash trees just beyond. Dylan could just make out, at the end of the wall by the gates, that there was a sign. He furtively made his way along the outside of the church wall, the rear section of which ran parallel to the first few feet of the white wall, until he could make out what the sign said. This was the UK office of Loddon Security Products.

That was all Dylan needed to know for the

moment. Of course he couldn't just walk in there after Chas. He would instead have to adjourn to the hostelry next-door to see what he could find out about the company from the locals and obviously enjoy a refreshing pint of something wet.

Dylan entered the Queen's Head public house and made for the bar. He perused the plaques on the beer pumps. Amongst the ales on tap he could see that there were three available from the local brewery - one of which was the winner of a considerable number of awards.

'A pint of Colley's Dog please, landlord,' cried Dylan, as the person in question approached.

Full-bodied, bald-headed, double-chinned and with at least two teeth missing, the landlord gave the impression of being a jovial man. This was unlike some of the miserable wretches holding tenancies Dylan had the misfortune to have encountered. He whistled a jolly tune as he pulled the pint, and held an unforced smiled as he did so. He placed the glass of ale on the bar in front of Dylan.

'That'll be £2.70 please, sir,' he said, maintaining the smile.

'Colley's Dog. What's the story behind that one then?' Dylan asked him.

'Oh, just a local myth, sir, as these things always tend to be. Apparently this chap, Colley, led a band of men on something of a misguided witch-hunt around these parts a few hundred years ago. They were responsible for the drowning of an elderly woman who was later found to be completely innocent. They also killed her

253

husband. Colley was later arrested, convicted and hung.'

Dylan, who loved hearing tales of local myths from which ale names were derived, listened with interest.

'And the story goes that Colley's spirit roams around here in the form of a large black dog. Don't ask me why.'

After a short pause the landlord changed the subject.

'Would you like to order anything to eat, sir?' he said enthusiastically.

When Dylan said that he didn't the landlord just smiled and moved back to the other end of the bar, whereupon he continued to read the newspaper that he had abandoned moments earlier.

Dylan looked around and there was only one other customer in the pub, but it was not quite lunch time yet. He picked up his pint and looked for somewhere to sit. The solitary customer didn't look altogether approachable; a dishevelled man in a tattered old tweed jacket which looked like it had been rejected from a charity shop at least forty years ago. The hair on his head, for that was all Dylan could see, as he stared, face down, into an almost empty pint glass, was grey and matted and probably hadn't seen hot water or shampoo in a month of Sundays.

Dylan chose instead to move to the other end of the bar and interrupt the landlord, who was probably the best person to get local information out of anyway. The landlord looked up cautiously as Dylan approached, but when he spoke he did so in a cheerful manner.

'Yes, sir? Changed your mind about the food, have you? Chef's not quite ready yet. It'll be another ten minutes or so before we start serving.'

Dylan was quick to quash any hopes that the landlord had of getting a food order.

'No, no. I haven't changed my mind about the food. I just wanted to ask you a few questions about the people next-door.'

With his thumb Dylan pointed through the pub and out of the side window which looked out on the rear of the premises occupied by Loddon Security Products.

'You mean the security company?'

'Yes, that's the one.'

'I don't wish to be rude, sir, but why do you want to know?' His manner suddenly not as jovial as it had been.

'It's just that I'm looking to do some business with them and I wanted an outsider's opinion on what kind of company they are.'

'With all due respect, sir, I'm just a publican, I don't know anything about security. Surely you'd be better off asking someone in the trade rather than someone like me?'

'That's a fair point. But when I work with a company I like to know everything about that company and not just about the people at the top, or their accounts. One of the main things that I look at is the kind of people who work there: the operational people; the people I'll have to deal with on a day-to-day basis. And I imagine that, as there's not much else around here, a lot of them come in here at lunchtimes. So, who better to ask than your good self?'

'Well... I suppose so. You're obviously a very serious and thorough man when it comes to your business. There's nothing wrong in that. It's all too rare in this day and age, especially in someone as young as yourself.'

'Well, I try to be.' Dylan's expression was suitably serious. 'I do intend to make an appointment with one of the sales chappies of course, but I thought that I would pop in here first to see if I could get an opinion on the real bones of the company from an outsider before I do.'

'All I can tell you, sir, is that the owner of the company is a gentleman called Edward Loddon. A very nice gent, although he doesn't come down here very often himself - only when they're all in here at Christmas for their company celebration. We've spoken to each other on occasions, about local issues and the like, and I've always found him pleasant enough to deal with. For instance, when they first moved into the building. It used to be the old vicarage before they turned it into offices and there were a series of tunnels that connected the three buildings...'

'Three buildings?'

'The vicarage, the pub and the church over the road.'

'That's very interesting.'

'Yes. Apparently it was constructed around the time of the plague on the orders of the vicar, so he could move from the church to the vicarage safely. Well, that's the story anyway. And, as these were the only three buildings here at the time I suppose he thought there should be a tunnel to the pub as well.' He gave a sly wink. 'But as soon as they moved there, they blocked their end off. The church end of the tunnel and our end here were blocked off ages ago, way before my time, and I've been here thirty years. Anyway, Mr Loddon came round to ask me about the tunnel before he blocked it off. He wanted to see if the other two ends were already blocked.'

'Why do you think he would want to know that?'

'I don't know, sir. I didn't really feel inclined to ask. I just told him that our end was definitely blocked off and that, as far as I knew, the church end was as well, but that he'd have to check with the vicar.'

The thought occurred to Dylan that if Lola was being used by Chas and Loddon for some purpose, and was now held against her will, these tunnels sounded like just the kind of place for the job.

'And do you know if the vicarage end was definitely blocked off?'

'Well, I don't know for definite. I've never been in there, but they say it was. Not my business really, sir. All I know is that on the odd occasion that I've had cause to have dealings with Mr Loddon, I've found him to be pleasant enough. But you know what people are like. When someone is successful they start dredging up stories about them being involved in this and that.'

'Really? Like what?'

Could this be what Dylan was waiting to hear?

The landlord, realising he had possibly said too

much, was now nervously looking up at the clock on the wall opposite, which was fast approaching twelve o'clock. He glanced across at the other customer, who didn't give any impression that he had been listening - still sitting with his face down, gazing into his glass.

'Look,' said the landlord, 'if you hang around a few of them are going to be in here soon for their lunch. You can judge them for yourself. Now you really must excuse me, I've got to go and speak to chef about the food. You sure I can't interest you in a spot of lunch, sir?'

Dylan shook his head and with that the landlord disappeared through the door and into the kitchen.

Dylan looked across at the table occupied by the only other customer and just as he did so the only other customer looked up from his now empty glass and across at Dylan, viewing him with suspicion. He had a dishevelled face, perfectly matching his un-coiffed hair. Red-nosed and full-bearded, he clearly looked like a man in need of another pint. Dylan didn't want to be too presumptuous, but in all probability it did seem that where this man was at that moment was far more agreeable than anywhere he had to go back to afterwards. And, if each pint bought with it a period of shelter from his reality outside of the four walls of the pub, then Dylan was only too willing to help.

TWENTY SEVEN

When the landlord re-emerged from the kitchen Dylan was quick to point out that he still hadn't changed his mind about the food.

'I'd just like a pint of whatever the gentleman over there is drinking, please, and another half of the Colley's Dog.'

The landlord looked towards the table where the dishevelled man sat, slouched over his empty glass.

'Terry? I wouldn't go bothering him, sir,' said the landlord. 'You start him off and you'll be opening a whole can of worms for yourself. You'll find that most of what he comes out with is pure fantasy anyway. If you're thinking of asking him about the security people, I warn you that he's a bit biased. You see, he was squatting for a time in there before they moved in and had him forcibly evicted. So he won't have a good word to say about them. And I certainly wouldn't be basing any business decisions on what he tells you.' He shook his head. 'You won't get any truths out of Terry. He's best left alone if you ask me, sir.'

Dylan knew that being a good private investigator was not achieved by leaving things alone, best or otherwise. Besides which it was exactly what he wanted to hear - a man who held a grudge against Loddon was a man he needed to speak to. Biased he may be, but at least there was a fair chance that he would have a story or two to

259

tell.

Dylan carried the pint of beer warily over to Terry's table. As he placed the glass down a grey head rose up, revealing two piercing, rheumy eyes that had, to all appearances, looked out on life for the best part of three score years and ten. When he spoke, his voice was deep and gruff.

'Look, old chap,' he said, in an accent that belied his appearance. 'I don't wish to be inhospitable, but kindly piss off will you. There are plenty of other tables.'

He looked around the pub at all the other tables at which customers were conspicuous by their absence.

'You won't be wanting this then.'

Dylan took up the full pint glass and feigned retreat. This provoked an instant change of attitude.

'Not so hasty, old chap, not so hasty.' Neither was his voice so gruff any more. 'Sit down, sit down... yes, it's... erm,' He looked Dylan up and down. 'I don't seem to remember your name presently, but I know I've seen you around here before. Yes, sit down here next to me.'

He pulled out the chair next to him and patted the seat, inviting Dylan to sit. On his hands were gloves cut to the knuckles. His eyes were on the pint of ale that Dylan held in his hand. Dylan sat and placed the glass back down on the table in front of him.

'There you go... Terry,' he said hesitantly, not sure whether being so familiar at this early stage was the right thing.

'Terrance, please, old chap. I simply detest

abbreviation of names. I was christened Terrance, and Terrance I shall remain until my final breath and beyond. I'll come back and haunt the bastard that sanctions the engraving of Terry on my gravestone.'

'Oh, sorry. It's just that the landlord called you Terry and so...'

Dylan wasn't allowed to finish.

'Oh, him. The less said about him, the better,' he growled, lifting the glass of beer and taking a good, long quaff.

'Now, let's see if I can't remember your name. I know that I've seen you around.' He looked at Dylan, scrutinizing every inch of his physiognomy. 'Is it young Philip from the butchers on the High Street?'

'No, I'm not Philip from the butchers. Actually...'

Dylan was again interrupted.

'No no no, don't tell me,' he insisted, holding up a hand. 'I'll get it. Just give me a minute.' He took another, smaller sip of beer. 'Is it Michael? No, I know. I've got it now. Of course, it's Christopher, isn't it? Vernon's lad. How is your father nowadays? Is he still in the ironmongery business or has he retired now? I haven't seen him for donkeys' years. I don't get over to that part of town much any more. Still, do please give him my very best regards, won't you? We were at school together. And dear Susan. I-i-is your mother still alive? Oh, please don't think me insensitive, dear boy. It's just that I heard she was quite ill a few years back, and I haven't seen her in quite a while.'

He took yet another sip of beer and then leaned towards Dylan, speaking quietly into his ear.

'Perhaps I shouldn't really tell you this, but I knew your mother very well. We were at school together you see. Did I mention that already? Anyway, although nothing untoward occurred between us after she married Vernon, it didn't stop people around here gossiping. You know how people are.'

He grabbed the sleeve of Dylan's jacket and pulled it towards him. He glanced around the still empty pub, empty that is except for the landlord who was back at his newspaper but quite obviously concentrating on their conversation.

'When you came along...,' he whispered, '.... and I am sure that you will laugh at this, dear boy, but there were rumours that I, Terrance Penhaligon, was your real father.'

He let out a short burst of laughter.

'However, I can assure you now, that everything between me and your dear mother was strictly above board.'

He placed a hand on his left lapel, above his heart.

'Look, Terrance... Mr Penhaligon... I really am not who you think I am. You don't know me. I'm not even from around here. I've come up from London.'

'What? London?' He suddenly looked very confused. 'Not Vernon and Susan's boy? I did start to wonder, because I was pretty sure that you weren't Welsh before.'

'No. I'm not Christopher, Mr Penhaligon. Which I think is for the best really. Maybe you shouldn't be telling the real Christopher what you've just told me. Probably not the sort of thing he would want to hear, really.'

Penhaligon looked a little disappointed at the fact that Dylan wasn't who he thought he was, and a little embarrassed at having just been castigated by the younger man. With his head down he took another mouthful of beer, then, all of a sudden, he sat bolt upright in his chair. The disappointment and embarrassment of the last few moments having completely subsided, he enthusiastically questioned Dylan.

'So, what is your name then, young man? Whom do I have to thank for this fine pint of the golden nectar?'

'Dylan is my name, Mr Penhaligon.'

'Oh, please do call me Terrance. Dylan, eh? Fine Welsh name: Dylan. I knew a Dylan once. A writer he was. You may have heard of him, surname of Thomas. Used to drink with him when I lived down in London.' A sharp intake of breath. 'Going back a bit now of course.'

'You knew Dylan Thomas?' Dylan asked incredulously.

'Oh, yes,' he boomed. 'Used to drink with the man. We would end up three sheets to the wind on many an occasion. Invited me to his house at Laugharne once, to meet his wife and see his writers' shed, but I didn't go. I mean, why did I need to go all that way to get drunk when I could have done it perfectly well on my own doorstep? Never asked me again. Always one to bear a grudge he was. Then of course he went and died, across the pond. I think they said it was drink. It

263

certainly came as a bit of a warning to me. Didn't stop me bloody drinking though.'

He nudged Dylan's arm with his elbow and sniggered.

Dylan Thomas had died in 1953. Even if Terrance Penhaligon was at the top end of the age range that his appearance indicated, then it would still have meant that he was sub-teens when the great man had died, thought Dylan. As he had already caused him one moment of mild embarrassment he didn't wish to provoke another, so he said nothing. At least he knew now that the landlord hadn't been lying.

'Terrance, I just wanted to ask you about the people next door actually. The people at the security company.'

'What? Next door? That bastard Loddon?'

He suddenly became animated. There was a real anger in his demeanour.

'He threw me out of my home, the bastard. Him and those heavies of his. They threw all my belongings out into the road. Granted I didn't have much, but... I went to the police. They didn't want to listen. I was squatting legally. He just came along and inflicted violence upon my person. What was an old man to do? Fortunately the vicar let's me sleep in the church sometimes, when it's really cold. Now there is a good man. A man of God, yes, but a good man.'

'Not a believer in God then?' Dylan asked, over the rim of his glass.

'God? I should say not. He's not been here for me when I've needed him.'

'But you just said yourself that you're allowed

to sleep in his house sometimes, so he's given you shelter when you've needed it.'

Dylan was not a believer himself, or at least he was undecided, but felt that the point had to be made, if only to get Terrance's response, which was sure to be entertaining.

'Don't be fooled, young man. A God may be worshipped anywhere, just as a football team may be worshipped anywhere. A church, just like any other building is mere bricks and mortar, just as a football stadium is also mere bricks and mortar, or whatever blasted stuff they use nowadays. They are simply places for like-minded people to come together. But never be fooled into thinking that there is necessarily substance to those things being worshipped. They are merely there to control, and to direct people away from that which is considered evil.'

He took another draught of beer.

'I have been a Tottenham Hotspur supporter for many a year now, young Dylan, and I have had to worship from afar. The temple of the White Hart is unfortunately the home of Mammon nowadays and has been beyond my financial, as well as physical, reach for some time. They too promise miracles that have yet to be seen.' Dylan smiled. 'It is believed that if God is not in your heart there is a danger that you will move towards the devil. If Tottenham Hotspur were not in my heart, then, in all probability, I would have veered towards the Arsenal.'

He leant over and spat air towards the floor.

'I am allowed to sleep in the church because of the goodness of the vicar and no other greater power. If the vicar tells me that his goodness is derived from what he sees as a much greater power then I will respect his belief. But when I settle down for the night, within the four walls of the church, I will hold onto my own belief that there can be no greater good than that which the human heart is capable of, when, and if, it chooses to display that goodness.'

Dylan looked at the glass that Penhaligon was clutching and saw it was empty.

'Would you like another, Terrance?'

'Now you, young Dylan, are a very good man indeed.' He placed his glass into Dylan's waiting hand.

*

By 12.07 the lunchtime crowd were starting to drift in. This included a few employees of Loddon Security who were not difficult to distinguish from the other customers. They were all sitting together at one large table and, although most of them wore suits and formal office attire, some wore black polo shirts with a yellow Loddon Security insignia embroidered on the left breast. Dylan had moved away from Terrance Penhaligon's table and was now occupying a smaller table on his own. He noticed that the landlord had whispered something in the ear of one of the men that had gone up to get the drinks, after which the man turned his head and looked towards where Dylan was sitting. After handing out the drinks to his colleagues he came towards Dylan's table. Wearing a navy blue suit and tie, he looked every bit the salesman.

'I understand that you're looking to do some business with us? The name's Drake, Alan Drake. I manage the sales department at Loddon Securities.'

Dylan stood up and leaned across the table to shake Drake's hand, introducing himself as David Morgan. The salesman reached into the inside pocket of his suit jacket and took out a card.

'Give me a call. We'll see what we can do for you.' Dylan took the card. 'Where did you hear about us, anyway?'

Dylan answered, looking for a reaction to gauge. 'From Chas. I'm a friend of Chas's. He said that you may be able to help me with my requirements.'

'Chas? Not sure I know him.'

'Chas,' Dylan reiterated. 'Scottish? With chains all over the place.'

There was an instant sign of recognition in the salesman's face.

'Oh, Charlie. Eddie's mate. Okay. He was in the office earlier. Only left a few minutes ago, I think. Did you come up together?'

'No, no, we came up separately. Look, I don't want to take up any more of your lunch hour, but I don't suppose you have any appointments for this afternoon, do you?'

'Yes, sure. After all, you are a friend of a friend of the governor. I've got one or two things I need to finish off when I get back but I can see you around two o'clock. That okay for you?'

As Dylan finished his drink and was leaving the pub Terrance Penhaligon shouted across the now busy bar area to him.

'Farewell, young Dylan - the last of the good men. Farewell.'

His cry rang out as he held his glass aloft. This drew the attention of everybody in the pub, including Alan Drake, who looked first at Penhaligon then towards Dylan.

When Dylan got outside he looked towards the end of the cul-de-sac and saw that Chas's car had indeed gone. This made things easier for him as there was now nobody to recognise him - or was there? After all, he didn't know what this place was that he'd be walking into, and he didn't know who this fellow Edward Loddon was. All he knew was that he owned a security products company, that he was a friend of Chas's, and that he may or may not be involved in certain activities of an illegal nature. For all Dylan knew, Loddon may also have been the person behind the whole Lola story - even possibly the person behind his abduction. And, if this was the case, Loddon was sure to recognise him as soon as he walked into the office, and the whole charade of being there on the pretext of business would be shot.

Dylan walked back to his car and sat looking out of the window formulating his plan B. Good old plan B. The desperate man's last resort, well unless there was a plan C of course, but when did anybody ever have a plan C?

He telephoned Tony to let him know exactly where he was so that, in the eventuality that he disappeared again, Tony would know exactly where to look for him this time. There was no answer. It was then that he remembered that Tony would probably still be sitting on the back of his cousin's moped following Mrs Puckett.

Dylan left a message on his voicemail with the address of the security company, and another teaser which he'd quickly Googled.

'Se mi succede qualcosa, si prega di spargere le mie ceneri in cima del Monte Snowdon.'

Dylan looked at his watch - it was now 12:37 and he had just under an hour and a half until his appointment with Alan Drake. Ample time, he thought, for popping into the church for a word with the vicar.

Lunchtime worshippers were obviously thin on the ground in the parish. When Dylan walked into the Church of St John the Baptist he found it devoid of customers. He could see someone standing at the rear of the church fumbling about with sheets of paper in the chancel. Dylan made his way down the aisle, stopping at the front row of seats. Hearing Dylan's footsteps, the person in the chancel looked up. His expression suddenly changed from blank to one of delight. He practically threw down the sheets of paper and started walking hurriedly towards the Welshman.

As he walked through the arch and down the two steps that brought him into the nave, his black cassock swung loosely around the emaciated frame upon which his even thinner head sat. He looked to be in desperate need of a few extra square meals to help keep him upright, thought Dylan. In fact, had he of had a hood and a scythe he would have evoked the recognisable image of Death.

'Welcome, welcome,' he enthused. 'It's good to see a new face... Well it's good to see any face at all nowadays to tell you the truth. Our numbers are ever dwindling. It's becoming somewhat of a major cause of concern for the vicar.'

'Oh! You're not the vicar then?'

'No, no, bless you. I'm the verger here. Unfortunately Mike has had to visit one of our elderly parishioners who is approaching the end of her journey. I was just about to shoot off somewhere myself. But maybe I can help you?' He brought his hands together with a smack.

Consequently, the verger was most forthcoming with information about Edward Loddon and his company. The consensus of opinion around town was that Loddon was indeed involved in far more than just running a security products company. He explained that the vicar would probably know far more than himself, but that he was loathe to speak ill of him as Loddon was quite the local philanthropist; generous to the church and local charities, he was known to have helped many a person down on their luck. When Dylan mentioned Loddon had been less than beneficent to the homeless gentleman he'd just encountered in the Queen's Head, he was surprised that the verger had no idea who Terrance Penhaligon was.

TWENTY EIGHT

At exactly two o'clock, Dylan was sitting in the reception area of Loddon Security Products. The receptionist, an extremely pleasant looking girl with red hair, and in her early twenties, announced his arrival to Alan Drake and was now on the phone busily chatting away to her boyfriend, judging by the content of the conversation. Every time the conversation got a little amorous she would look across to Dylan before lowering her voice. Dylan did a splendid impression of someone reading a security products catalogue, pretending not to listen – which of course he was.

A door opened at the far end of the corridor that led off past the reception area and Drake emerged in some state of anxiety. When he spoke he sounded flustered.

'I am really sorry about this, Mr Morgan, but it completely slipped my mind that there was an outside sales call that I had to make this afternoon. One, I'm afraid, that I can't get out of. So, unfortunately, I won't be able to see you myself. But there's no problem, I mentioned it to Mr Loddon and he was quite keen to see you himself. It seems that you're going straight to the top. He's not quite ready to see you yet I'm afraid, but he asked me to arrange a tea or coffee for you while you're waiting.'

Drake turned to the receptionist who had quickly curtailed the conversation she was

271

having.

'Sandra, will you sort that out for me, please? Get Mr Morgan here whatever he would like to drink and maybe a few biscuits.' He turned once again to Dylan. 'Mr Loddon won't keep you too long, he knows that you're waiting. But I'm afraid you really will have to excuse me now as I'm already quite late.'

He shook Dylan's hand before rushing out of the main door to attend his meeting, taking nothing with him - no briefcase, no folder, nothing.

Sandra returned from the kitchen, placing the tea and biscuits down on a small table by the side of Dylan's chair that was full of trade publications. The door to the front office opened and out stepped Edward Loddon. He was an imposing man in his middle years, around six and a half feet tall and built like a brick outhouse. His shirt looked as if it were at bursting point, each muscle rippling through the thin cotton material. He was a well-groomed, handsome man who obviously took great care of his appearance.

'Mr Morgan, I'm so sorry to have kept you waiting. I'm Edward Loddon. Please come through.'

Dylan stood up. Shaking Loddon's hand he flinched, feeling the considerable power in his grip. He reached over to take up his tea and biscuits.

'Don't worry about that,' said Loddon, then turned to the girl. 'Sandra, will you bring Mr Morgan's tea through, please?'

Dylan entered Loddon's office and sat by a

beautiful, black marble-topped desk with white leather panelling. It was considerably more cluttered and busy looking than his own desk. Loddon made his way to his own chair and fell into it.

Dylan glanced around the office; on the pastel blue walls hung framed trade certificates and awards. Whatever else this business may be a cover for, thought Dylan, it was certainly giving the impression of being a very successful and professional security products company.

Sandra placed the tea and biscuits on Loddon's desk and quickly departed, closing the door behind her.

'Now, what is it that we can do for you, Mr Morgan? What is it exactly that you are looking for?'

The tone of Loddon's voice and the half-smile on his face led Dylan to wonder whether the game may already be up. Chas had, after all, been and gone.

'I'm in the property development business, Mr Loddon. My company is currently working on several projects at the top end of the market and I am looking at offering these properties with the most up-to-date security systems available, which is what I'm hoping you can provide.'

'Property developer, eh? Do you have a card on you?'

Dylan didn't have a card on him of course. He continued with the charade by searching frantically around his jacket pockets for the non-existent business card. Handing over a Beaumaris Investigations business card at this juncture would not have helped.

'I'm afraid that I don't, Mr Loddon. To be honest, it didn't occur to me that I would have to be handing cards out today, so I came out without any on me.' He gave a slight shrug of the shoulders as Loddon just stared. 'Silly really, I should know to always carry some on me... just in case.'

The smile that had been on Loddon's face disappeared.

'So, how did you hear about us, Mr Morgan? Or may I call you Dylan?'

He appeared equanimous, but his question indicated an awareness of the charade.

'What? Dylan? No, my name is David.'

The first real indication that Loddon knew the truth. Dylan's innards knotted up.

'Oh. It's just that Alan said someone in the pub had called you Dylan. It did make us wonder.'

'Oh, I see, yes. No. The old fella seemed to think I was the son of a friend of his. I couldn't get it through to him that I wasn't. Then he told me that he'd actually met Dylan Thomas, so I think he was just getting a little confused.' Dylan was relieved that this seemed to be all that was troubling Loddon. 'Anyway, where was I?'

'You were telling me how you heard about our company.'

'Oh, yes. You know, trade publications, word of mouth, a bit of on-line surfing, that sort of thing.'

'Which is it? Word of mouth, internet or trade publications? How did you first find out about Loddon Security – I'd be very interested to

274

know?'

'I've got friends also in the property development business and they recommended your company.'

Dylan was panicking now. He knew that his answer, offered in a moment of duress, invited the inevitable next question.

'Who are your friends, Mr Morgan? It's just that Alan Drake also told me...' here it comes, thought Dylan, '...that you were a friend of Charlie's.'

The game was now surely over.

'More of an acquaintance really,' Dylan said nonchalantly. A response that was weak and he knew it.

'More of a pain in the arse I would say..., Mr Morgan.'

And there it was.

Dylan shifted uneasily in his chair, considering his next move. Loddon was surely in no position to make a move with the receptionist sitting just the other side of the door. All Dylan would have to do is shout for help. And even if Loddon did make his move right there, there was no other way out, except for the large bay window behind Loddon's desk which looked out onto the car park. He would have to keep Dylan, or his body at least, in the office until everybody had gone home before he could move it out of there.

Dylan stared hard at Loddon and Loddon stared with equal intensity at Dylan. For what seemed like an age, but was in reality just a handful of moments, they sat staring at one another. Like a Mexican stand-off. All that was needed was for Eli Wallach to walk in so they could play out the culminating scene of The Good, The Bad and The Ugly.

A sudden feeling of claustrophobia came upon him and Dylan was forced to break his stare. He looked instead past Loddon and out of the window. His attention was held by a large willow tree that dominated much of the lawn adjacent to the parking area at the front of the building, until he was suddenly jolted by a heavy rap on the door. Without invitation the door swung open.

It wasn't Eli Wallach.

Another extremely large gentleman, sporting a scar which ran from beneath his eye to just above the side of his chin, leaned his enormous upper frame into the room. He looked not too far removed from a primate of the Oligocene period. He glanced first at Dylan then over to Loddon, who hadn't moved and was still glaring menacingly at Dylan.

'Just to let you know, boss,' said the primate, 'I've let Sandra go for the day, so I'll be just outside on the desk if you need me.'

Dylan knew the information was as much for his benefit as Loddon's. Loddon didn't respond, and the primate didn't wait for one. He left the room, closing the door behind him.

It was only then that Dylan noticed, out of the very corner of his eye, behind him was another door, in the part of the room that had been out of his line of vision when he'd been ushered in.

He looked back at Loddon, whose eyes were still on the Welshman. As intimidating as it had been sitting across the desk from Chas, with all his chains and tattoos, the prospect of tangling with the man in front of him now was infinitely more terrifying.

Without expression, Loddon finally spoke.

'Here we are then, Mr Morgan, or whatever your name is. You, the proverbial pain in the arse, and me with a drawer full of pain reliever. Now, I'm a fair man and so I'll ask you before I make any move, do you perhaps have an alternative suggestion for easing my pain?'

Not a situation conducive to levity, Dylan thought that he'd try anyway.

'I thank you for giving me the opportunity, Mr Loddon,' Dylan said boldly. 'I would obviously like to make this as easy as possible for myself, and for you, because, and I won't lie to you, I'm a little bit shitting myself here. Now I am sure that you have the potential to be quite a... let's say... belligerent man, and so I appreciate your allowing me to come up with an alternative solution to solving any problems we may have, without the necessity of you having to deploy your weapon. I-I'm assuming that's what you're talking about when you say pain relief.'

Loddon maintained his stare but his features softened. Dylan then unwittingly made the crucial mistake of smiling. Although irreverence wasn't his intention Loddon had obviously misconstrued it as such.

'Now look here, Taff!'

'Steady on,' pleaded Dylan. 'You don't have to start getting....'

'SHUT UP!' roared Loddon.

Dylan shut up.

'Now tell me... Mr Morgan... what it is exactly that you want, because I know, and you know, and that pigeon sitting in that tree out there knows, that you're no fucking property developer.'

He leaned in closer to Dylan. His arms extended as far as they would go, his palms flat on the desk with fingers straight as they could possibly stretch. His whole upper body taut and straining, like a dog on its leash being taunted by an out of reach cat; the same provocative position that Chas had assumed the previous day.

Dylan knew that there was no margin for error in his next words, there seemed no point in lying any further. Deciding to go on the offensive, having nothing now to lose, he replied without hesitancy.

'Okay. I'm sure then that Chas would have told you that it's Lola that I'm looking for. As soon as I mentioned the name it seemed to have an effect on him. So, I'm pretty sure that he, and probably yourself, know exactly where she is. I followed him and he led me here.

'Before I arrived here I wasn't sure whether you had anything to do with all this, Mr Loddon, whether you were involved, but I have to say that your attitude and your actions have only gone towards proving to me that you are... involved, that is.'

Loddon sat back in his chair listening. Dylan relaxed as he continued speaking.

'Now, I am willing to forgive about the whole abduction thing and pumping me with those drugs. The doctor at the hospital said that, in the wrong quantities, they could have been very

278

dangerous, but as you obviously had someone who knew what they were doing.... But, as I say, I am willing to forgive and forget, and all that. I've not been pissing any more than I should be, and I've had no palpitations. That Indian chap still shows up every now and again but, to be honest, I don't mind, I'm getting quite attached. I still don't know what all the business about the phone was, but never mind, eh? As I said, it's water under the bridge now, although I was a bit miffed when the bubble came back.'

Loddon listened, perplexed.

'But I should just warn you that I have notified my people I'm here,' he said quite confidently, 'so that if anything happens to me again I can be found this time. So, Mr Loddon, I'm here to do a job and I would like to know where Lola is. What can you tell me about that?'

Loddon's response, when it came, was quietly delivered.

'Mr Morgan, I'm going to try to remain calm. The doctors have warned me already about my blood pressure, so I've got to watch it. I really haven't got a fucking clue what the hell you're going on about. Indians? Bubbles? I don't know anything about any drugs, but after listening to you speak I imagine that you must be on something.

'One thing I do know though, is that coming around here and shouting about Lola has done you no favours whatsoever. You shouldn't have come here. I don't know how or what you know about Lola, or what you're trying to gain, but I can tell you that Lola doesn't want to be found. And so

279

now we have a situation. I can't exactly let you leave, it wouldn't be sensible. This thing has been going on too long for me to allow it to end here, like this. Nobody would thank me for that.'

Confused, Dylan could only sit and watch as the big man reached for his top drawer. There was only one possible thing to do, he thought. Just as he had done in Chas's office yesterday, his only option was to run, but he knew that he wouldn't make it far outside the main door from the office as the formidable primate was just outside. His only chance was to try to make it through the door behind him. He had no idea where it went but he didn't hesitate.

Dylan quickly reached across and grabbed the large glass paperweight that sat on the corner of Loddon's desk. With one fluid movement he lifted it up and threw it at Loddon, who with quick reflex lifted both hands to stop it from hitting him full on the temple, but the force pushed him back in the chair and stunned him momentarily.

Without stopping to see how much damage it had done, if any, Dylan made for the other door. He pulled it open and once inside quickly pulled the door shut behind him. It was pitch black, not even the faintest chink of light could be seen. Fumbling around hastily in the dark, he found a lock and slid it across. The bolt felt quite chunky and sturdy. He thought that it would probably hold fast for at least a minute or so while he considered his next move. He knew it was only a matter of time before Loddon would be kicking down the door.

Dylan groped around trying to locate a light

switch and found it just to the right of the door. He flicked the switch and the room illuminated. *Shit, a toilet!* Dylan saw immediately that there was no window. It was probably a converted store cupboard.

He heard Loddon murmuring something as he got up from behind his desk. He heard the main door open and the primate enter the office. And he heard a few mumbled words. He listened intently as both men approached the small en-suite and started to pound heavily on the door. But then something caught his attention. Feeling the floor beneath his feet give a little in one section he realised that it was anything but solid.

Reaching down, Dylan pulled up the loose beige carpet, held firm only through its sheer weight, and underneath it there was a metal hatch. He had possibly found his way out, but being honest with himself he couldn't shrug off the feeling that all he was doing was delaying the inevitable. The only decision to make now was: did he want to be captured in a dark, dank tunnel that in all probability he may never get out of, or was a light and airy office that looked out upon a gently weeping willow a more fitting end?

TWENTY NINE

As Dylan descended the few stone steps that led to the floor of the tunnel, the foreboding that he had felt in Loddon's office suddenly and inexplicably lifted, and an unaccountable and overwhelming sense of bliss came upon him. An elation propelled him along through the darkness of the tunnel, his cares seemingly left somewhere behind him.

This was not the first time that he had experienced such a moment of euphoria - he had experienced them before and they had lasted for as long as, well, just that - moments. However, when they had occurred previously, they'd done so during more carefree times, and not whilst being pursued by a couple of missing links. But there was something of the child in Dylan that had never left him. The less than acute sense of danger that spurs children on without due consideration to consequence also plagued Dylan. Although this condition had not, so far, been detrimental to his well-being on the whole, he was aware that the situation he currently found himself in was, without doubt the most alarming he had ever been faced with, and therefore not really open to a lack of cognition.

As he moved through the tunnel he smirked to himself, but knew that he had to keep moving. He reached into his jacket pocket and took out his mobile phone. Just like at Gerald De Vere's house he knew that it would give him enough light so as to see what was ahead of him.

He could make out that the tunnel, around six feet in width, went on for a distance of thirty to forty feet before the light began to fade. Walking on further, he could see that there was a fork where the tunnel split and went in two different directions, dividing, presumably, to go one way to the church and the other to the pub. He couldn't tell how long each tunnel went on for after the split, but he guessed that all three sections would be of similar length, one hundred to one hundred and fifty feet, from the intersection.

He also made out, at regular intervals along the tunnel, alcoves, eight feet in width and around six in depth, cut into the stone wall. As he moved past each alcove he pointed the light into them revealing crates, most of which looked appropriately shaped for housing framed paintings. There were a few articles, bronze sculptures, porcelain figurines etc., which were loose and not crated up.

One thing that he did not see was where they may have been keeping Lola. If she had been down there he was pretty certain that he would've seen a doorway leading off somewhere, but apart from the alcoves there was nowhere likely to conceal a human being, in this section of the tunnel at least.

Though loathe to do so he knew the crates that housed the works of art, if scattered across the width of the tunnel, would provide a suitable obstacle to his pursuers. One by one he pulled a few of the larger crates out from the recess and dropped them onto the tunnel floor until there were enough to ensure Loddon's passage would be a little more difficult to negotiate.

Reaching the fork, he heard behind him the sound of his pursuers breaking through the door to the en-suite and knew that he had to make an instantaneous decision which direction to go. Dylan stood silently, knowing he had no time for deliberation, and after a few moments took the tunnel to the left, which he remembered from the topography of the three buildings at ground level should lead him to the church. The entrance to the pub he knew to be blocked, because the landlord had already told him as much.

Passing more alcoves filled with yet more crates, the nearest of which he scattered on the floor behind him, he eventually came to another set of stone steps leading up to a small wooden door. He could hear in the distance that Loddon and the primate were now in the tunnel, but unless they had some source of light their progress would be hampered and slow. There would of course be some light coming down the hatch but after ten or twenty feet this would fade to nothing - and they couldn't know which tunnel he had taken at the fork. This would hopefully delay them a little. Then the obvious occurred to him - one, if not both of them, was sure to have a phone on him, and as there were two of them they would take a tunnel each. Doh!

He heard them cursing him as they stumbled over the first set of crates that he'd thrown down.

He quietly tried the door but it was obviously locked and there was no way of telling what was on the other side. A door alone he just may be able to break through, but if it was also bricked up on the other side his escape would be near impossible.

On pure impulse he began rushing at speed up the steps in an attempt to charge the door. He came to regret this as soon as he pulled away from the undamaged door and felt the excruciating pain in the shoulder. He bemoaned his fortune once again as he rubbed it vigorously. Luckily though, his jacket had dampened most of the noise that would have been made and the door seemed a very tight fit and so hadn't rattled at all when he'd hit it.

If he could just go back to the nearest alcove, only ten feet or so from the bottom of the steps, he thought, there may be something heavy enough to use, but he would have to hurry as he may already have given himself away. Loddon and Scarface were making a concerted effort to be quiet in order to distinguish any tell-tale sounds; he could hear their occasional whispers and the noises of wood upon wood as they attempted to make their way past the strewn works of art without causing them further damage - the sound carrying further than normal by the acoustics of the tunnel.

He made it to the alcove and amongst the crates there were a few loose pieces, including a large bronze of a woman reclining on a bed attached to what looked like a thick and sturdy marble base - a foot and a half in length and very heavy, he picked it up. It certainly felt solid enough to penetrate an old wooden door, which is what he was hoping was the only thing that lay between the confine of his subterranean prison and freedom. Everything else being either too small, too fragile looking, or crated up, he took it.

Hauling the bronze back over to the steps, ignoring for the moment the pain in his shoulder, he climbed again. Whilst still holding onto the bronze, he managed to manoeuvre his left hand around just enough to enable him to drop the phone into his jacket pocket, which lit up as the light shone through the fabric. He would need both hands in order to put as much force into his thrusts as was required to break though. He knew for certain he'd be heard once he began smashing away, but there was no getting away from it. He just had to go for it, and as quickly as possible.

Swinging his arms with as much force as he could muster he smashed the base against one of the panels of the door. This was followed swiftly by a second effort, causing the panel to splinter satisfyingly. It made a noise that was surely enough to awaken those that were laid to rest in the small cemetery above, and would certainly serve to alert his pursuers as to which tunnel he was in. He raised his arms once more and brought them down just as quickly causing more splinters.

Dylan couldn't see through to the other side yet, but even in the darkness he knew, from the weakness in the panel, that he had nearly broken through. He quickly repeated the action for a fourth time and felt part of the sculpture break through the crack it had created. Dylan could now see a little light coming through. At the fifth attempt the crack was gaping. He turned the sculpture over and hit it with the bronzed lady herself, as she lay recumbent and oblivious to it all. The hole was now big enough to put his hand through but the light coming through was subdued, as if there was something else behind the door.

As much as he tried to ignore the pain, his shoulder ached terribly. He didn't have the time to dwell on it though. He dropped the bronze sculpture, which bounced heavily down the steps, throwing up stone chips in its wake, and reached through the gap enough to feel something rough and wooden on the other side. It felt like the back panel of a piece of furniture which, as he shoved it, slowly toppled away from the door. It came crashing down with an almighty din onto the large rug that covered the stone tiled floor beneath. The noise would surely have been heard in every corner of the church, and possibly beyond. Dylan could now see that it was a bookcase, as some of the books had been sent sprawling on its descent.

The light now came cascading through onto the steps and away into the tunnel. It would take Loddon no time at all to get to him now. Dylan quickly reached through the panel again and round to where the lock of the door was, praying to everything he believed in that there would be a key. Incredibly, there was. He tried to twist it; it was quite stiff, but eventually turned in the lock. The church end of the tunnel hadn't been permanently sealed off. The extent of the sealing was a locked door, with the key still in the lock, obscured from view by an old bookcase placed in front of it; as fortunate as he felt that this was all that was keeping him from freedom, now was not the time to reflect on good fortune, now was the time for haste.

Dylan pushed open the door as far as the base of the old bookcase that was laying prostrate on the ground would allow, and squeezed through. He made his way hurriedly out of the musty atmosphere of the tunnel. Judging by the amount of ledgers and theological books contained within, the room that he now found himself in served as the church office.

Rushing to the door, he found it too was locked. Why lock a room in a church, he thought, before reality dawned on him that nothing was considered sacred any more. The house of God, it seemed, was just as prone nowadays to unwanted intrusion as were the houses of his flock.

There was a window a few feet from the doorway so Dylan made for it. Turning briefly to peer back into the semi-darkness he had just surfaced from, he could hear that his pursuers were now nearing the steps. He released the catch and lifted up the sash window, but didn't go through. Instead he turned and looked around him for anything that could be thrown through the gap and down the steps in order to obstruct his pursuers progress further. They would already be hindered by the bookcase and the magnitude of their girths - Dylan himself had only just squeezed through. In the end, and even considering the circumstances, his conscience would not let him damage or destroy any more than he had already. He climbed out of the window and ran as quickly as his legs were capable of towards his parked car. The little blue

Japanese car started instantaneously and he put his foot down hard on the accelerator.

For the briefest of moments Dylan allowed his mind to wander towards the idea of a possible connection between defeat in wars and the ability to make well-made, reliable cars. He considered whether the Germans and Japanese had sat down together one day, towards the end of the Second World War, and decided that world domination would be more easily achieved through the manufacture and sale of dependable, and therefore more commercially viable, automobiles. This would surely hold a lot less consequence to human life (although with the number of idiotic drivers on the roads these days, the difference, Dylan suspected, had by now been considerably eroded).

He screeched out of the car park and had a quick look in his rearview mirror, but couldn't see Loddon or the primate anywhere. Turning right he negotiated the bend in the road that would take him back through town, the way that he'd arrived.

He had covered a distance of no more than a few hundred yards when he noticed that his route had been completely blocked off by a large red van parked across the whole width of the road a little way ahead. He slammed his foot hard on the brake. He felt the pain in his shoulder again as the seatbelt tightened with the force of the car coming to a sudden halt. There was no going forward. Glancing in his rearview mirror to make sure that the road behind him was clear, he put the car into reverse gear and again put his foot down hard on the accelerator. But Dylan was no

Steve McQueen, who probably would have done the whole journey backwards, so as soon as he reached a space wide enough with a dropped kerb he made a speedy two-point turn and headed back in the direction from which he had come. As he went back around the bend in the road he had another look towards the church and down the cul-de-sac to see if there was any sign of his pursuers. There wasn't.

He carried on with no idea where the road would lead him. He had come through the town on his way in, but of course he'd been following Chas and took no real notice of any of the town's landmarks. There was no time now to start fiddling with his Tom Tom for an alternative route out, he had to keep driving... anywhere. Sooner or later there would be a sign to show him the way back to the main routes out, and ultimately back to London - or so he hoped. He knew that he had to get back onto the A41 which ran to the south of the town but he also knew that the church was at the northern end of the town, and that now he was heading even further north it seemed, into open country.

Dylan assumed that the reason that Loddon hadn't chased him out of the church, and that his main route back had been blocked by the van, was because he was being steered somewhere more convenient for his pursuers. As it turned out it was a very cogent theory indeed. Having travelled no further than a mile out of town he saw ahead that his route had been blocked yet again, at a point just past a narrow turning on the right. Not much more than a dirt track, it veered off eastwards. Eastwards was in totally the wrong direction for where he was sure he needed to go, but quite obviously it was the direction that someone wanted him to be headed.

With no other option left open to him Dylan took the right turn and as soon as he did he saw in his mirror that the car which had blocked his path also turned into the lane after him. There was no point attempting to lose it because there was sure to be another roadblock further down the lane. He couldn't turn off anywhere along the track because there was dry-stone wall either side the whole length of road.

Instead Dylan fumbled in the pocket that he'd dropped his mobile phone into earlier. No better time for an emergency call he thought, but when he pressed the standby button nothing happened. He took his eyes off the road momentarily and looked down at the phone. The screen was still black. He pressed the button again, but again the phone failed to respond.

'Come on, damn you,' he shouted. 'Turn on, you bastard.'

But it wasn't about to; it had run out of charge.

'FUCK!' he yelled, throwing the phone down onto the passenger seat before it bounced off and landed in the footwell.

'Shit!'

He reached across to retrieve the phone, then prized open the glove compartment and took out his in-car charger. As he came back up he saw that there was now another vehicle, which was blocking the road ahead of him just as he had expected. He threw both phone and charger back down. No point now, he thought.

Dylan slowed the rolling car and came to a stop.

'Oh well,' he said to himself as he opened the door and got out. 'Let's see what kismet's got in store for me then, shall we?'

There were fifty feet or so between him and the car in front, and the car that had come up from behind stopped at a similar distance. He stood by the side of the little blue car with his left hand resting on the bonnet and awaited the inevitable. The passenger door of the car in front opened and out got Edward Loddon. The primate emerged from the driver's side. They both started walking towards Dylan who, under the circumstances, gave the impression of being extremely calm indeed. He was managing to conceal the inner turmoil that he was truly feeling, although why he was bothering he wasn't quite sure. It was so powerful a feeling of turmoil that, as he stood there, motionless, small sections of his life began appearing spontaneously in front of his eyes. It was the kind of moment often spoken of in life or death situations that Dylan had always been so sceptical of, but which now he knew to be true.

Friends from his childhood in Porthmadog appeared before him, happily laughing; the beautiful face of his mother, ultimately flawed and psychologically distracted, yet still the source and origin of all he was to become, floated in and out of view; he saw once again the mountains of Snowdonia, rising to peaks and plunging into valleys to form the unmistakable landscape that was forever in his soul; he saw the little train that chugged and hissed as it crossed the road at Penrhyndeudraeth on its short journey to the slate grey town of Blaenau Ffestiniog; he saw his friends, Malcolm, Jonathan, and Aidan, waiting for him as they propped up the bar in the Roebuck; he saw Victoria, a part of his life that was now to remain forever unfulfilled; and finally, he saw the morally and ethically upstanding Tony who, though he didn't know it, had done so much to enhance Dylan's, now soon to be spent, life - unfortunately though, he still saw him, comically, clinging on to the back of the little red, white and green scooter.

All these things slowly disappeared from his private view as reality surged back in. Loddon and the primate were converging on Dylan and each had a firearm aimed directly at him. He took a cursory glance behind and there were three more men advancing on him from the rear. He turned back towards Loddon and flashed him a big exaggerated smile. Might as well leave them with a bit of humour, thought Dylan.

'Okay, Mr Loddon,' he called out, 'you've had your chance now. Are you going to tell me where Lola is, or am I going to have to force it out of you?'

In truth, the courageous façade that he was putting up masked the fact that he was, at that moment, feeling very faint. So faint in fact that his senses were oblivious to anything else that was happening around him, including the sound coming from above which grew louder with each passing moment.

Dylan closed his eyes, waiting for the ineluctable bullet, and after several seconds when it hadn't come, he opened them again only to see that everybody was now looking up to the skies and not at him. Then he heard it - the rhythmical whirring of helicopter blades. It was coming in to land on the road just behind Loddon's car. And a little further back Dylan saw that there were at least three police vehicles also pulling up. He looked behind him again and similarly there were more police vehicles converging from the rear.

Dylan fought back the inner feeling of languidness and was filled once more with a renewed sense of foolish bravado.

'Well, Mr Loddon?' he shouted mockingly. 'What's your answer then?'

Edward Loddon lifted his weapon, which had dropped to his side whilst watching the in-coming helicopter, and pointed it once again towards Dylan. Everything he had achieved or obtained, by fair means or foul, was now evidently at stake. The one thing he could ensure in maintaining however, was his reputation. He lined up the sight of the gun with Dylan's chest.

'Here you go, Mr Morgan,' he called out, loud enough to be heard above the helicopter's blades. 'Here's my answer.'

Dylan heard the sharp crack of the bullet as his whole body involuntarily relaxed under him, causing him to fall against the bonnet of the little blue car, smashing once more his damaged shoulder and finally coming to rest slumped against the off-side front wheel.

THIRTY

The bullet entered Loddon's left leg through the back of his knee, shattering his patella and sending him crashing to the ground in a heap, conscious but quiescent.

In a matter of seconds the police officers, including DI Cranshaw, descended upon Loddon and his associates and quickly nullified the potential threat of the primate, who had dropped his weapon instantaneously. Five of the officers rounded on Loddon's remaining three accomplices before they could pull out any weapons or make any attempt at escape.

When Dylan finally came to, he saw the face of Terrance Penhaligon hovering over him.

'Lucky for you, Mr Beaumaris Morgan, amongst my talents, of which I have many I might add, is that of a trained marksman. Because I think that mouth of yours will continue to get you into some big trouble.'

'Terrance?' murmured the dazed Welshman.

Dylan struggled to lift himself off the ground, then up to his full height with a little help from Penhaligon. He looked him directly in the eye.

'Is this your doing?' he asked him.

'I'm afraid so, my boy.'

Dylan looked around him at the swarm of officers.

'What the hell is going on here? I knew there was something strange when the verger at the church told me he'd never heard of you, but I never imagined...' He felt a sudden jolt of pain in his shoulder and lifted up his right hand to gently massage it. 'Who the bloody hell are you?'

'I think that you deserve a few things explained, but not here. Come with me and we'll have a nice chat.'

He led Dylan towards the helicopter.

'Hold on, what about my car?'

'Oh, don't worry about that. I'll have it driven back to London. It'll be back home before you are.'

'But I'd rather take my car, if it's all the same. I don't think I'll be very good up in one of those things.'

Penhaligon motioned to the helicopter pilot.

'Okay, Dylan, we'll have it your way then. Are you alright to drive or do you want me to?'

Leaving the scene of Loddon's capture behind, Terrance Penhaligon drove off in the little blue car with Dylan beside him in the passenger seat. They had agreed they would pull into the first watering hole that they came across and Dylan would be told everything. Indeed, no sooner had they settled down at a table at the Golden Lion pub than Dylan started interrogating his saviour.

'So, come on then, who are you really? 'Cos I don't think that you're Terrance Penhaligon.'

'Okay, it's true, I'm not Terrance Penhaligon. The thing is, in my line of work you don't get far being who you actually are. Unfortunately, I can't tell you who I really am. Let's just say my name is...' He paused, smiling. '... Why not just call me Mr Stone!'

The corners of Dylan's mouth dropped. He slowly leaned in to cross-reference Terrance's features with what he remembered of Mr Stone.

'You... are Mr Stone?' he gasped, falling back in his chair.

'I'm afraid so.'

'You're the rude, obnoxious, arrogant bastard that came to my office?'

'Yep. That was me...., I suppose.'

The strange thing was that, looking across the table at him now, Dylan thought of him as being quite avuncular.

'So, what? Was that just a disguise as well then?'

'Well, a bit of a disguise I suppose, but the suit is mine though, and to be honest I quite like it.'

His tone and features betrayed a little hurt at the fact that one of his favourite suits should be so denigrated.

'But I did have to do some acting. You see, the whole idea at that point was to dissuade you from getting involved in all this by attempting to scare you off.'

'What you succeeded in doing though, was to fire me up even more.'

'Scare tactics have stood me in good stead in the past. Foolishly, I didn't legislate for your recalcitrance. Perhaps I subconsciously went a little too easy on you.'

'I was actually thinking of jacking the job in before that, what with dead bodies and everything.'

Dylan looked around, making sure nobody was listening to his talk of dead bodies. No-one was.

'I was starting to wonder whether I was really cut out for this business, to be honest,' he continued. 'Then you came along. I have to admit that I disliked you so much that I thought I'd carry on.'

'I appear to have stirred some negative emotions in you.'

There was a sense of achievement in Mr Stone's voice which was not lost on Dylan.

'You did. But why did you want me off the case? It's quite clear now that it was Loddon you were after all long, and I didn't even know about him then.'

'Not so, Dylan. Mr Loddon and his accomplices just came along as an added bonus - not so much for me, more for the police.'

'So you're not with the police then?'

'No.'

'Well then, who are you with?'

The erstwhile Mr Stone glanced briefly around him, then answered quietly.

'I really can't tell you too much about that, but let's just say I work for an organisation whose remit it is to ensure that the national status quo is maintained at all times, and that the great big machine that is Britain continues to run smoothly. In order for that to happen cogs and wheels need greasing, and I'm one of those people with the grease gun.'

'Oh... right. So, whatever it takes then?'

'Whatever it takes.' His answer so resolute it left no margin for misunderstanding.

'I don't understand though, where do I fit in to all this?' asked Dylan.

'That was something of a coincidence. I'd been doing a spot of freelance, work for the Met's Arts & Antiques Unit, trying to locate a collection of artwork stolen years back from a Montreal museum. For repatriation back to Canada. If you read the papers you'll have read that there's a big oil deal going down. Anyway, the Canadians have been threatening that the success of this deal is dependant on us getting the paintings back to them. It's become something of a point of principle for them. I think that Detective Inspector Cranshaw may have clued you up. Gerald De Vere was an important piece of the puzzle in locating these paintings. But, as we both know, Mr De Vere was murdered. And that's where you came in.'

'And the coincidence?'

'I was just coming to that. My main work often brings me into contact with rich and influential parties in the Middle-East, people unhappy at the constant unrest in the region that would just like to enjoy their wealth without having to deal with neighbouring religious or political strife. A great deal of that strife is cultivated outside of the region before it goes on to feed the factions within that perpetuate it. One such area of cultivation is Britain. We want a well-oiled machine, they want a peaceful environment in which to enjoy their wealth, so we work together to try to achieve this. And that's where the coincidence comes in. One such family I came into contact with some time ago...' He hesitated. '...was that of your late father.'

Dylan's ears pricked up. 'My father's family?'

'Yes, Dylan. You see, the circumstances of your conception have never soured their opinion of you. In fact they show great concern as to your welfare - blood is blood to them. I know that they'd like to meet you one day.'

Dylan's face softened.

'That is where I came in,' Mr Stone continued. 'The family wanted someone to watch over you, and so I took on the personal task of doing just that. And trying to keep you from getting into any trouble. A little moonlighting, let's say.'

'What?' Dylan couldn't believe what he was hearing. 'You've been watching over me?'

'Relax. It wasn't like Big Brother or anything like that. I really don't have the time anyway. It's just that, because of the kind of work I do, I could keep a watchful eye on you. Just enough to report back to the family that you were doing okay and not coming to any harm. But, of course, then you decided to become a private investigator, and even then I thought that you couldn't come to too much harm. Until, that is, I saw your name linked with the De Vere murder, and that was when I knew I had to intervene and try to keep you out of trouble.'

'It didn't work though, did it?'

'No, it didn't - but you walked each time, didn't you?'

'I did wonder about that. I thought that may have been down to DI Cranshaw. I sort of got the impression that he believed me.'

'He did. But you were still, officially, the major suspect. We spoke to him and his superiors. At first they were just looking for someone to pin it all on, and you blundered along - the perfect patsy.'

'I was rather, wasn't I?' Dylan said, self-pityingly.

'But then we decided that somehow, in your own naïve way, you were our best bet for getting to the bottom of everything. I had to keep tabs on you so I planted the tracker in your mobile phone.'

'My phone? So it was you who broke into my flat and took it?'

'One of my colleagues actually. More of a 'breaking and entering without actually breaking' expert than me. It was his voice on the message arranging the meet at Kenwood House. The thing was, I wasn't sure where you'd disappeared to during your abduction or when you'd be back. So I waited until you came back on our radar and we switched the phones while you were at the hospital. It was just around the corner, but A&E being as busy as they are, we knew that you would be a few hours. And we had someone watch you there. But somebody else, it transpired, had already broken in to plant an SD card complete with photographs taken during the abduction.'

'And what about the person there that picked my pocket?'

'A female colleague. I thought that with your penchant for the fairer sex you would be more titillated by a beautiful girl brushing against you than you would be concerned about where her hand was going whilst she was doing it. It was me that gave the phone to the young lad to give back

301

to you though.'

'Young Josh? He said you were wearing a disguise that wasn't very good. And that you were too old to be wearing a hoodie.'

'I am. Dreadful things. But when there's a job to be done...'

'Hold on though. So, the photographs on my SD card that the police found - you knew that they were on there and just left them?'

'When we took the phone to plant the tracker we knew that they were on there for a reason. So did the police, when I notified Cranshaw. We knew that once you were shown them you would probably come out fighting and be even more determined to find whoever was doing all this to you.'

'Who abducted me then?'

'We don't know for sure yet, but we're thinking possibly the Canadians behind the De Vere murder.'

'Who the hell are these Canadians?'

Again, Dylan look around. Nobody seemed interested in the pair's conversation; too busy with their own lunchtime assignations to be concerned with anybody else's.

'Okay. This is the full story, minus one or two loose ends we've got to tie up. As I said, this big deal was dependent on us locating the stolen Canadian paintings. The Canadian government received information from some of its sources abroad that, after lying dormant for quite a while, the collection was going to be moved into mainland Europe to one of the big collectors there, but they weren't sure where exactly. So, in order to elicit the help of the British government in tracking the collection down before it was moved, they stalled on the oil deal. We made sure that the press reported this. We knew that whoever had the paintings would start to panic if they thought that they were in the way of a big deal going through. They would know that those looking for the paintings would get the big guns out.

'The British government and the organisation I work for solicited the help of Gerald De Vere who, as well as being a very prominent art dealer, was also known to have contacts in various international underworld organisations - this included the Canadian outfit we think was responsible for your abduction. They were the ones that masterminded the theft of the paintings from the museum in Montreal and arranged their shipment to Britain. The story goes that it was De Vere who arranged for the collection to be stored until it was ready to move on. In order to make sure that De Vere's loyalties were kept in check they arranged for someone to keep a close and personal eye on him, a female escort - your Miss Douglas.'

Dylan's eyes widened. 'Lola? Hah! I knew she had to be involved in all this.'

'Lola? No... Victoria.'

'Victoria? Her name isn't Douglas, it's Henson,' barked Dylan.

'It's Douglas, Dylan. Victoria Douglas. We know all about her. Henson is her boss.'

'What, Chas? That can't be right. It can't be. Victoria asked me to put flowers on her parents' grave. I put them on Reginald and Margaret Henson's grave.'

'They were Charles Henson's parents.'

There was sympathy in Mr Stone's voice.

'That's why he was there that day,' muttered Dylan, slowly working it all out in his mind. 'She knew that he'd be there and wanted me to see him. She knew that I would follow him.'

'I hate to say it, Dylan, but the lovely Miss Douglas has been playing you all along.'

Dylan was a broken man. He perched on the edge of his chair, his hands covering the humiliation he felt for allowing himself to be led so naively. His gullibility mocked him and the sense of shame burned inside. He was sure that he could feel the derision of the other customers as they sat at their tables lost in their own conversations, oblivious even of his existence.

'Why did I not see it?' he asked himself through barely parted fingers. He pulled his hands away from his face and sat back in his chair once again. 'Well... that's not strictly true. I think that I was starting to suspect but I really didn't want to think that of her.'

'Before you tear yourself up too much,' piped up Mr Stone, 'we don't know yet what her full involvement is in all of this. However, we *do* believe that she may have been used as well. We know that she was present when De Vere was killed.'

Dylan felt crushed beneath a pile of emotional rubble.

'We suspect that she was meant to be there in order to cover the tracks of the people who killed

304

him, and to lead police off the scent. We're not quite sure how she got away, but once she did she knew that she'd be in the frame and that she'd have to find a way of getting the heat off of herself.'

'And on to me, you mean? So there never was a Lola. She played me.'

'Look, you really shouldn't take it so personally. It could have been anyone. It was just that, and this is only my theory you understand, she knew that you were soft on her, and she also knew that someone in your profession may have been able to help her with her predicament so she came up with a plan.'

'A plan?'

'I think that she couldn't tell you what she was doing as you wouldn't have played along...'

'I would have helped her, if she'd only told me the truth,' Dylan interrupted.

'Yes, but the problem was that you were just a rookie, and she probably thought that if you knew what you were getting involved in... the kind of people you would be coming across... then you'd run a mile. You're not in it for the rough stuff and she knew that.'

'So, you're sticking up for her now? Is that it?'

'No, Dylan, that's not it. I think she'd worked out that if she led you down the garden path then you'd slowly lift up the stones covering the things that needed uncovering. She was being constantly watched and couldn't do it herself. They had something on her, she was present during De Vere's murder. Her life was in danger and the one thing that she probably knew about you, the thing that I found out myself, is that when you are threatened you go on the attack. That's what happened, isn't it?'

'I suppose so.' Dylan's reply came like that of a scolded schoolboy. 'But where did James Braddock come in to all this?'

'We know that De Vere liked women, but that he also had a thing for transvestites and transsexuals. Again, this is only a theory, but we suspect that when it became public knowledge that De Vere was asked to help the government in retrieving the very paintings that he was helping to hide, the Canadians weren't sure whether they could trust him any longer and so had to find a way of discrediting him, hoping that would secure his silence. They had the photographs taken of De Vere and James Braddock on the beach at Brighton and sent them into the newspapers. When only one, less than veracious, newspaper published the photographs they probably decided that discrediting him was not enough and that was when they decided to kill him.'

'Why did they kill James Braddock?'

'Again, it's one of the grey areas. We're not sure why he was killed, we think that maybe it was because he knew too much. De Vere may have shared secrets with him.'

'And I just happened to be the first person to find his body.'

'Also engineered, I imagine, but I don't know if that was Miss Douglas's doing. She was out of the country at the time. The chief constable, who was also on the scene with his wife, is an old friend of mine by the way. I did ask him to keep an eye out

306

for you when I found out that you were headed down to Brighton.'

Dylan shook his head in disbelief.

'I can help you with one thing though. When I was down in the tunnels that run between Loddon's office, the church and the pub, I did see lots of crates that looked like they could contain paintings. That could be what you're looking for. Unfortunately I had to use them as an obstacle when I was being pursued, so I don't know if any got damaged.'

'We've already got the paintings that we're after. We received a tip-off as to where they were being stored. And our Canadian friends are now in custody. I'm sure that the police will be searching Loddon's offices thoroughly though, to see what he's got stashed down there.'

'So where does all this leave me then?' Dylan asked.

'I would say that first of all you need to go home and rest, oh and maybe pull your assistant off of the Puckett job.'

'One of yours?'

'One of mine. Actually, Gary Puckett's a good friend, and he and his wife are very happily married, as far as I'm aware. Just for the record, she knew nothing about the tail. We wanted it to look real. The other jobs were real though. I spoke to one of my friends who runs an investigation agency. I just asked him to divert a few jobs.'

'Hmmm. We did wonder. And so the case of Professor Braddock's missing son was just...?'

'Probably part of Miss Douglas's master plan. I

think that once you have rested you may want to track her down and get the rest of the answers that I'm sure you're looking for. Do yourself a favour and don't do anything foolish though. I may not always be able to get you off the hook.'

'And what about Victoria. What'll happen to her?'

'Technically, apart from not telling the authorities about De Vere's death, and helping in the movement of stolen art, which they don't have enough real evidence for anyway, they have nothing on her. There is, of course, your abduction, should you wish to press charges, but I'm not sure how much evidence there is with which to mount a viable prosecution case. And... look, maybe I shouldn't be telling you this, but we cut a little deal with Miss Douglas. She was the one who told us where the paintings were, in exchange for the police dropping any possible charges against her.'

He noticed the expression of disgust on Dylan's face.

'Don't look at me like that, Dylan. Police cut deals with people all the time. It may be frowned upon but it's considered as being for the greater good. As I said, we didn't really have that much on her anyway, so it was a good deal. I think that it's just her conscience that Miss Douglas has to live with, and you may know better than me whether she will find that easy to do.'

Dylan was no longer sure that Victoria actually had a conscience at all.

THIRTY ONE

That evening Dylan dined with Tony and his family.

He had accepted his assistant's telephone invitation readily, as he didn't want to spend the evening alone at home brooding over how he would deal with Victoria. The knowledge of her deceit, although he'd had an inkling of it, tore at him. While it had only been a flimsy suspicion milling around in his mind, there was still the chance that paranoia may have been a factor, however, now that her duplicity had been laid out clearly in front of him, it gained a gravitas he could no longer deny.

He didn't want to sit around on his own tonight. Tonight he needed company that would help relieve his mind of burden, and tomorrow he would decide what to do about Victoria.

'So, what is all this about throwing your ashes on Mount Snowdon then, boss?' asked Tony, as they sat around the dining table in Tony's Islington home, tucking hungrily into the feast prepared by his wife, Lucia.

'Ahhh, so you understood my request then?'

Dylan had left the message in Italian along with the address of Loddon Securities shortly before presenting himself for the meeting which had turned out so eventful.

'No. Nico he translate it for me,' Tony answered, looking across the table at his youngest son.

Dylan's excitement was brief and quickly dampened. However, he didn't allow the disappointment of his failed attempt to taint his meal. Instead, he cast the failure instantly aside and, with the merest hint of a scowl born of defeat, tucked into his dish of Manicotti alla Romana.

Lucia, all five foot one of her, had worked tirelessly all evening, bringing more and more dishes out to the table. Her work ethic was incredible, her energy boundless as she moved from kitchen to dining room and dining room back to kitchen. The enthusiasm with which she threw herself into conversations was boundless also. Tony's daughter, Daria, had offered assistance, but Lucia insisted her daughter remain seated at the table along with her three brothers, who had offered no help at all, and get acquainted with their father's employer.

At first Dylan had mistaken Lucia's insistence as a possible gesture of her matchmaking between the two of them. Daria was twenty-five and had inherited her good looks from her mother; in her mid-fifties, Lucia was still a very attractive woman. Although Daria held obvious aesthetic appeal for any potential suitor, Dylan was not the courting type and felt a little awkward in the situation. However, it soon became apparent that it wasn't matchmaking on Lucia's mind, but more a desire for her children to get to know the man their father worked for. And in doing so show him, through them, the sort of person their father was. It was a question of respect. Showing due respect to Dylan and to each other reflected well upon Tony. It was evident that this family held traditional values which in some societies were considered outdated, but these were the values bred in them all and which helped create the strong family unit that existed. Dylan's inability to relate to the relationship the Spinetti's had did nothing though to diminish his appreciation of it.

After the meal was finished the four younger members helped their mother clear the table, then politely excused themselves, going their separate ways. Tony chatted with Dylan about the events of the last couple of days whilst Lucia prepared coffee.

At just after ten o'clock Dylan thanked them for a wonderful evening, and Lucia kissed him affectionately on both cheeks. Shaking Tony's hand, after rebuffing his attempt at a kiss on both cheeks, Dylan departed, satisfied and fully fed, for his flat in Hampstead. It had been a long and tiring day; a day of revelation from which he wanted to rest and recover before the arrival of the new day, during which he would have to tackle the question of Victoria.

*

Victoria hadn't given Dylan the full address of where she would be staying, but it was in the village of Bishop's Hendron in Hertfordshire. She said she would be staying with Lola's parents, but in all probability it was pretty certain now that they were her own.

Hertfordshire was one of the connecting factors in this whole business: Victoria's parents

311

house, De Vere's house, Loddon's business, the cemetery where Charlie Henson's parents were buried, and possibly the De Vere family too, all located there. Having scoured the map, however, he was unable to find Bishop's Hendron in Hertfordshire, or anywhere else for that matter.

He turned on his laptop in order to Google Bishop's Hendron – this was sure to throw something up. As soon as he entered the name Bishop's Hendron into the search engine and pressed the return button the answer jumped out from the screen and hit him. Bishop's Hendron was a made up name - it did not exist. It was the name of a village Graham Greene had created for a short story entitled *The Innocent*. The imaginary Bishop's Hendron was in fact believed to be Greene's home town of Berkhamsted. Dylan thought it as good a starting point as any in his search for Victoria.

He remembered her telling him that she had found a book of short stories by Greene when she'd searched Lola's room. It was just one of many pieces of string she had laid down for him to follow; one of the clues he would investigate at the end that would lead him to her.

She wanted to be found.

He Googled *The Innocent.* One site offered the opportunity of reading the whole story. When he entered this site and glanced at the first page of Greene's short story he saw that on the very first line there was mention of the name Lola. She was slowly revealing herself to him. He read the remainder of the story, a mere handful of digital pages, but none of the rest seemed relevant. Or, at least not as he could make out.

He had to find an address for Victoria's parents. He had the town, at least there was a very good chance that it was Berkhamsted, and he had a name of Douglas. He remembered Victoria telling him that Lola's parents were called Sidney and Prudence, and he had no reason to think that they weren't the real names of her own parents. That was where he would begin his search.

There were nine listings for Douglas in Berkhamsted, but only one was a Sidney. And this Sidney Douglas ran his own furniture making business in the town. He remembered her saying that Lola's father was a carpenter. Dylan checked the commercial directory for Berkhamsted and came up with an address. He would find Victoria through her father. He put the address into Google Maps and it zoomed in on a road that didn't look as if it were located in a commercial or shopping area, but rather in a residential one. Dylan clicked on Street View to reveal that the address he was looking for was indeed a private house.

'Bingo,' he cried out loud. Surely now he had found her.

THIRTY TWO

All that could be seen of the property that Dylan was looking for was an expanse of scrub land with a rough gravel drive at one edge which led to the house that sat back from the road.

During the winter months, when the trees at the front of the property will have shed their leaves, the house would be fully visible. In the height of spring, however, the very top of the house and the roof were the only things that remained unobstructed by the blazing green of the foliage. At the point where the drive met with the road there was a sign indicating that this was indeed the premises from which S Douglas Carpentry & Joinery operated. An arrow directed customers towards the rear of the premises.

Dylan slowly made his way along the drive, gravel crunching underfoot. He reached an intersection where a small path branched off toward the front of the house and the door. The main driveway continued on to the rear of the house and a rather large outbuilding at the very end of the garden in which Sidney Douglas presumably crafted his furniture. Dylan took the smaller path and arrived at the front door. Underneath the brass numeral 23 was a door knocker of an Arts and Crafts design, and on the frame of the door was a solid looking bell push. Dylan rang the door bell and after a few seconds the door opened and there stood Victoria, resplendent in a green and red dressing gown.

Having no make-up did nothing to diminish her appeal in Dylan's eyes.

She smiled, clearly anything but surprised to see him.

'So, you made it.'

She turned away and started walking back into the house.

'Come in,' she called nonchalantly behind her.

Dylan followed her into the living room.

'I'll just get us a drink. I take it you want one?'

Her early morning, husky drawl once again sucked him in.

'Please,' he said, quietly. 'It might help soften the blow.'

Dylan watched Victoria as the flimsy gown described with each sway the contours of her body. He knew that her every move and posture was calculated but he couldn't stop himself from wanting her. It was a gait refined over the years to acquire the desired reaction from men. It certainly worked with Dylan, and she knew it.

She returned with the drinks and sat down on the sofa next him.

'How did you find me?'

'I just followed the clues. It wasn't difficult in the end.' He looked around him. 'So, this is your parents' place then. I see your father works from home.'

'Hmmm. They're away at the moment. I decided that it was best to send them on a little holiday while all this business got sorted.'

'And is it sorted?'

Dylan was hoping that their talk would finally put an end to all the madness of recent weeks. He wasn't expecting her response.

'Yes, but it'll only be completely over for me once Lola's been found.'

Confusion clouded Dylan's mind. Why continue the charade? Why was she still prolonging the pretence that Lola even existed? Simply by virtue of the fact that he was here, having followed the clue of Greene's vignette, was surely indication enough that he knew Lola was just a character in a book and not a flesh and bone form.

'What are you talking about, Victoria? I know now there never was a Lola, except in your imagination. Unless of course you're talking about James Braddock, and you know that I found him. You made sure of that.'

Victoria became animated.

'For the record, I didn't know that was going to happen,' she said.

'So, you're saying that you had nothing to do with that?'

'No, I'm not saying that. I did help to get you down to Brighton, but you have to believe me when I say that I didn't know that they were going to kill him. They just said that I had to get you down there so that they could photograph you and James together. I can only think that James found something out, that Gerald had told him something... something too dangerous for him to know, and that's why they killed him. I suppose the fact that you were there meant they could then implicate you in his murder as well as De Vere's.'

'And you helped them?'

'Yes, but I was frightened.'

316

'Who are these people, Victoria?'

'I'll tell you. I may as well, now.'

She paused for thought, before continuing.

'Some time ago members of the Canadian underworld broke into the Museum of Fine Art in Montreal and stole various pieces of artwork, including seventeen priceless paintings. Soon after the robbery, they smuggled the paintings out of Canada and into Britain. They arranged for them to be stored for a while, the intention being to move them eventually into mainland Europe. This was all arranged by Gerald De Vere.'

'I know all of that,' Dylan interrupted her. 'Tell me something that I don't know, like what your part in all this was.'

'Two Canadian guys contacted the agency one day asking for an escort,' she continued. 'Someone to show them around and, well, just generally look after them while they were in London. It was Gerry that had put them onto Chas. They were only going to be in the country for a few days so Chas sent me. They seemed like really nice, ordinary guys, and we had a really good time.

'Then, some time after, they contacted Chas and told him they wanted to meet up with me again. I went to meet them and they told me they had a proposition for me. They came right out and told me all about the stolen paintings. I suppose they thought I was someone who wasn't going to go running to the police. They said that they needed my help. They told me all about this big deal going down between the Canadian and British governments, something to do with oil, and how the Canadian government had asked the British for help in retrieving the stolen paintings. These two guys told me that their contact over here, Gerald De Vere, had been recruited to help find the paintings. The government people knew the paintings were in the UK and knew that Gerry had a lot of underworld contacts. What they didn't know was that he was the one who had the paintings.

'Bill and Jean-Paul, that's the two Canadians, weren't sure whether Gerald could be trusted to keep the pretence up and so they asked me to get something on him. Because Gerald was a customer of the agency too, I had already met him a few times, and they said that they would pay me to get close to him and keep an eye out for anything he said or did and report back to them. They said that they would pay me more than I could ever dream of making as an escort, so I foolishly agreed. Chas obviously knew nothing about it.'

She shifted uncomfortably on the sofa.

'Then one day they said that they were getting really worried and felt that Gerald would buckle under all the pressure that the government people were putting on him. They said I had to help them discredit him, involve him in a sex scandal with which they could blackmail him. That was when they stopped being nice and started to get heavy. I said no at first, but then they threatened to blackmail me too. They threatened to send a video that they had made, of me with them, to my parents. My parents have no idea that I'm an escort, Dylan. They think that I have a high-powered job in the City. It would kill my father. I'd made the mistake in the first place of telling them that my parents knew nothing of my real work. This gave them the ammunition to make sure I did what I was asked. And I just got in deeper and deeper.'

She took a tissue from her gown pocket and wiped a tear from her cheek. Dylan had no control of his hand as it reached out to comfort her. He knew that he would crack sooner or later but he'd hoped to hold out for a little longer than he had.

'I knew that any sex scandal involving Gerald would sooner or later have made the news, so I obviously didn't want it to be me. They agreed that I could find someone else, someone that didn't know what was going on. That was when I introduced Gerald to James Braddock.

'I bumped into James at Regent's Park Zoo. I was there with the Canadians and I recognised him. I knew that he was gay because I'd met him once in a Soho gay club and knew that he was Chas's boyfriend's best friend. The Canadians, after meeting him that day, decided that he was the perfect set up. Things just clicked into place.

'So I then had to arrange for him to meet Gerald. Gerald was bisexual. He liked transsexuals and cross-dressers, and went on trips to Thailand supposedly on business, but really it was for the ladyboy sex. Anyway, James was quite taken with him, and Gerald was definitely taken with James - spoiling him rotten, buying him lots of expensive gifts - so it wasn't difficult persuading James to do anything that would keep Gerald happy. And he did look great dressed as a girl. His features were very feminine, so it worked.

'They went on trips down to the south coast and that was when the photographs were taken and sent to the newspapers. The Canadians knew that most of the newspapers wouldn't print them, but even they knew the one that would. And that was the newspaper that they were really aiming for. The seedier the tabloid, the better. Especially one with a huge circulation.

'But obviously it turned out that just discrediting him wasn't enough as everybody, including the government people, knew the sort of things that Gerald was involved in, but they didn't care as long as he did the job that they were putting him under pressure to do. The one thing the government people didn't know, as I say, was that Gerald was the person actually in possession of the paintings. The Canadians were really worried that Gerald was going to crack and reveal where the paintings were so that this oil deal could go through, and he could get the government people off his back. That was when they decided to kill him.'

'And you were there when they did it? You played a part in it?'

'No, please believe me. I was used. On the night that it happened they didn't tell me what was going on. Gerald had been trying to get in touch with James, who was supposed to be coming up from Brighton, but James wasn't answering his calls and Gerald got angry. He called me. He said he needed me to go round to the house. I knew it was to spite James. I called the Canadians. They told me to keep an eye on him, because in his angry state he could do something stupid and ruin everything. I didn't know they were going to kill him that night - I didn't even know anybody else was in the house. They'd laced the whisky with GHB. It knocked me out for the count, but Gerry had respiratory-arrest, and he had a heart-attack. They knew that he suffered from heart problems. I found out later, of course, that they had a doctor working for them that could do that sort of thing.'

Dylan raised his eyebrows at this.

'But when they did it, and then threatened to frame me, I knew that I was in deep trouble. I'm not sure whether they were expecting me to die as well that night. It was only because I took just a sip or two of the drugged whisky that I didn't. It just knocked me out.'

A clenched fist covered her quivering lips and she strained to get the words out.

'I'm convinced that Gerald suspected they would make some sort of move. I'm not sure but, when he gave me those pins to put in my hair, I think that some sort of sixth sense warned him that they would do something. But he can't have known whether I was in on it or not, after all it was meant to be James he was seeing that night, not me. He was the one that was supposed to be in the frame, or dead, not me. But I was there, trapped without means of escape, or so they assumed, and so I became the substitute sacrifice.'

'And me?' asked Dylan.

'That's where you came in.'

'Yeah, thanks for that, Victoria.'

'Please don't be like that, Dylan.'

'What do you want me to be like then?'

Dylan was hurting, but the strong yearning to reach over and caress her that he was fighting at that moment, made the aloofness he displayed on the face of it all the more impressive.

'It was obvious that you had a bit of a thing for me, and not just an escort/client thing. You can't hide your true feelings very easily; you're emotionally transparent. Like now, I can see that you're trying to remain detached, but I know that's not how you're feeling inside.'

'Am I that obvious, Victoria?'

Dylan felt vulnerable and exposed.

'Don't beat yourself up about it. I promise you, it's not a bad quality. I actually find it quite endearing.'

Dylan looked away towards the far end of the room.

'And the false Professor Braddock?'

'Oh, just someone who owed me a favour.'

'So you used him as well? He was pretty convincing though. Had me fooled.'

'Look, Dylan, I was up against it. I had to use every resource I had. I didn't have much going for me, but the one thing that I did have was that I knew where the paintings were, and the Canadians didn't. Gerald had moved them all. He never really trusted them.'

'No honour amongst thieves, eh?'

'They threatened to set me up for Gerald's murder unless I found someone else to pin everything on. They had all the evidence. They took the CCTV footage from Gerald's bedroom, showing us both in bed, but left just enough to implicate me. I couldn't go to the police as they would have known that I was there that night. I was the prime suspect. It was the classic Sid and Nancy scenario, and I had to act fast. I came up with a plan - a plan which unfortunately had to involve you.'

Dylan remained impassive.

'I thought that you would be the perfect person because of the business you were in. I just had to ensure that, whatever happened, you came out of it unscathed. That was when I came up with the search for Lola.'

'Why could you not have let me in on it?'

'Because I was frightened that you wouldn't do it, and that if you did your actions would have been unnatural and contrived. Also, I didn't want to make you an accessory, which you would have been in the eyes of the police. You were really my only hope. I thought that if I could set you out on the trail for Lola you would be able to slowly uncover the truth and help me out of my dilemma.'

'How could you know that I wouldn't get into big trouble? After all, wasn't it your doing that those photographs got put on my phone, which then got into the possession of the police?'

'Yes. That day in your office, when I showed you the SD card and told you it was Lola's, I took information from your SD card without you knowing. I then took the photographs to put on there together with all the information that you had on there already, and after your abduction I put it back into your phone. I knew that all the

323

photographs together wouldn't add up to much more than circumstantial evidence and failing to report a dead body, but it served a purpose.'

'Now you come to mention the abduction. How could you, Victoria? That was serious stuff. Those drugs you used could have killed me.'

'Firstly, I had to do something to show the Canadians that I was serious about implicating someone else, so I went along with it. They assured me that their doctor knew exactly how much of each drug to use without doing any real harm. Even the chloroform they used at the restaurant was carefully measured. They were used just to keep you out of it for a while. It was only supposed to be overnight but when you didn't have your mobile on you it took them a while to find the right opportunity to break into your flat in order to get it.'

'Was the doctor Indian by any chance?'

'Well, yes he was as a matter of fact. Why do you ask?'

'And did he have long silver hair?'

'No. Why?'

'Oh, no matter. And who was the girl in the photographs that was made to look like Lola?'

'Me.'

'Please tell me that you're not going to charge me for that session?'

Victoria's face morphed into an embarrassed smile.

'There was something in one of those photographs that I was hoping you wouldn't spot. I was doing that thing that you like done, you know the one. I wasn't thinking. It was just instinctive and could've blown everything apart had you realised it was me at that point.'

'To be honest, Victoria, I didn't really look at the photographs that closely when the police showed them to me. I just couldn't bring myself to.'

'I know how you must be feeling. I'm not feeling great about it either. I feel really shitty about what I did.'

'You still haven't explained how Chas and Loddon fit in to all this,' said Dylan, brushing Victoria's remorse aside.

'Loddon? That vicious bastard? He's a villain, a real villain. He's a good friend of Chas's. Chas would send him girls and the bastard would always send them back damaged. He beat the shit out of me once, but the problem was that Chas was scared of him and wouldn't do or say anything against him. He would just sweeten any girl that he sent to Loddon with extra money to make up for the pain.'

A reflection of that pain was evident in Victoria's face as she spoke.

'I knew that Loddon was a big underworld figure and I made a point of finding out a little about him - to use just in case I ever needed it. The coincidence was that he also dealt, amongst other things, in stolen art. When I found out that he'd been given the contract by the Canadians to kill James Braddock, his fate in my eyes was sealed. That was really when he became part of the plan. Gerald, who knew anybody and everybody there was to know in the art world, legal or not, had once told me that Loddon was in possession of something which was considered to be the holy grail of the art world.

'The Canadians needed some kind of diversion for the police until they could get their paintings out of the country and into Europe. They were negotiating the sale of the paintings to some big Middle-Eastern art dealers in Paris – a meeting that I had arranged. That was why I had to disappear for a few days, because they wanted me to keep the potential buyers sweet. So, I thought the opportunity of killing two birds with one stone was too good to miss. Loddon would become the diversion they asked me to get, and you, unwittingly, would bring him down.'

'Hold on now. How did you know that he wouldn't bring *me* down? He's a nasty bastard. In fact he was that close to shooting me,' he said, exacting the point with his fore finger and thumb pressed together. 'He had his gun pointed straight at my chest, until someone shot him first.'

'I had a fair idea that you'd be okay, Dylan. You see I know that you have a little guardian angel.'

'You know about Mr Stone? How?'

'Mr Stone? The guy that you told me visited you at the office? Well, to be honest, I didn't know it was him, but I knew there was someone.'

'So, tell me how you knew.'

Victoria stood up and reached out for Dylan's hand.

'Come with me.'

Victoria led Dylan upstairs to a room on the door of which hung a green plaque engraved *Lola's*

Room in gold.

'Lola's Room? This is *your* bedroom then?'

Victoria let go of his hand and sat down on the edge of the bed. As Dylan walked into the room he felt a stifling heat.

'Christ, Victoria, it's really hot in here. Feels like a jungle. Why don't you open a window?'

'I can't. It's jammed. In the afternoon, when the sun comes in, it bakes in here.'

Dylan looked around him, overwhelmed with an intense feeling of déjà vu. There were small round cushions of varying colours scattered all over the bed and on the wicker chair next to the dressing table. He couldn't quite put his finger on what it was, but there was a definite sense of familiarity.

'Sometimes, when things aren't going right, we need to be somewhere else... or someone else. When I was young, and found life difficult, I would retreat to my room and pretend I was Lola. I'd read Graham Greene's story and associated with the Lola character. Unwanted, with no real purpose is how I often felt. I know now it wasn't true, my parents always loved me, but that's how I felt. So, I would become Lola when things got tough. She wasn't an imaginary friend, she was me. This became Lola's Room. I think my parent's just accepted my alter-ego after a while. As I grew up I kept Lola. When I didn't want to be me I became Lola. She had nothing to do with my problems; she was my place of retreat. Then later I used her as a shield, and anything I couldn't deal with ceased to be my problem and became Lola's.'

Dylan put an arm around her shoulders, her head resting on his chest.

'I don't know whether you believe me or not, Dylan, but I am being genuine with you now. I have no further reason to lie.'

'I know, sweetheart,' he said, as he ran his free hand up and down her silky arm. 'I think I know. But have you told me everything? I mean, are you sure there aren't any other Lola's to come out of the woodwork?'

'Well... only the real one,' she replied, almost inaudibly.

THIRTY THREE

'Why are you still persisting with the lie that there's a real Lola?' cried Dylan.

'Because there is,' replied Victoria. 'As I said earlier, this thing being completely over depends on whether Lola's been found or not. For me anyway.'

'I don't believe it. So, who is she?'

'Not *who* exactly, but what.'

'What...?'

She pulled away, assuming an upright stance. His posture stiffened, as he waited for her revelation.

'Yes... what. Lola is actually a painting.'

'A painting? Not one of the paintings that they're all looking for?'

'No. This one's different. Probably more precious than any of those.'

'So tell me,' Dylan pleaded. 'Put me out of my misery.'

Victoria began her attempt at doing just that.

'Here goes the history lesson then. About seven hundred years ago there was this group of cardinals who gathered to elect a successor to Pope Clement the Fifth. They chose some Frenchman called Jacques Dueze. Proclaimed Pope John the Twenty-Second, it was decided that he was to take up his papacy at Avignon in France. Everyone had expected it to be Rome and so this upset a lot of people in Italy, and for a short time they actually installed an anti-pope in

329

Rome. In opposition to this decision. Anyway, the cardinals commissioned the painter Giotto di Bondone to produce a painting which was to be presented to the new pope, as a kind of welcome to the job present.

'The problem was that Giotto had no wish to publicly endorse the new French pope, as he had many friends who believed that the papacy belonged in Rome and nowhere else, but he was put under certain pressures to fulfil his commission. When the painting was finished he refused to put his name to it for fear of reprisal. His depiction of the Virgin Mary he named *Maria de los Dolores*, which translates from Spanish as Mary of the Sorrows. He sent the painting on its way without signing it, and with the strict proviso that it not be revealed, outside of the papal circle, who the true artist was.'

Dylan listened with interest, but he was beginning to wonder what all this had to do with Lola. He said nothing, allowing Victoria to continue with her tale.

'Unfortunately, somewhere between Giotto's studio in Florence and its destination in Avignon, the painting was stolen by bandits who knew full well the origin of it. The hijack of the painting was rumoured to have been at the order of Louis IV of Bavaria who was then the Holy Roman Emperor and the person who had installed the anti-pope in direct opposition to Pope John XXII. He had apparently found out about the painting through a small group of corrupt cardinals. Of course, bandits being bandits, the painting disappeared and from that day onwards was never seen again.'

'Victoria, what has all this got to do with Lola?' Dylan asked, impatiently.

'I'm getting to it,' she replied, with a trace of irritation. 'As I say, this painting has not been seen since that day, officially. But unofficially, amongst the art underworld of Europe it has become something of a Holy Grail. The painting brings its possessor great prestige, and is something, when required, to be traded at a very high price. It's priceless because of its reputation. It has been moved on from hand to hand, as and when needed, for centuries.'

'And Lola?' asked Dylan, almost pleadingly.

'As I say, Giotto called the painting Maria de los Dolores, and a latter-day abbreviation of the name Dolores is Lola. And for the last hundred years or so that is what the painting has been referred to as. A kind of code name.'

'So Lola is this painting,' murmured Dylan, relieved at finally knowing the truth.

'That's right. A painting which I found out from Gerald, Edward Loddon was the current possessor of.'

'So it was probably one of the pieces that I saw crated up down in the tunnels.'

'I hope so. I knew about the tunnels because Gerald had told me about them. I asked Chas about them once too, but he just got angry and said that they were just a myth and not to mention it again. But it was too good an opportunity not to use in my plan. I knew that once you started asking about Lola, both Chas and Loddon would get restless. Hopefully the police now have Lola

331

along with all the others. And that will be the final nail in Loddon's coffin. Bastard!'

'But you still haven't told me how you knew about my guardian angel.'

'He was told that if he followed you then you would lead him to the paintings that he was looking for. When you went to the cemetery to put flowers on my 'dead' parents' grave, what you didn't know was that your guardian angel was with you all the way. I also told the Canadians, that was the best day to check on the paintings before arranging movement from their resting place, the Devere family crypt.'

'Amazing. I knew there was something about that crypt. So, you made sure that everybody was there at the same time.'

'And, I knew that Chas would be there as it was the anniversary of his parents' death. It's a ritual that he visits them on that day, at exactly the time they were killed. When he first told me I knew that he wasn't as hard as his exterior implies.'

'That was probably why he was crying in his office, when I followed him that day.'

'Mmmm, probably. Anyway, I said that it was *my* parents because I knew that you wouldn't let me down. I just gave you a slightly earlier time.'

'That's right, Victoria. I'm just your little predictable puppet.' She saw the look of resentment on his face. 'But how did you know that Mr Stone was following me?'

'This is the reason I bought you up here... Well, I found out about him whilst in Paris. I'd set up a meeting with two brothers from the Middle-

East to buy the paintings, but they were unaware at that point that the paintings were stolen. The Canadians returned to London to organise the movement of the paintings and I was to stay and keep the customers entertained. This is what I wanted. It gave me a chance to work on the brothers.

'I made a point of mentioning to them that they bore a striking resemblance to somebody I knew. Knowing the truth I asked if they had any family in London. They said they did, a half-brother they'd never met. When I pressed them further, they told me his name was Dylan Morgan.'

'...My brothers?'

'That's right.'

She looked at him with doleful, sympathetic eyes, and it was now her turn to put a consoling arm over his shoulders.

'I remember you telling me once about your father's wealthy family. I had to do some serious research but I found out all about them. I found out that amongst all their business interests they also collected art. So when Jean-Paul and Bill, the Canadians, were looking for buyers for the paintings I said that Gerald had once mentioned a certain Saudi party that were always interested in buying art collections, and that if they wanted I could set up a meeting. Of course when I did, I didn't tell them that it was stolen artwork or the plan wouldn't have even got off the ground.

'Even though they had never met you, your brothers spoke about you with great affection. They told me that before your father had died he had made them promise to make sure that, whatever it took, you were never to fall upon hard times. They told me that they had even hired someone to keep a watchful eye over you – your Mr Stone. Coincidently, it turned out that this person was also involved in the search for the stolen paintings. I then came clean to them about what was happening, that the paintings were stolen and that you were being set up by the people who had stolen them, and who were now looking to pass them on. I told them I desperately needed their help and they agreed, without hesitation, to help me.'

Reaching across to the small bedside cabinet, she opened the top drawer and pulled out a photograph.

'This is them. We were all a little tipsy at the time but I wanted something to show you, when all this was finally out in the open.'

Victoria handed Dylan the photograph. He glanced at the two faces either side of Victoria. There was a definite familiarity about them both.

'We agreed on a plan whereby they would tell the Canadians that they wanted the paintings on a certain day, so that Bill and Jean-Paul would have to come back to London to arrange the transport. I would arrange for Mr Stone - I never got to find out his real name - and the police to be at the cemetery just at the time they were checking on the paintings. I made a deal with Mr Stone that he would get any charges against me dropped.'

Dylan stood up and walked towards the window. He needed to take all this in. He had expected some revelations when he arrived at the house, but he hadn't expected anything like this.

334

He had already found out of course that Mr Stone, or whatever his name was, had been keeping an eye on him at the request of his 'other family', and that he was also looking for the stolen paintings. He knew all that because Mr Stone had already told him. To now be told that he had two brothers somewhere, who spoke of him with affection and whom Victoria had actually met and entertained, was a lot for Dylan to take in. Together with finding out that the father he'd never known, and now never would, was dead, threw his emotions into a state of turmoil. His gaze was firmly held by the view outside the window, although his thoughts were most decidedly not.

'Dylan... please... They said that they would get in touch with you one day, when they felt the time was right. You now know the whole truth. Everything has turned out fine, hasn't it? I've finally got the Canadians off my back. Mr Stone and the British government have got back their paintings to negotiate with. The police have got Loddon and his organisation, and Chas too, as an accessory. I'm a little sorry about Chas. He wasn't all bad - but he was sending the girls to Loddon knowing what was happening to them, so...

'And if it was still in the tunnels when the police searched them, the world has finally got Lola after seven hundred years in the wilderness.'

'Yep!' Dylan cried, turning around to face her. 'Everybody's happy and all's well that ends well, eh, Victoria? Except me, the person whose life it seems is being controlled by everyone but himself.'

He looked down again at the photograph then

folded it up and put it in his jacket pocket. Giving Victoria a look that bellowed treachery and deceit, he turned away and began walking towards the door.

'Can you ever forgive me?' she asked.

'I'll tell you what, Victoria. You call me, once you've forgiven yourself, and I'll see what I can do, eh?'

He walked solemnly out into the hallway, down the stairs, and out of the house.

*

Dylan turned the key in the lock of the front door and entered the house in Hampstead Hill Gardens. As he walked through the main hallway everything was eerily quiet on the ground floor. There was not a sound to be heard from Don's flat, or the flat belonging to Tom and Sally McGuiness. He climbed the staircase to the first floor where, outside Bikram's flat, he was almost certain that he could hear the delicate and soothing sounds of a sitar recital from within. As he continued on, ensuring he moved stealthily past Mrs Sumner's door, he reached the staircase that would take him up to the top floor.

It was as he climbed the final set of stairs up to his flat that his nostrils suddenly picked up a hint of something that was somehow familiar to him. By the time he reached the top step, and as if to taunt him, his nose had filled with the faint, but sweet fragrance of Indian agarbatti which seemed to be coming from somewhere above.